EURO QUEST INTELLIGENCE AGENCY MISSION DOCUMENT

Agency location: Prague, Czech Republic

Specialty: Creating femme fatale spies—special women with killer instincts who can take their place in the world of global espionage.

Mission: Uncover the hideout of Holic "the Butcher" Reznik. Seize his future-kills file. Assassinate the assassin.

Recommended agent: Nadja Stein, age 29, 5'9", brown eyes, blond hair. Code name: Q

Notes: Q's sexy appearance is an asset for taking a quarry off guard. Her mental acuity and quickness are matched by a surprising tolerance for pain. A former Olympic skiing hopeful, Q spent three years in rehab after an accident that could have left her paralyzed. She recovered almost fully, but cold weather can affect her performance. However, her personal connection to this case—a connection she is not yet aware of—will give her an edge and determination that won't allow for failure....

Dear Reader,

Silhouette Bombshell is dedicated to bringing you the best in savvy heroines, fast action, high stakes and chilling suspense. We're raising the bar on action adventure to create an exhilarating reading experience that you'll remember long after the final pages!

Take some personal time with *Personal Enemy* by Sylvie Kurtz. An executive bodyguard plans the perfect revenge against the man who helped to destroy her family—but when they're both attacked, she's forced to work *for* him before she can work against him!

Don't miss *Contact* by Evelyn Vaughn, the latest adventure in the ATHENA FORCE continuity series. Faith Corbett uses her extrasenory skills to help the police solve crimes, but she's always contacted them anonymously. Until a serial killer begins hunting psychics, and Faith must reveal herself to one disbelieving detective....

Meet the remarkable women of author Cindy Dees's *The Medusa Project*. These Special Forces officers-in-training are set up to fail, but for team leader Vanessa Blake, quitting is not an option—especially when both international security and their tough-as-nails trainer's life is at stake!

And provocative twists abound in *The Spy Wore Red* by Wendy Rosnau. Agent Nadja Stefn is hand-picked for a mission to terminate an assassin—but getting her man means working with a partner from whom she must hide a dangerous personal agenda....

Please send your comments to me c/o Silhouette Books, 233 Broadway, Suite 1001, New York, NY 10279.

Best wishes,

Natashya Wilson
Associate Senior Editor, Silhouette Bombshell

Please address questions and book requests to:
Silhouette Reader Service
U.S.: 3010 Walden Ave., P.O. Box 1325, Buffalo, NY 14269
Canadian: P.O. Box 609, Fort Erie, Ont. L2A 5X3

WENDY ROSNAU

THE
SPY
WORE
Red

Silhouette®
BOMBSHELL™

Published by Silhouette Books

America's Publisher of Contemporary Romance

SILHOUETTE BOOKS

ISBN 0-373-51346-1

THE SPY WORE RED

WENDY ROSNAU

resides on sixty secluded acres in Minnesota with her husband and their two children. She divides her time between her family owned bookstore and writing romantic suspense.

Her first book, *The Long Hot Summer,* was a *Romantic Times* nominee for Best First Series Romance of 2000. Her third book, *The Right Side of the Law,* was a *Romantic Times* Top Pick. She received the Midwest Fiction Writers 2001 Rising Star Award.

Wendy loves to hear from her readers. Visit her Web site at www.wendyrosnau.com.

Chapter 1

Winter smog hung thick over the city of Prague, as well as a fresh layer of wet snow. Neither, however, could be blamed for Nadja Stefn being late. Twelve minutes, to be exact.

Red wool swirled around her as she dashed up the stone steps to the Vysehrad Museum and through the heavy mosaic front doors. Inside, she kept moving as routine and familiarity took over. She pulled off her black leather gloves, her calf-high boots clicking out a hurried tempo on the slate floor as she made a right down the corridor, then a left.

In a narrow passageway she stopped and faced a slender mirror next to an elevator. Once the retinal scanner identified her, the doors opened and she stepped inside and placed her right hand in the fingerprint recognition mold on the wall. An electronic charge tin-

gled her fingertips. A computerized voice welcomed her
by name, then the elevator took off, descending into the
underworld beneath the museum.

Polax would be having a hairy cow by now, Nadja
thought as she buried her gloves in the outer pocket of her
slim black briefcase. He would be cursing her in ten lan-
guages for holding up his all-important morning meeting.

Today a Quest agent would be chosen to accompany
an NSA Onyxx agent on a mission into Austria.

A milestone mission, Polax promised when he had
called her yesterday with the news that she was one of
the candidates being considered. He hadn't offered her
any particulars, and none would be shared unless she
was the agent packing a bag at the end of the day and
flying out of Praha Ruzyne Airport at midnight.

That's how it worked at Quest: everything was done
on a need-to-know basis.

Nadja's technique set her apart from the other agents
at Quest. She was ranked number one among sanctioned assassins—had been for the past four years.
Then, too, it was hard to miss at point-blank range when
you were straddling your victim.

Though she rarely did handstands to get noticed at
Quest, the difference today was that she was eager to
be chosen.

A week, or a month—the mission's term didn't matter. All that mattered was finding out what had happened
to Ruger. Her last three letters had been returned un-
opened, and his had stopped altogether. She didn't believe that he had left Austria. He would have told her if
he had, and he certainly hadn't changed professions.
No, never. Ruger loved his work, which meant he would
still be in residence at Wilten Parish in Innsbruck.

Still, something was wrong and she meant to find out what.

An uninterrupted hour with Father Ruger, that's all she needed. A soul-searching session with her brother to assure her that all was well—that their secret was safe.

The elevator continued on its way into the underbelly of the Vysehrad Museum. That's where EURO-Quest had been conducting its secret intelligence operations for the past ten years. Where femmes fatales such as herself were trained to their fullest potential according to their expertise.

She shrugged off her wool cape, and that's when she saw the fat wrinkle blazing a path across the front of her thighs. How it had gotten there, she had no clue. She studied it for a moment and decided she looked like she'd slept on a bar stool all night.

She hadn't.

She'd gone to bed on time.

Only she hadn't fallen asleep right away. She'd gotten caught up in all the possible reasons why Ruger had stopped writing. She had succumbed to exhaustion, only to awaken hours later and realize she'd slept straight through her alarm.

Nadja slapped at the wrinkle, then swore when it sprang back into place as if it was spring-loaded. Facing the mirror that decorated one wall inside the elevator, she looked for a way to camouflage the wrinkle. If she dropped her hand just so, when she walked into the meeting room, maybe she could conceal it.

She went through the motions as she studied her white blouse and black jacket.

The blouse looked good.

Her jacket…was missing a gold button.

It suddenly occurred to her why this particular suit looked so awful. It was the one she'd intended to drop off at the cleaners.

"Shit."

She dropped her cape to the floor, swearing three more times before pinching her briefcase between her knees to peel off her jacket. Briefcase back in hand, she draped the jacket over her arm to hide the wrinkle, then examined herself once more in the mirror.

"Better, but…"

She gathered her blond hair into one hand and pulled it back from her face. Wishing she hadn't overslept, disgusted that she had no clip to make even a bare-bones improvement where her hair was concerned, she dropped her hand and shook out the mass.

Her hair wasn't the worst of it. Her eyes were bloodshot. Glasses would disguise her lack of sleep and lack of makeup—there simply had been no time for eyelashes and lipstick.

Not even time to pee.

Again she pinched her briefcase between her knees in search of the reading glasses she kept in her jacket pocket. Of course they weren't there—it was the wrong suit jacket. Angry with herself, she grabbed the briefcase unaware the metal clasp had caught on her silk stockings. When she felt the unmistakable tug, she glanced down to see a large hole circling her knee.

In a matter of minutes the elevator would stop, the doors would open and she would be greeted by two inhouse agents. Kimball and Moor had squarish faces, pug noses and no sense of humor. But then, why would agent hopefuls who had fallen short be in a good mood? Ever.

The "butlers," as Nadja called them, would flank her as she left the elevator and doggedly escort her to the conclave where Pasha Lenova and Casmir Balasi—the other two agents vying for the Austrian assignment—would already be waiting.

As stringent as Polax was about being punctual, he was twice as neurotic about professional neatness. Which meant arriving late looking like she'd been on an all-night bender would definitely get her a look, but not the job or a trip to Austria.

She would be skipped over in favor of Pasha's promptness, or—she glanced down at the fat wrinkle tracking her thighs, then the hole that had targeted her knee—Casmir's flair for always looking like she stepped off a Paris runway.

She dropped her briefcase to the floor, pulled off her boots and jerked her skirt high. It would take only a second to unhook her stockings from her garter belt. No one in the business could get in and out of their clothes faster than Quest's bedroom assassin.

Nadja Stefn had the best hands in the business.

The sexy garter belt was red, the flat-screen monitors in Polax's office recreational size.

After studying the first two Quest agents on the monitor as they entered the elevator, Bjorn Odell had slid his ass onto the corner of Polax's desk to watch the third, and final, candidate. She was late, and Polax had pissed and moaned about that for the entire twelve minutes.

Arms crossed over his chest, Bjorn watched as the brown-eyed blond peeled off her silk stockings and dropped them to the floor next to her briefcase. He put to memory every detail of her performance. Studied every move she made, every article of clothing on the floor and left on her body.

The Italian-leather holster strapped to her thigh was also bad-girl red. Inside was the prettiest pearl-handled mini-compact .45 Springfield he'd ever seen. The Springfield was a dandy—a one-of-a-kind, just like the femme who owned it.

She had long thoroughbred legs and beautiful thighs. Satin-smooth skin.

The sweetest ass in Prague—Bjorn would wager his own concealed 380 Beretta Cheetah on that.

"I know the deal is you get to choose from my top three operatives, but for this mission the logical choice would be Pasha Lenova. You really don't want Stefn."

Polax's comment sent Bjorn's eyes away from the monitor to where Quest's slightly overweight, bald commander stood with his hands in his pockets.

"And why don't I want her?"

"What I meant is that each of my agents have a specific talent. Pasha Lenova is our endurance agent. As you say in the U.S., she's as tough as shoe leather." Polax grinned. "She can match any man you've got. My personal favorite for a physical mission such as this. But if you're set on a blonde my second choice would be Casmir Balasi. She's our actress—slash model—but she wasn't recruited just for her pretty face and amazing body. Her role-playing skills are flawless. As for Q, you can see—"

"Q?"

"That's what I call Stefn because she's Quest's question mark." Polax looked back to the monitor to all the clothes on the floor in the elevator. "As you can see she's a bit scattered at times. But like cream, Q always seems to rise to the top. However, she's not an endurance player—which is what you'll need for this mission."

Bjorn's gaze returned to the monitor. *Scattered* was a good word for her, he thought. Polax's "cream" had turned the elevator into her own private dressing room.

"Here at Quest we call Q our 'candy queen,'" Polax continued. "She's got a sweet body, and she's not shy when it comes to sharing her sugar to disarm her target. I can assure you that every man who finds himself in Q's bed ends up with one helluva toothache. But then, if my number was up and I had a choice, I'd elect to die high on sugar, wouldn't you?"

With a hearty laugh, Polax pressed the zoom button on his remote and double-sized Nadja Stefn's sweetness—making all her treats larger than life.

Without conscious thought, Bjorn fit people into three categories: the doers, the talkers and the assholes. Polax was of the asshole variety. He had an obsession for electronic gadgets, as well as super-sexy female spies.

The wall-size monitors had pulse-sonic sound and a state-of-the art room feature that could find a grain of salt in a sugar bowl. And then there was Polax's desk chair. The motorized yellow leather contraption was voice sensitive, and had been following him around the room for the past hour like a pet puppy. On the chance he felt like sitting on a second's notice, all he had to do was plop.

He'd plopped twice since Bjorn and Merrick, his Onyxx commander, had arrived.

Bjorn glanced at his commander. Adolf Merrick was leaning against the wall with his arms crossed over his chest. His attention wasn't on Q's ass or show-stopper legs, however; he was staring directly at Bjorn—watching him with an intensity that would have made a lesser man squirm. Bjorn didn't squirm. He didn't even flinch. He turned back to the monitor at the exact moment Polax zeroed in on a chocolate-colored mole on the candy queen's inner thigh.

The commander of EURO-Quest more than enjoyed the fringe benefits of his job. Bjorn had come to that conclusion an hour ago when he and Merrick had followed Polax as he paraded through the agency corridors like a sheik with a harem. A sheik with itchy fingers— he was now fiddling with the super-sensitive sound control, tuning into Nadja's rapid breathing as she worked quickly to strip off her naughty little red garter belt.

Bjorn raised his eyebrows just as Polax looked over his shoulder.

"What's wrong, Agent Odell? You did ask to examine the candidates. I thought a profile expert such as yourself would accept nothing less than a head-to-toe private audit of what we offer here at Quest."

Bjorn kept his ass on the corner of Polax's desk as he looked on. It was true he had requested a private viewing of each candidate before they actually met them. As a profiler he didn't base decisions on file stats alone. He considered body language and mannerisms as well as data. He listened to voice tone, verbal communication and motor response. But more importantly, the silent communications that lay hidden under the surface.

"Our goal is to impress you with our product." Polax sent his drab green eyes over Bjorn's broad shoulders, down his solid chest and athletic long legs. Taking his measure, noting the obvious differences in size and height, and possibly the importance of keeping the bigger man happy, he added, "Speaking of impressed, I've read your profile, Odell. You're a damn hard man to kill."

"You say that as if it's a flaw."

"On the contrary. I respect any man who can survive seven years in the hot seat. But then, I'm not surprised. Only the best are commandeered to join Onyxx. And only a handful of those become rat fighters. Merrick's elite are simply the best anywhere. That's why I feel it's important that we select the right partner to complement your consummate skills. My agents are also quite talented. Quest trains only the top two out of every hundred that make it to the evaluation stage. Stefn…" Polax motioned to the monitor. "I interviewed her as a favor to an old friend. I never believed for a minute she'd meet my criteria."

"Meaning?"

"Her injuries automatically made her ineligible. That's the reason I gave her the name Q. Once I read her profile… Well, the gift she'd been given was far too remarkable to ignore."

"Gift?"

"Stefn has an incredible tolerance for pain. Both emotional and physical. As you know, one of the obstacles agencies face in finding suitable operatives is their ability to survive whatever comes their way. A tolerance for pain goes hand-in-hand with survival. Nadja is not only our candy queen, but she's also the queen of pain. Her pain threshold is simply the best I've seen in all my thirty years in the business. That kind of discipline makes her a sought-after commodity in the intelligence world."

Bjorn picked Q's file off the desk and opened it. "It says here that she was born in Switzerland. That she was an Olympic gold medal hopeful. You mentioned injuries. What sort of injuries?"

"A skiing accident. It's all there in her file, every surgery. The gory details. Her grandfather was a gold medalist. Q was supposed to follow in his footsteps. At age eighteen she was expected to win gold. Instead she crashed on a slope in Zurich doing sixty miles an hour. She broke damn near every bone in her body."

Polax walked up to the monitor—his pet chair on his heels. He angled his head as if searching for something, then ran his hand over the screen, touching Q's right knee. Slowly he moved his hand upward over the screen, stroking her leg like a man who knew her intimately. Or a man who had lain awake nights contemplating the idea.

"She has a tattoo that is quite spectacular." Polax turned and looked at Merrick, then Bjorn, before he sat on his pet chair. As it took off and rounded his desk, he said, "It's located in an area I call the 'dead zone.'"

Bjorn ignored the comment and asked, "These old injuries—do they limit her in any way?"

"Not in her percentages. But only because I've tailored her missions. That's what it's all about, you know. Finding your agent's gift and exploiting it. Right, Merrick? Isn't that how you became so successful with your rat fighters?"

The commander of Onyxx only nodded. Adolf Merrick wasn't known for inane conversation, or explaining his stratagem.

"If a femme wants to work at Quest," Polax went on, "she's got to have something special we can market."

"And what is that something special that Agent Lenova has?" It was the first Merrick had spoken since they had cloistered themselves in Polax's office to examine his agent lineup.

"Pasha's durability is extraordinary— my rain-or-shine agent. Desert heat, or arctic cold, Lenova will match you every step of the way. Q's something special is getting on top quick in the bedroom. Since this mission will be a chilly affair, you're going to want an endurance player."

"It says here Stefn trained for the biathlon." Bjorn scanned the file for more data.

"That's true, but Lenova is the true biathlon queen. She shoots ninety-eight percent," Polax quoted from memory. "You're going to need that, going up against Holic Reznik."

It had been a month since Bjorn had apprehended Holic in Santorini, Greece. He'd managed to capture the country's most wanted assassin during a hotel fire that had sent him and Holic off a crumbling balcony into a burning ballroom full of screaming people trying to escape the chaos.

Three days ago he'd learned that Holic had successfully slipped through the National Security Agency's fingers and escaped his well-guarded prison cell. When he'd heard the news he'd been so angry he walked out of Merrick's office.

Normally he was a good-tempered guy. Reasonable, even during upsetting times. And smart enough to know that Merrick wouldn't listen to him if he was shouting and throwing furniture.

He'd spent an hour walking off his rage, then he'd returned to Merrick's office to discuss what action the

Agency intended to take now that Reznik was once
again a free man.

Seated in front of his commander's desk, he'd asked,
"Has the Agency issued a new objective?"

"They have, and your name was mentioned for the
assignment. It's yours, if you want it. But there are conditions, and additions."

"I'm not a field agent any longer."

"Reinstatement would be a simple formality. You've
studied Holic Reznik's habits, know him better than
anyone. That makes you the most qualified for this mission. I want you on the job, Bjorn. That is, if you'll take
it."

It was true, he and Holic had a history. Bjorn had profiled the man nicknamed 'the butcher' as well as faced
him in the field.

He listened while Merrick detailed the situation.
Holic had been seriously injured falling thirty feet off
that hotel balcony at Cupata. Because of Holic's many
injuries, the Agency believed he would return to his
homeland of Austria to heal and grow strong again.

They hadn't been able to pinpoint where he would
go exactly, but they felt confident it would be someplace
familiar to him. Someplace remote and isolated. Someplace hard to reach.

"We know that before the Chameleon died, he con-
tracted Reznik and hired him to eliminate a list of his
enemies. He was promised millions and—"

"Eva Creon as his mistress to sweeten the deal,"
Bjorn interjected. "Yes, I know."

"Since that part of the contract fell through when
Holic was captured, and then since his recent escape,
we're not sure what he intends to do with the kill-file

or how many of our agents have been targeted. The truth is Holic Reznik could start picking off our operatives at any time. So you see how important this is. If you should decide to take the assignment, your mission will be to infiltrate Austria, uncover Holic's hideout, seize the kill-file, then assassinate the assassin—with one catch."

"One catch?"

"The Agency wants to partner you with a female operative from EURO-Quest."

Bjorn liked the new objective, except the part about a partner. Still, Holic was the most reliable killing machine on all seven continents. He had to be stopped.

When Bjorn resurfaced from his private musing, Polax was still tossing out reasons why Pasha Lenova was his choice for the mission. He listened to the Quest commander while watching Nadja Stefn slip her tall black boots back on her pretty feet.

When Merrick cleared his throat, he glanced at his boss. "You say something?"

"I asked you which one you've decided on. You know Reznik better than anyone—which one of these women would be your biggest asset?"

"The one with the sweetest ass," Bjorn said, knowing that next to his obsession with killing, Holic's second favorite pastime was enjoying beautiful women.

"The question you've got to ask yourself, Bjorn, is which one of these beauties do you want to share your days and nights with for the next few weeks? Merrick said. "I don't care who or why, as long as she can do the job. So do you fancy the rain-or-shine brunette, the angel faced actress or the bedroom playmate with the candy-cane legs and cotton-candy ass?"

"My recommendation—" Polax began.

"We know." Bjorn turned his piercing blue eyes on the Quest commander. "Your choice is Lenova. You've made that clear. A little too clear."

Polax climbed out of his chair and puffed out his chest. "As I said before, my job is to match the mission with the best possible agent. For this one you need an all-around sexy ball-buster who chews ice cubes in place of gum, and that would be Lenova. Quest is still working on earning its stripes in the spy world. This agency can only survive if money changes hands. For that to happen, my femmes need to shine on every mission. With Pasha Lenova at your side in Austria, a win is inevitable for both of us."

"What you're forgetting is, it's not your choice," Bjorn reminded. "It's my call."

He glanced back at the monitor. The elevator had stopped and Q's skirt was no longer hiked clean to her amazing ass. He watched the doors open, watched her greet the two men waiting for her. She handed her red cape to the shorter man. Then, like a resilient cat who had just landed on her feet, she started down the corridor. Her briefcase in one hand, and her jacket draped over the other so that the missing button and the wrinkle across her thigh were hidden from view.

The only evidence that something was amiss was one lone silk stocking left on the elevator floor.

Chapter 2

Bjorn was left alone in the office with his choice of water or gin to keep him company while Merrick followed Polax out into the hall to take a walk. When the door closed, he reached for the gin, ignoring the early hour.

He hitched his ass back on the desk, sipped the gin and spent the next twenty minutes cooling his heels, watching and waiting, and keeping his ears on what was being said inside the sterile boardroom between the curvy femmes.

He was conscious of his eyes going back to Nadja more often than the others. That was understandable— he liked natural blondes with long legs and cleavage.

Quest's bedroom assassin had the winning three. There was no reason to argue that point, nor would he. Q's body type, her voice and the way she moved had already been logged into his subconscious.

A profiler's best friend was his database memory, and he had one. Onyxx had, however, refined his talent. They had polished his telephoto memory and added instant-recall capabilities.

Like Q, he was at the top of his game, although he was willing to bet she was enjoying her work far more than he was his.

It was a god-given gift, Merrick had told him—Bjorn's so-called database genius. But there were times when it didn't feel that way. With his talent came the price of remembering everything—good or bad—and never forgetting any of it. Not his youth, his first mission, every man he'd killed, or every woman he'd slept with. It was all there, every bit of it crystal clear.

As clear as the past five minutes.

His greatest challenge at Onyxx had been keeping all the data organized so he could remain focused. And right now he needed to do just that. He didn't want any old memories messing up this assignment, or his goal. And that goal was to put a bullet through Holic Reznik's black heart—after he recovered the kill-file, of course.

So the question was, which femme did he choose to assist him? Based on the facts, the task should be simple.

Polax was right, an endurance mission required an endurance player. But not when they were going after a man with a fetish for beautiful women. And it was a known fact that Holic was partial to cleavage and tangle-me-up-in-a-knot long legs.

When Merrick and Polax returned, it was Bjorn who took a walk with Merrick. They rode the elevator up to the main level, and as they stepped out and headed for the art gallery, Merrick said, "You want the bedroom beauty, yes?"

"What makes you say that?"

"The look on your face when she stepped into the elevator."

"I like blondes."

"Casmir Balasi is a blonde."

"Then I should have said I like blondes and cleavage," Bjorn amended. "Balasi is too petite for my taste."

"I got the feeling there was more to it than that. For a moment I thought you recognized Stefn."

"Every man recognizes the woman in his dreams. She's got looks, a helluva body and a mind."

"And she's good in bed," Merrick added. "So what's the problem? If Polax's candy queen appeals to you, then pick her. The nights in Austria are going to be damn chilly and I know how you hate cold weather."

Bjorn glanced at his boss. "Advocating I use a Quest agent as a bed warmer, Merrick?"

"If that's the only way you can keep an eye on her every move, yes. The goal is to get our hands on Holic's kill file. Whatever you have to do to achieve that goal is acceptable."

"What's Quest's interest in Reznik?"

"The same as ours. They're worried that some of their agents have been sanctioned. That's why it's so damn urgent that we get that file. Who knows who's all on it?"

"If this is so urgent, my first thought is we're two days off the pace. We know Holic flew to Austria, so stopping off in Prague to pick up—"

"—your partner—"

"—only puts me further behind."

"I know that, but the Agency—"

"Is kissing Quest's ass for some reason," Bjorn said. "I sure would like to know why that is."

"I'm not at liberty to discuss that. They just feel this will be advantageous for a future mission."

The "they" Merrick was referring to were the top brass in the upstairs office at Onyxx. The big boys who made the final decisions—right or wrong, smart or stupid.

"These spy games are never black and white, Bjorn. The Agency is still upset that the Chameleon's death hasn't slowed down the anarchy, and they're feeling pressured to turn things around quickly."

"Will we ever get rid of the Chameleon?" Bjorn mused out loud. "He's dead, and yet he lives."

"It's certainly the truth. We have the son of a bitch's corpse under lock and key in the Agency morgue and still we don't know shit about who he is…was."

"No confirmation yet?"

"No. And I'm told it's going to be a while. We know the body underwent multiple plastic surgeries. His goal was to clone Paavo Creon. Our experts have even time-lined those surgeries. But some things still don't add up. We just have to be patient."

Bjorn glanced at Merrick, noting the conviction in his commander's voice. If anyone deserved peace of mind where the Chameleon was concerned, it was Adolf Merrick. The Chameleon had killed Merrick's wife years ago. He'd strapped C-4 to her curvy body and sent her to hell while Merrick had watched it un-fold on the computer screen in his office.

Bjorn suspected his commander still blamed himself for his wife's death, and it was that blame that contin-ued to drive him where the Chameleon was concerned. Even though his longtime enemy had been killed weeks ago, he wanted the man's entire international operation wiped out.

"Then you believe everything Eva Creon said?" Bjorn asked.

"Yes, I do. She said the Chameleon admitted to her that he had purposely stolen her father's face. He admitted to cloning Paavo Creon's likeness surgically, and slipping into his life for the sole purpose of revenge."

"A lot of trouble to go through for a little revenge."

"My question is, who is he and why? There are days when I think he's laughing at me from the grave," Merrick admitted. "It's not over yet. Hell, maybe it'll never be over."

"What makes you say that?"

"Something Sly McEwen said before he took off to go fishing." Merrick stopped and looked at Bjorn. "McEwen said I shouldn't put off my surgery. I should have the operation because I was going to need to be a hundred percent soon. I think he was hinting that when we get the identity on that body, all hell is going to break loose."

"You think he knows who it is?"

Merrick shook his head. "If he does, he's going to have a helluva a lot of explaining to do when he decides to surface with Eva." He rubbed his jaw. "I'm tired of this shit. I've been playing this game with the Chameleon for fourteen years and I'm ready for it to be over. I want to bury it along with him, and his identity, whoever he turns out to be."

"Have you decided to have the surgery?"

"Not yet, but…" Unconsciously Merrick moved his hand to his left temple. "I haven't had a headache in a week. Maybe once this assignment is in the bag I can take a month off. But right now I can't afford to be on my back while you're in Austria. I've decided that I'll be your controller on this one. While you're in the field you'll report directly to me instead of to one of the technicians in the Green Room. Anything you need, I'll see that you get."

Merrick had been diagnosed with a brain tumor and had put off his surgery too long, Bjorn thought. Bjorn had noticed certain things in the past week, the way his boss blinked more and squinted in bright light. The temple massaging.

It all added up to one thing—the tumor was growing, and putting pressure on the retinal nerves behind his eyes. To tolerate the pain he had started mixing pills and booze. That wasn't smart, but there would be no convincing Merrick to have the surgery until he was ready.

They started to walk again. "Ordinarily I'd remind you that personal contact with an associate or suspect is frowned upon at Onyxx," Merrick said, "but on this mission anything goes as long as we recover the file and Holic Reznik ends up on a slab next to the Chameleon. There is some concern that Holic might contract out the assassinations in that kill-file. That is, if he doesn't get the use of his hand back. You've profiled him. What do you think?"

"If there's killing to be done, and he's capable of doing it, Holic's going to be the one pulling the trigger. The question is, will his hand be up for it? Multiple fractures and nerve damage…" Bjorn shrugged. "It doesn't sound good. If there's a God upstairs, Holic's assassination days are over. If not, at least his victims will be up against better odds. Holic's MO is taking out his victims with one shot."

"He could decide to contract the work out."

They had been strolling through the museum, and so far neither had looked at a single painting. Bjorn, still matching Merrick's steps, said, "That would mean he would have to trust someone. From what I know about him, Holic trusts damn few. That's why he's been so elusive."

"Then if he doesn't hire someone to pull the trigger, what do you think he'll do? A useless hand isn't going to get the job done."

"He'll retire. He'll find a buyer for the kill-file, sell it for a few billion, then enjoy his money and his myriad of mistresses until he's too old to find his zipper."

Merrick stopped in his tracks. "Sell the file? You think that's a possibility?"

"That's what I'd do. Holic's life revolves around two things, killing and women. If he can't do one, then he'll bury himself in the other. No pun intended. His reputation is flawless, and if that's all he has left then he'll want to preserve his legend status. He's got a big ego."

"Then the sooner we locate him the better, before he starts shopping for buyers and the perfect getaway. Which brings us back to the question of the hour. Which lucky lady is going to keep you warm in Austria? It doesn't matter to me who goes, so make your choice."

It would matter, Bjorn thought. If Merrick knew that he and Nadja Stein had a history and he decided to take her along, there would be a dozen questions. Questions he wasn't prepared to answer. He'd never mentioned her in his report five years ago when he'd gotten back from Vienna. She'd had no bearing on his mission while he was there, and he'd wanted to forget her.

But that had been impossible for a man with a telephoto memory and instant-recall capabilities.

* * *

Normally Nadja wouldn't have minded cooling her heels. She could use the time to pull herself together. But nature was calling and she needed to use the rest room because her morning routine had exploded into chaos the minute she'd opened her eyes and realized she had overslept.

She stood and glanced at Pasha Lenova across the room, then down at her friend, Casmir. "I'm going to the little girl's room. If I'm still gone when our almighty commander decides to show himself, tell him I went for coffee. Still take two creams, Cass?"

"Two creams, no sugar. I don't get paid for being super-sweet like you do. I'm the ruthless bitch, remember?"

Nadja smiled. Casmir was good at playing a ruthless bitch, just like all the other roles she had perfected in the name of Quest. But that's not who she really was. Out of character, she had a beautiful smile, was extremely generous and had impeccable manners, thanks to her Russian mother, Ruza.

"I thought that was Pasha's job," Nadja teased. "Presenting attitude."

Pasha blinked open her eyes and gave Nadja and Casmir the finger. "I do my talking behind a gun, that's a fact. I don't play dress-up, or straddle my victims. Being a hard case suits me just fine."

Pasha's words had Casmir on her feet and on the defensive. She was the slightest of the three, but fiery nonetheless.

Nadja stepped in front of her friend before she did something stupid—like knock Pasha off her chair. They were all friends, but sometimes the pressures of the job put Cass and Pasha at each other's throat, and they took things too far.

If Polax walked in and found a monkey pile on the floor…again…they were all going to be sitting this one out.

She said, "Sit down, Cass. You two have already been caught fighting once this week."

Casmir touched the faint bruise on her cheek, the last bit of evidence that there had been more than words exchanged with Pasha, then settled back in her chair. "Why aren't you wearing your jacket? Polax is going to say something."

"It's missing a button."

Nadja glanced at Casmir's crisp white shirt beneath her immaculate black suit jacket, then at Pasha who was wearing a similar outfit. "If I'm lucky, he'll be satisfied with seeing it. If he does say something, I'll complain about being too hot."

Casmir's gaze shifted to Nadja's chest. "I wish my blouse fit me half as good as yours fits you." She made a show of sticking out her chest, her modest 32B no match for Nadja's full-figured 34C. "Maybe I should have implants. What do you think?"

"Men like petite women." Nadja pushed Cass's long honey-colored hair off her shoulder and it rippled down her back to tease her waist. "You have gorgeous hair, and rescue-me-please eyes." She fluttered her own to emphasize the fact. "Just look what that combination accomplished with Yurii Petrov, a man rumored to have no heart. He fell in love."

"He wasn't in love with me," Casmir argued. "He was in lust. Anyway, I want to forget that mission. Him."

"I'm sure you do, but he will never forget you. I'm

sure of that." Nadja pointed to the diamond-and-ruby ring on Casmir's finger. "I see you're still wearing the ring he gave you. Why is that? If you're trying to forget—"

"I don't ever want to forget." Casmir held up her hand and studied the priceless bauble on her slender finger. "This reminds me of what can happen when you start to enjoy your work too much. Luckily I came to my senses in time. Yurii was not a nice man."

"There are no nice men, Cass. They only exist in a weak woman's mind."

"I'm beginning to believe that. Who do you think will be going to Austria?" Casmir asked, changing the subject. "I hope it's not me. I just got back from Munich and I'm still trying to catch up on my sleep."

"Unlike you, I was hoping it would be me," Nadja admitted. "But I overslept this morning, and you know how Polax feels about scheduled appointments. He's probably already crossed me off the list for walking through the front door late."

She gave Casmir an oh-well shrug, though in her heart she felt sick about the lost chance. She needed to be on that plane bound for Austria. It was the only way to find out what had happened to Ruger.

"I'll be back with the coffee," she said.

It had been five years since he'd seen her. But Bjorn remembered that night in Vienna like it was yesterday.

He'd been on Onyxx business, and Nadja was most likely on similar business for Quest. Although at the time, who she was or where she worked hadn't been important. The only thing he had cared about when he'd seen her was celebrating the end of a long four-month field mission by getting laid.

He had gone out to a *keller* for a bite to eat and had just finished his meal when she'd entered the small restaurant wearing knee-high black boots, snowflakes in her wild blond hair.

She was breathless, her nose and cheeks as red as her wool cape. It wasn't the same wool cape she was wearing when she stepped into the elevator today, but the similarities had been uncanny. So much so that it had put him back in Vienna in a blink of an eye.

That night she had made a quick search of the *keller*, located the rear exit, then left as quickly as she had appeared. He'd read the signs, knew she was on the run. He'd paid for his meal, then followed her, his plan self-serving. Help her out of her tight spot—whatever it was— then later, if she was willing, out of her clothes.

With that in mind, he'd stepped out the back door just as gunfire erupted in the alley. As bullets ricocheted off the brick walls, he had grabbed her hand and raced for cover.

On the run, she had pulled her .45 from her thigh holster and returned fire. Her smooth moves and unruffled response had assured him that she was no novice at dodging bullets and getting out of tight spots.

It had been cold as hell that night, and after they had eluded the gunman, he had hot-wired a car and driven them to an inn on the outskirts of the city. Inside a spartan room, safe from the outside world and the nasty weather, Nadja had expressed her gratitude as she had pulled the red cape from her shoulders.

He'd suggested a hot shower to warm her up—she

was shivering—and when she'd agreed, he'd gone into the bathroom and turned on the water.

On his way out, and on her way in, she had given him a look. Her sexy soft-brown eyes...the door left ajar...

An invitation?

No man would have seen it differently.

From the bedroom he'd enjoyed the show as she re-moved her boots, then the custom-made Springfield along with the red leather holster strapped to her thigh. He'd watched her slip off her silk stockings and red garter belt. Then her panties and bra.

With each piece she dropped to the floor, his blood had surged hotter and hotter, until... Until he'd stashed his two .38's under the mattress and entered the bathroom.

His plan of sweeping her off her feet hadn't been necessary. He had stripped and stepped into the shower, and had been backed up against the wall immediately. She had put his cock inside her so damn quick that he hadn't lasted three minutes the first time. But then, nei-ther had she. She'd gone off like a firecracker.

The second time had been almost as quick.

But the third...

Polax was wrong about Nadja's endurance.

Looking back on that night, she had never broken a sweat. Not while they had been on the run, or after an hour in the shower. When she'd stepped out, he'd stayed inside. He'd needed a minute to recover from the most amazing sex he'd ever experienced.

He'd shut the hot water off and stood under a blast of cold to clear his head, then emerged from the bath-room minutes later determined to start round two. But to his surprise and disappointment, she was gone. Gone but not forgotten.

With his gift for remembering details, the woman in red had been engraved in his memory for all eternity.

They continued to stroll the museum now, Bjorn in tailored navy blue pants and a navy Henley sweater, his flaxen hair brushing his shoulders. His look—that of a man who had seen more in his thirty-eight years than most men twice his age. Merrick was dressed in his usual all-black attire. A stark contrast to his silver hair and neatly trimmed steel-gray beard.

On the way back to the elevator, Bjorn stopped in front of a narrow window. There, overlooking the River Vltava, he silently considered the situation. He could think of a hundred places he'd rather be in January. It was snowing again, and the temperature was a bone-chilling twenty-two degrees. Austria would be no better.

He hated cold weather. As a kid in Copenhagen, he'd spent too many nights freezing his ass off in dark alleyways. Worse, he hated what those cold nights had forced him to become.

Still, this chilly trip had proven to be interesting. It really was good to see her again. To see that she was alive and looking so well.

He had never met a woman who could match his sexual appetite. But that night she had more than done so. She had driven him over the edge, and followed after him without any hesitation or reservations.

Normally he didn't care about conversing with the women who fell into his bed. But over the years he had never been able to forget the lady in red and the wild, hot sex they had shared in that shower in Vienna. And often he had wondered what she would have said the next morning if she had stayed to wake up beside him.

They were in an elevator headed back into the under-world of the Vysehrad when Merrick said, "It's settled then. We'll tell Polax you've made your choice, and you want the—"

"Brunette," Bjorn injected. "My choice is Pasha Lenova. Polax's rain-or-shine femme."

Chapter 3

Nadja left the conclave and walked to the end of the hall. She was just rounding the corner when she spied *him* standing next to a bank of elevators with his back to her. She knew it was *him*. Knew because there was no way she would ever forget that stance, or that ass— bare or otherwise.

In his sleek dark pants, he owned the stance. Solid and sure, his fair hair grazing his shoulders.

He was talking to a man dressed in black. The man was older, and she recognized him—who wouldn't recognize the all-impressive Adolf Merrick, the legendary Isis from Onyxx?

Nadja slipped back around the corner and leaned against the wall, her thoughts completely suspended. After the initial shock waned, her brain began to toss out questions. The first being, what the hell was *he* doing here with Adolf Merrick? The second, did he know she was an agent here at Quest?

The memory of that night in Vienna and of him washed over her. He'd been amazingly resourceful. On the run together, he'd proven to be a quick thinker, and an even quicker man of action. And at the inn…

Nadja unconsciously licked her lips as her stomach did a flip. She was recalling him in the shower. The size of him and his performance, how she'd reacted to him.

She was suddenly short of breath, and her stomach was alive with butterflies. She hadn't had *that* feeling since…him. Understandable, she reasoned. The man was not only gifted in that area, but he knew how to use what he'd been blessed with. As a result he'd become a professional player. It was the only explanation she had for how she'd responded to him. He could kiss like the devil. And the way he used his hands and fingers…

No man had ever touched her like that—touched to own and possess so completely.

It was true—he had easily owned her that night.

She glanced around the corner to make sure she was seeing everything clearly, but nothing had changed. Merrick was still there, and so was that amazing memorable ass, along with his cocksure stance. She flattened out against the wall once more as the world around her tilted, then plummeted.

Even though she was in shock, she forced herself to remember Vienna. He had come out of nowhere to help her that night. He'd faced exploding gunfire in a back alley and hadn't flinched. Not once.

Of course he hadn't, he was a professional—of another kind. One of Onyxx's special weapons. One of Merrick's rat fighters. Men who were on the left side of human, Polax had once said. Men who ate lead like candy and slept with both eyes open. Men with endless stamina.

Endless stamina.

The kind that could go on all night long…and he would have if she had stayed that night.

Truly shaken, Nadja sucked air slowly. It didn't help. She was going to be physically sick.

"I'd like you to relay my decision," Bjorn said. "I'll wait in Polax's office."

"Are you sure you don't want to meet Polax's beauties before you make your final decision? Ask them a few questions?"

"No. I've made my choice."

"What did I miss? I watched you watch the leggy blonde. You liked what you saw."

"Like I said, I like blondes."

"Most men do."

"Not McEwen. Sly's into redheads with green eyes. Heard from him and Eva?"

"No. Not yet, but I'm confident that when the final lab reports are in, and we're able to confirm the Chameleon's identity, Sly and Eva will suddenly surface from whatever Greek island they're sunning themselves on."

"They're not fishing?"

Merrick snorted. "Would you be fishing if you were with a woman who looked like Eva Creon?"

"It's true. Sly hooked a beautiful femme."

"Are you sure you don't want Q?"

"Like Eva, Nadja Stefn has it all. But that doesn't mean I want to carry around a spring-loaded cock day and night on this mission."

"I see your point. Still, I was sure you were going to choose Polax's candy queen."

Bjorn kept walking. This was for the best, he told himself. He needed to focus on Holic and the file.

"The brunette is Polax's recommendation. She's pretty," he said as if saying it out loud would convince him that he'd made the right decision.

"Have you asked yourself why Polax wants Lenova on this mission? Or maybe a better question is, why does he want his cotton-candy queen left behind? He seemed awfully taken with his bedroom assassin. Maybe he's got something going with her."

"He's not her type," Bjorn said, then wished he hadn't spoken so freely. "Uh, he's too short, don't you think?"

Merrick raised a gray eyebrow. "Short? What does that have to do with it?"

"You're right, it doesn't."

"If Polax isn't screwing her, he wants to."

"We can't fault him if he's got a sweet tooth," Bjorn said, using Polax's own words.

"Someone else who has a sweet tooth is Holic Reznik. I can't imagine Holic walking away from the candy queen. Q is definitely a better choice bait-wise."

Bjorn couldn't argue with that. Holic would be drooling. What man wouldn't be? To deny that their night in Vienna haunted him would be a lie. And that's why sharing a mission with the woman responsible for the picture-album of memories he'd been carrying around for five years would be crazy.

Emotional baggage had no place on a field mission. It was the quickest way he knew of to get your ass fried. And once it was fried, the mission usually ended up in the toilet being flushed, along with the agent assigned to it.

Being fried and flushed held no appeal. He had gotten used to certain things in his life—hot food, clean air to breathe and a bed of his own. The vital three is what he called them.

No room for error. Nadja was out and Pasha Lenova was in.

He needed a kick-ass partner with an ugly attitude, not a ball-handler with velvet-soft hands. A natural blonde, no less, with amazing breasts and hug-me-tight thoroughbred legs.

There was also that lie he had told in Vienna that needed to be skirted. He'd told her he was the owner of a shipping company in Denmark.

Not a complete lie. He had worked on the docks as a boy, and he had lived in Denmark. But as far as owning anything… He hadn't owned more than the clothes on his back for the first eighteen years of his life.

As Merrick turned left and headed for the conclave, Bjorn turned right and started back to the Quest commander's office. Over his shoulder, he said, "Tell Polax that Lenova better be everything he claims she is. Tell him I want her at the airport at midnight. And tell Agent Stefn, Bjorn Odell thanks her for the peep show. It was a pleasure."

Bjorn was in Polax's office staring at monitor C, wondering why the chair that Nadja had occupied minutes ago was now empty, when the door swung open. He turned, expecting to see one of Polax's flunkies enter, but it was Nadja.

He'd just sat down, and now he eased back up and

stood as she kicked the door closed and locked it. She had her Springfield in her hand and it was aimed at his chest.

He said, "This is a surprise."

"Somehow I find that hard to believe, Agent Odell. Bjorn… Hmm… I never really thought you looked like a Lars." She glanced at the wall monitors that could disappear into the wall at the flick of a switch. "Surveillance cameras in the elevator. I should have suspected as much."

"With sound and zoom. If you're curious, even in diffused elevator lighting your ass is still beautiful ten times its natural size."

She digested his words, and Bjorn could tell she was going over in her mind her recent ride into the bowels of the Vysehrad. She had put on quite a show, and she knew it. "I'm not the enemy, Nadja. Put the gun away."

"Why Pasha Lenova?"

She had heard him in the hall. That didn't explain why she was there, but it did explain her question. "Polax says she's top-notch."

"And I'm…?"

"Not an endurance player. Polax's words. He says he handpicks your missions."

"So it's all about endurance with you, then. Are you saying I lack stamina? Did I lag behind in Vienna…at any time?"

She never blinked—not a single eyelash fluttered—even though she knew that her question would require two separate answers.

He glanced back at monitor three. Merrick and Polax had joined the other two women, and Polax was asking Casmir Balasi where Q was.

Her answer was, out getting coffee.

Bjorn turned back to face her.

"It looks like you forgot the coffee." He wondered how much of his conversation with Merrick she'd overheard.

"I heard enough," she said, as if she had telepathic capabilities to go along with her long legs, sweet ass and memorable treasure chest.

"You're a liar, Agent Odell. Either that, or you sold your shipping company in Denmark for more excitement playing spy games. Somehow I doubt that, though."

"You would be right."

"How long have you been working for Onyxx?"

"Long enough. You? How long with EURO-Quest?"

"Long enough to know that if you're with Merrick you're a rat fighter. A real tough guy, *da?*"

Her tone, as well as her quick on-and-off smile, mocked him. Speaking of tough, Bjorn thought, she had developed a crust of her own. And more curves.

She had to be close to thirty now, but the years had only made her more beautiful.

"Do you have an interest in this mission, or did you draw the short straw, Agent Odell?"

"I agreed to the mission."

"So there was a choice? Which means you have a personal stake?"

Bjorn didn't answer.

"Who's the lucky pigeon?"

"The target is Holic Reznik."

She offered no expression on hearing the name. "I read the transcript that came in on his capture in Greece. Were you there?"

"I was there," Bjorn admitted, seeing no reason to

elaborate on the subject, or the part he played in Holic's capture.

"So now you're hunting my fellow countryman again."

Bjorn's ears perked up. "Countryman. I thought you were born in Switzerland, not Austria."

"I was, but I moved to Austria to live with my grandfather at the age of eight. At the time Kovar's home was in Langenfeld. Do you know where Langenfeld is in relation to Holic's home in Otz?"

"Yes."

"That's where Holic Reznik was born."

"Holic is listed as an orphan. His birthplace has never been confirmed."

She shrugged. "He knows much about Otz."

"We know he lived there for a time."

"Do you know where exactly?"

That was the question every agency hunting Holic wanted to find out, but no one knew the exact location of Holic's hideout in the Otzal Alpine.

"I'll take your silence as a no. That's too bad. I could find that cabin in the dark, drunk."

Bjorn studied her face, then her stance. He saw nothing alarming. Nothing to make him think she wasn't telling the truth. Still, he asked, "What kind of game are you playing, Nadja? If you know so much about Holic, why isn't that listed in your file?"

"Because no one's ever requested the information."

"I'll ask again. What's your game?"

"My game is simple. I want to be on that plane bound for Austria. What do you say? Why not grant me my heart's desire, Lars...uh, Bjorn? Let's say...for old times' sake."

She wanted to go with him. To be his partner. Why? What wasn't she telling him?

"I've already made my choice."

"The wrong choice."

"Whether you think so or not. It's my call."

"In the end it will be your call. To your commander to tell him you've changed your mind."

"But I haven't."

"Only a fool would leave behind the map to Holic Reznik's mountain hideout, and I have it." She tapped the side of her head. "It's in here. Let's see…he's been on the run for two days. That should place him very close to his destination. He's no doubt made a phone call already and asked to be picked up."

"Holic trusts no one."

"That's where you're wrong. He trusts someone, and that someone will see to it that he's tucked into a warm bed very soon. He'll be waited on, hand-fed, and within a week he'll be back to his old self."

"Not likely. His hand was seriously injured in Cupata. If Quest has information that can advance this mission, then Polax should forfeit it."

"He can't give up what he doesn't know he has. Like I said, I've never shared this with anyone, until now."

"But you'd share more with me if I chose you for the mission?"

"Grateful is what I would be, and grateful people can be generous."

"And will you be?"

"Yes."

"Why do you want on the mission so badly?"

"I've got a small personal matter in Innsbruck that I need to take care of. It won't take long—a few hours is all."

"Personal shit has no business on a mission."

"I agree, but this can't be helped. It won't interfere with my work."

"Back to Holic, how well do you know him? The truth."

"He spent time at Groffen."

"Groffen?"

"My grandfather's ski lodge. You must not be much of a skier if you haven't heard of Groffen. It's powder paradise. Everyone dreams of skiing Groffen."

"And Holic was there skiing? When?"

"He spent two winters at the lodge out of the four missing in his file."

Bjorn went over the data on Holic that he'd stored in his memory bank. The assassin was an orphan, believed to have lived, at least for a time, in the Otzal Alpine. His file was full of holes, however, and if he remembered correctly—which he always did—the amount of time Nadja said he was missing fit.

"I suppose you've kept abreast of Holic's exploits?"

"Of course. He's listed on the top ten most wanted in the spy world. A legend to some, the devil's son to many."

"And to his wife," Bjorn mused out loud. "I wonder how she feels about his murdering ways."

"I don't know. You would have to ask her."

"And while I'm at it, I should ask her how she feels about her husband's appetite for variety in the bedroom."

She was too cool when she said, "Whatever you think relevant."

"What kind of woman marries a man with no remorse or morals?"

"One who loves him, I suppose."

"Or perhaps one who has been kept in the dark all these years. But then that would make her unbelievably stupid or very smart. Holic is a wealthy man. His debauchery affords her an excessive lifestyle."

"She is neither stupid nor a woman who sanctions debauchery."

"Is that so?"

"Yes, that's so."

"Because you know her so well, right? If you say yes, you would be the only one. She's as elusive as he is." When she didn't answer him, he said, "I wonder if love is worth it."

"Excuse me?"

"You said she loves him."

"No, I said *maybe* she loves him."

"And if she doesn't?"

"Then his death could be a celebration."

"And if she does love him?"

"The gift of freedom can be a wonderful present to an imprisoned soul."

"You don't believe in fate, then?"

"Living a life determined by fate is for passive dreamers who lack the confidence to embrace change and make healthy choices."

"Is that your definition of Holic's mystery wife?"

"Mady Reznik is not a dreamer. She's a brave woman, caught in a storm of circumstance."

Mady... Bjorn's memory zeroed in on the name. In Reznik's file there was no information on the woman he had married. Nothing, but that he had a wife and a child. He said, "They had a kid, right?"

"She was named Prisca after her grandmother. I've

often wondered if she is fair and slight like her mother, or if she's tall with hair as dark as her father's black locks."

The comment convinced Bjorn that Nadja knew things no one else knew. Why was that? Or maybe a better question to ask was, who was Nadja Stefn before she became Quest's bedroom assassin?

She glanced at the third monitor, and her interest made Bjorn look, too. Merrick was telling Polax that they should start without Q because her presence wasn't necessary to conclude the meeting.

Nadja motioned to the high-tech silver phone on Polax's desk. "Pick it up, Agent Odell. Ring Polax. There's a similar phone in the conclave. When he picks it up, ask to speak to your commander. Tell him you've changed your mind. Tell him you've decided on the blonde with the cotton-candy ass."

Bjorn hated to admit it, but he'd be a fool not to take her with him. If she could pinpoint Holic Reznik's hideout, then that would put him back on schedule. Possibly ahead of schedule.

"Pick up the phone, Bjorn. Tell your commander you've had a change of heart. Tell him you've decided to carry around a spring-loaded cock after all." Her eyes found his crotch. "And here I was worried that you might have injured yourself in Vienna. It's a relief to know there wasn't any permanent damage."

Merrick was standing now, clearing his throat to deliver Bjorn's choice. Without further delay, Bjorn picked up the phone and pressed the red button on the panel labeled "Conclave."

Polax's voice sounded. "Yes, who is this?"

"It's Bjorn Odell. Put Merrick on."

"But we're in the middle of—"

"I know what you're in the middle of. I'm watching from a monitor in your office. Put Merrick on the phone."

"A moment."

When the phone was pressed to Merrick's ear, Bjorn said, "The blonde is the better choice. Tell Polax to get Q ready to fly. Tell him—" Bjorn's eyes locked with Nadja's "—she'll need plenty of wool panties to keep her sweet ass warm. The temperatures have been in the deep-freeze there in the past few days."

The minute he hit the button and disconnected the call, she said, "Very good, Agent Odell. Now turn around and face the wall."

"What?"

"Do it." She aimed the Springfield at his heart. "Turn around and face the wall."

He turned and faced the wall just as Merrick announced that Nadja Stefn would be joining the Onyxx mission to Austria. A second later the scent of Alpine heather told him she had come up behind him. She leaned in, and her full breasts pressed into his back. Her gun hand moved over his hip, then down his thigh, letting him feel the hard steel against his leg. She took her time, moved across his thigh and stroked his crotch with the short barrel of her pearl-handled .45—worked his cock until it was stiff.

"It's chilly in the Alps," she whispered close to his ear. "Wool panties are a good idea. Better pack an extra sock for yourself. You wouldn't want to freeze off anything you can't live without. The airport at midnight, then. *Auf bald.*"

Bjorn left the Vysehrad Museum cursing his crystal-clear memory, and the snow that had gotten worse throughout the day. He hated winter. The cold shriveled your dick and made you aware of all your aches and pains. Reminded you of your vulnerability. It made him feel old, and then not old enough because he could still remember what it felt like to be alone and cold.

To be a hungry snot-nosed kid on the streets of Copenhagen.

Still, he didn't hail a cab, opting to walk instead to his hotel in Old Town even though the chill in the air was bone deep. In his room he spent time at the window thinking about Holic, then thinking about Nadja. She had looked amazing today. Curvy and beautiful. So goddamn beautiful.

At six o'clock he joined Merrick in the dining room at the hotel and they shared an evening meal. When the waiter arrived, he ordered a gin martini while his commander requested his favored bottle of Glen Moray. Over food and drink they finalized the last details of the mission. Before Bjorn left the dining room to return to his room, he ordered a bottle of gin to take along with him.

It was nine when he arrived back in his hotel room. More time was spent at the window, more time remembering her, while he smoked half a pack of cigarettes.

He packed after that, and just before he zipped his duffel bag closed, he took a second look inside, his eyes lingering on his socks.

Better pack an extra sock for yourself. You wouldn't want to freeze off anything you can't live without.

Chapter 4

He was going to make it. But then, he had known he would. Holic Reznik smiled even though he felt like shit. But he would eventually feel better. By tomorrow he would be warm and safe, sleeping in a familiar bed, waking up to familiar surroundings.

He used the image of a crackling fire and sweet-smelling pillows to put one foot in front of the other as he came out of the alley. The black SUV had pulled to the curb and he could see the driver's blond hair through the window.

Mady was on time.

The significance in that made his smile widen. His wife had never let him down. Not ever. Why would she? Mady loved him. Would forever love him, no matter what.

And because she loved him she would do whatever he asked of her.

That was why he had married her. Not because he had loved her above all else, or because she was curvy and had a nice ass and firm tits.

The real reason he'd married her was her loyalty. Loyalty was everything. He had only to snap his fingers and she would be there ready to give her life for his if he asked it of her. Even though she knew about his mistresses.

It hardly mattered, though. Her loyalty was not contingent on his. Mady knew her place in his life. Knew that it was a man's privilege to take what he wanted— as much as he wanted, and as often as he felt like it.

Mady had known that from the beginning. Had known that he answered to no one but himself. Knew that whatever he desired, he would take.

Right now what he desired was to be out of the cold and in a hot bath, then a warm bed. He'd been on the run for three days and his hand hurt like a son of a bitch. He was hungry and tired, and anxious to have his wife tend to all of his needs, one at a time.

He pulled the drab gray stocking cap lower over his forehead as he left the alley behind. The dirty black coat he wore, he'd stolen only moments ago off the dead man who slumped against the brick building with his throat slit.

He didn't hurry as he headed toward the SUV. The pain attacking his muscles made every step challenging, but then he'd always been up for a good challenge. Still, he was in bad shape. Possibly the worst he'd ever been in.

His body was on fire, burning up with fever. He steeled himself against the dizziness that threatened to knock him to his knees.

Four feet from the vehicle, the door swung open. He ducked his head and eased into the front seat. He bumped his useless hand and swore crudely.

The word *useless* filled him with a surge of rage, followed by the need for revenge. An assassin with a useless hand may as well turn the gun on himself—but he wasn't going to. Instead he was going to find and kill the man responsible.

Bjorn Odell was going to die screaming. Die screaming while he cut him apart with a dull ice pick and fed him to a dog with a fork.

Mady reached across him and pulled the door shut. As she eased back behind the wheel, he caught the sweet scent of her. She smelled like lavender and a hint of lemon.

He studied her delicate features within the folds of her ugly brown scarf a shade darker than her wool coat. He had instructed her to dress warm, to borrow Jakob's SUV, and to come alone. She had done all three.

For a woman of thirty-six, Mady still had a youthful pixie face, and the blond hair peeking out of her scarf held no signs of gray. It was still a natural honey color, and as silky smooth as the day he married her.

"Drive," Holic demanded. Then he added, "You didn't tell anyone I was back, did you?"

"*Nein.* Not even Prisca. She will be excited, though. For weeks she has been asking when you were going to come for a visit. Are you sure you want to go to Groffen?"

"I'm sure."

She put the vehicle into drive. "We're very busy. It's the height of the season. What if—?"

"Someone sees me? You forget I can disguise myself easily if necessary."

"Why did you want me to meet you here in St. Anton, then? Why not Kitzbuhel or—"

"I have my reasons. Did you ready my suite? The one I requested?"

"I did."

"Then there is nothing to worry about. If I must flee, I will take flight. I always have a backup plan."

"Prisca will be so happy to see you."

"I do not want her to see me for a few days," Holic grumbled. "Not until I'm better."

"Your daughter will not care what shape you are in. Only that you have come home. And for once I think it will be good for her to see that you are human. You have filled her head with grand stories. She talks of you like you are a hero in a fairy tale."

"There is nothing wrong with that. She will never know the truth."

"I know the truth and I still love you."

"You are a rare breed, Mady. Some would say stupid, others would say blindly loyal."

"I'm neither stupid nor blind. You have seen to both. What I am is a woman cursed to love one man for all time."

They left the town of St. Anton behind, and as they began to head toward Zell am See, Holic asked, "How is she? Is my daughter well?"

"Prisca has grown into a beautiful young woman. Otto Breit has come home from Graz often, and swears that one day he'll take her away with him."

"He is ten years older. Too old for my Pris."

"She's nineteen. I was seventeen when you took me."

Holic scowled. "What are you saying, that Otto Breit is sleeping with my daughter?"

"*Nein.*"

"Good, 'cause if he is I will kill him, no matter if he is my friend's son."

"If you confine your daughter, she will grow restless. She must experience life. She is very smart and I trust her judgment. She needs something to nurture."

"Not a babe."

"No, I didn't mean a child, but something that she can be proud of. A career of some kind. We could send her to school."

"I will think on it. Speaking of nurturing, how is the runt? Is your brother's bastard still amusing Kovar?"

"Her name is Alzbet, Holic. And, *da,* she is still at the lodge. Kovar is teaching her to ski. Though she suffers from a cold at the moment. But don't worry, I will keep her away from you. You don't need a cold to compound everything else. What is wrong with your hand? You never told me when you called."

"A few broken bones is all. My hand will heal." Holic set his jaw at the thought of his hand remaining useless. Djorn Odell would pay either way.

He glanced out the window to the rugged countryside. He hadn't been back in Austria for months, and he realized he had missed it.

"Did you get the package I sent you six weeks ago?"

"*Da.*"

"And did you follow my instructions?"

"I bought the computer, and the money is in the safe at Groffen, along with the canister."

"Did you bring me a gun?"

"You know I hate guns."

"Did you bring it?"

"Yes."

Holic smiled. "Is it loaded?"

She glanced his way and frowned. "Of course it's loaded. It would do you no good if it wasn't."

"My thoughts exactly. And just where might this gun be hiding, Mady?"

With his good arm, he reached across the seat and slid his hand into her coat. He saw her suck in her breath as his fingers brushed over her breasts, then moved low over her belly and between her legs.

"*Bitte,* Holic. Not while I'm driving. It is reckless and—"

"Shh… I will touch you whenever, Mady, and wherever. You know I will. Now drive and stay on the road."

"The gun is in my coat pocket," she offered, as if that was going to stop him from his intent.

"A good place for it, for now," he said, finding the zipper on her jeans. Ten minutes later, he removed his hand from her underwear, pulled the dead man's hat off his head and tossed it in the back seat.

His long hair hung limp and damp with fever, slightly diminishing his well-noted rugged handsomeness. But he was still a virile specimen of male masculinity and he knew it—after all, he had the look of a pirate and the reputation to go along with it.

He reclined the seat and relaxed, the scent of Mady and her spent climax hanging in the close quarters inside the vehicle. When a shiver took him, Mady flipped the switch on the heater and a blast of warm air filled the front seat.

He was just beginning to doze off when he felt her hand on his forehead. If he wasn't mistaken, the SUV picked up speed after that, and he smiled again with the knowledge that she did love him no matter what he did.

As the miles came and went his thoughts turned to Groffen. They would arrive sometime tomorrow. Mady would get him there, he had no doubt. After all, she had taken a vow to obey her husband.

Loyalty then…it was the most powerful insurance a man could own. Mady was one of two people he could trust—she and Pris. Yes, his daughter loved him as much as Mady did. But unlike her mother, Pris wasn't afraid of guns.

A smile touched his dry lips and suddenly he had the answer to his daughter's dilemma, and possibly his own. Pris had the patience for it, and she valued perfection. Those were an assassin's two best friends.

Nadja stood below a spotlight a hundred yards from the Learjet that sat on the tarmac at Prague's Praha Ruzyne Airport. It was almost midnight and what gear she had packed fit into a compact carry-on. Whatever else she required she would purchase once she arrived in Austria.

A sharp wind blew out of the west, carrying more snow. Nadja wrapped her red cashmere cape closer to her body.

The weather forecast had predicted a major snow storm for the Alpine region. It would be good for the ski lodges, but not for much else. It could easily bring the mission to a halt for days at a time if the storm stalled out in the mountains.

"Our reputations, yours and mine, are riding on the success of this mission, Q. Do whatever is necessary to complete it as planned. Understand?"

"*Da*. Holic will die after the kill-file is recovered."

Polax nodded. "This mission could be tougher than

anything you've come up against so far. You're working with one of Merrick's best. Trust that, and his ability to back you up. He's damn good."

Yes he was, Nadja thought.

"What's in the file?" she asked.

"Names of agents and powerful people the Chameleon wanted executed. So you see why we must retrieve it. Questions, Q? You look like there's something on your mind. Ask it, so we can get this mission under way."

"Are we concerned that Quest agents are on that list?"

"We know it's likely, but not who or how many. Again I'll say there is a lot at stake here, Q. This mission is going to demand more of you than rhythm, a little moaning and good aim."

Nadja picked up on something in his voice and suddenly asked, "You wanted me on this mission, didn't you?"

"Of course. Except for your adversity to cold weather, you are the best agent for this job."

"But…"

"But why did I suggest Lenova over you? Men like Merrick and Odell don't like being told what they need. They believe they already know."

"It was a gamble," she said, knowing if she hadn't showed up in his office and faced Bjorn she wouldn't be taking the trip.

"Not to worry, Q. I always have a backup plan. There are, however, risks. You don't need to get caught in the middle of a storm, so don't. Don't forget your limitations. You know what they are and how vulnerable they can make you." Polax pulled a phone out of his pocket.

"This will make it possible to reach me if you have to, but only if it's urgent. It's my newest invention. No one knows about it yet, so it'll be our little secret. It's a phone, a computer and a little more."

He showed her the miniature plastic explosives behind a hidden compartment. "Don't make the mistake of thinking that they're too small to do the damage. One charge can put a six-foot hole in a wall ten seconds after detonation. Ingenious, yes?"

"Ingenious." Nadja took Polax's latest invention and slipped it into the inside pocket of her cape.

"I've loaded the necessary data you'll need into the computer chip. It can be accessed by using your PIN number. The data includes information on your partner, and the target. There's a high-frequency text messenger for fast communication with me. It's useless to anyone who doesn't know the codes, so if you lose the phone, Quest won't be compromised. But at the cost of two million a phone, try not to lose it, Q."

"No, sir."

"One more thing. Normally I would tell you not to trifle with a man of Holic's caliber, but as I said before, whatever it takes to recover the file is acceptable. Make the most of every opportunity. You've proven that there isn't a man alive who can resist your charms. It's your trademark, after all. Love 'em and leave 'em…dead, Q. Good luck."

Polax remained beneath the glowing security lamp when Nadja started across the tarmac toward the Learjet. She boarded the jet with false composure, but no one would have been able to tell. Since seeing Bjorn in the corridor at Quest she'd started to play the what-if game. A deadly game she rarely indulged in. But truthfully, seeing Bjorn today had shaken her.

Luckily she'd been able to fall back on her professional training. She'd managed to play the aggressor in Polax's office. She hadn't dared to show any weakness.

Six years ago when she'd joined Quest, she'd had no idea what she was letting herself in for. But she'd soon accepted her role. What choice did she have? She'd become single-minded: do her job—cancel the man beneath her—then return to headquarters. She'd followed the rules without question in Vienna. The bedroom assassin had found her quarry, canceled her target, and was on her way out of the city—when she realized she was being followed.

That's why she'd slipped into the *keller,* and Bjorn had come to her rescue in the alley.

She hadn't needed him to save her. But he had saved her that night in a very private way, and damned her, too.

The truth was, he knew the level of her passion. He knew how she looked naked. How long her legs were and the shape of her breasts. And he knew where she liked to be touched most, and to what degree. He knew where his lips could do the most damage. Knew she had a secret spot on her body that could render her helpless.

But what he didn't know was that all the other men who knew those same facts were dead. Every one of them. She had never had to look into their eyes after she'd given herself to them. Not an hour later, not a day or a year later.

Bjorn had changed the rules that night in Vienna. She hadn't been able to confirm that he was an enemy, and then there was that technicality as to where they had sex—she could honestly say she'd never had a sexual encounter in the shower before that night.

She could say that's what had altered the outcome

of their night together—why she'd let him live—but she would be lying. From the very moment he had taken her hand and led her out of the alley, she had lost some of her ability to think rationally.

She hadn't analyzed it at the time, but now, five years later, she knew what had made the difference, and she felt foolish—she'd been had by a professional, taken in by some of the most basic tricks a man could use on a woman—good old-fashioned experience.

She'd thought she was the one with all the experience, but Bjorn Odell was the master, his touch capable of lighting a thousand fires under a woman's skin.

And the way he used his lips...

Even now the memory of him coaxing her into climax sent raw chills up her spine. Helpless in his arms—that was the only way to explain how she had felt. Helpless and willing to forfeit everything to feel what she had never felt with any other man.

No, she had never wanted to see him again, didn't dare. Not after the way she had shattered in his arms. But that didn't mean she would ever be able to forget the man with the hot hands and the sky-blue eyes.

She wanted to turn around and run from the airplane, but she wasn't going to. She needed to visit Wilten Parish, and if Ruger wasn't there... No, he *would* be there, and he would assure her that all was well—that their secret was safe.

Then he would prove it by saying the prayer that produced miracles and moved mountains. Ruger had saved her once before, and he would do it again.

She came aboard wearing red wool and snowflakes, and the memory it evoked tightened Bjorn's gut. He watched her slip off the cape and toss it on a seat opposite him.

She was dressed all in black under the cape, and he sized her up. Her sweater moved along her curves as if it had been painted on. Her pants, too, fit like a sleek pair of expensive leather gloves. His eyes shifted to her narrow waist, then traveled to the flare of her hips. Then to the junction of her thighs.

He had boarded the Learjet ten minutes early. He had wanted to be seated, waiting for her when she arrived. He was glad he had; the memories of Vienna were making his pants damn uncomfortable.

She took the seat across from him. It required her to step over his legs sprawled in the aisle. He didn't move, but he did inhale the scent of her as she stowed her carry-on beneath her seat. The Alpine heather hijacked another hot memory, and he cursed it and her.

She avoided looking at him, finding something out the window to focus on. That amused him and he shifted in his seat to scan the airport for what had caught her attention. He saw Lev Polax standing in a long coat and flambeau hat below a spotlight. He lingered for only a minute longer, then jerked his hat low over his eyes to battle the nasty weather and walked away.

Still staring out the window, she asked, "When and where do we land?"

"Vienna, in one hour, thirty-six minutes."

His answer pulled her gaze from the window to look at him directly. He held his arrogant, relaxed posture, his legs angled and his ankles crossed, taking up the walkway.

He still wore what he'd had on earlier—his blue pants and sweater. In the seat across the aisle next to her red cape was his navy blue peacoat and a tan wool scarf. His elbow was propped on the arm of the seat, and his chin rested comfortably between his thumb and forefinger.

"Why Vienna?" Her voice sounded flat, and she directed her eyes back out the window.

"I thought it would be a nice way to start off the mission...on familiar ground."

Her head jerked back around. "Is this the way it's going to be with us the entire trip? At each other's throat?"

Bjorn shrugged for lack of an answer. He didn't know why he was pissed. Yes, he did. She had walked out on him that night, and he still felt cheated.

It was true that every man wants what he can't have. That night what he had wanted was more time with Nadja Stefn. More touching and tasting. More holding her and hearing those unforgettable moans that she made.

"Let's try to keep our minds on the mission," she said. "We'll be more effective that way. And for the record there will be no—"

"Heavy breathing? No moaning? No, 'right there, yes...there. Don't stop.'" Bjorn let the words roll off his tongue in his Danish lilt. The very words she'd breathlessly recited to him over and over again.

He'd played with those words in his mind a thousand times.

"Dreams are free," he said.

Her nose lifted, bringing her chin up. She tucked a strand of pale-blond hair behind her ear. She was a true blonde. He knew that because he'd been privy to seeing her naked. He hadn't been shy, no never. A shy man had regrets.

Polax mentioned a tattoo. He hadn't seen it that night

in Vienna, and that didn't make sense to him—he'd touched every inch of her body...looked hard at everything. Remembered everything.

The memory of her body moving against his caught and held him, sending more blood pumping through his veins—through his phallus. They had been tangled in a knot of lust in that narrow shower, and he hadn't ever been a part of anything that damn powerful in his life.

The plane's engine began to sing, and then they were taxiing onto the runway. The snow was blowing like hell and the temperature was steadily dropping.

He had been listening to the weather reports while waiting for her to come on board. It looked like they would be flying into a level-ten storm. That's the real reason he had altered their flight plan and decided to land in Vienna. The airports in and around Innsbruck were all closed.

Once they landed, he would check out the weather reports and see if any flights had opened up. If not, they'd rent a vehicle and drive to Otz.

"In Polax's office you said that you knew where Holic Reznik would head. Enlighten me."

She had heard him, but instead of answering him, she dodged the question and asked, "Are you sure we should be leaving in this weather?"

"I've flown in worse. We'll make it."

He said the words with confidence, though he didn't like the weather outside, or the fact that they could be flying into worse. He wasn't much on flying anyway, although he had done his fair share over the past seven years.

The plane's engine grew louder, and the reminder to fasten seat belts flashed overhead. Bjorn straightened and buckled up as the jet rolled out and headed down the runway. They turned, the plane's engines winding up, and suddenly they were racing down the runway.

Bjorn closed his eyes, hating that someone else was in control at that moment. That was what it was all about for him—giving over his control to someone he didn't know or trust, someone who might be having a bad day or just didn't give a shit if he lived or died at that moment.

The minute the plane was airborne, he opened his eyes and caught Nadja studying him. Their eyes locked briefly and he held her gaze openly.

"You're staring," she said. "Didn't your mother teach you that it's not polite?"

"I never had a mother."

She raised her eyes. "Everyone has a mother."

"It takes more than giving birth to earn that label" was all he said, and all he was going to say on the subject.

Once the plane leveled off, Bjorn unfastened his belt and stood. "I'm going to have a chat with our pilot. When I get back, we'll talk." He paused, gave her a warning look that his comrades had named the "gutted glare." "If you lied to me about knowing where Holic's hideout is, I'll ship you back to Polax the minute we land in Vienna."

Chapter 5

The headache came on halfway back to Washington. He hadn't had one for an entire week. Merrick pressed his fingers into his temples, the pain so severe he felt dizzy. He had taken a handful of prescription pain relievers, but it hadn't touched the shooting pain. It was a good thing he was sitting down.

He was on his third bottle of Glen Moray, but all that was doing was making him see double on top of everything else. But he continued to drink until the plane landed.

Because he was too drunk to drive, he took a cab to his apartment in Washington. He collapsed once he got inside, and ten hours later woke up on the floor to the aftereffects of too much whiskey and the tail end of the worst headache he'd had since he'd been diagnosed five months ago with a brain tumor.

The first thing on his agenda when he picked himself up off the floor was to phone his doctor. Paul was a personal friend, as well as a damn good surgeon.

"Sorry, Adolf, you're not going to want to hear this, but your time is up."

"Can't you give me something for a few more weeks? I'm in the middle of a—"

"You're always in the middle of something, Adolf. You've stalled long enough. You're gambling with your life and I can't be a party to that any longer."

"But—"

"I'm admitting you today."

"Not today."

"Then tomorrow."

"Give me two days."

"Two days, then. Get your affairs in order, Adolf. Then I'll expect to see you in my office at nine o'clock Thursday morning. If you don't show, I'm washing my hands of you. Those headaches are a warning. And they'll keep getting worse. You said this one was bad, but it'll seem like a walk in the park compared to the next and the next."

Feeling worse was hard to imagine. "All right, Paul. Day after tomorrow. Nine o'clock, your office."

When he hung up, he sat down and made a list of what had to be done before he admitted himself into the hospital. Sly was somewhere in the Greek Isles with Eva, and couldn't be reached.

I'll be found when I want to be found, Merrick. When there's a good enough reason to come back.

For the time being there was no reason for Sly to return to Washington. Pierce was in Hungary and Ash in Mexico. That left Jacy. The half Blackfoot Indian was recuperating in the mountains in Montana. But while he was sitting on his ass drinking green tea there was no reason why he couldn't become Bjorn's controller.

His decision made, he headed for his office to see to the details, and by late afternoon, he was in the air again, his plane headed for Big Sky country.

"Are you sure that Jacy Madox is going to let us bring all this equipment into his house? I heard he's kind of funny about people trespassing on his turf. Heard he was once in the Hells Angels or something like that."

"They call it territorial," said Vic Krandle, dusting a piece of lint off his dress pants. He was one of Onyxx's top physical therapists, but he was also a connoisseur of fashion. "And up here they don't call what he lives in a house. It's a log cabin, right, Merrick? Most likely a twelve-by-twelve with an outhouse out back. Which brings up the question of how we're going to fit all this equipment in such a small space."

"You'll have to make it fit" was Merrick's answer.

"I heard he's one of those loner types," Tommy the technician said, pulling his stocking cap lower over his ears. "The kind of guy you don't want to piss off or feed red dye number sixteen to."

Merrick glanced over his shoulder to the two men he'd brought with him to transform Jacy Madox's mountain *cabin* into a high-tech information center. Thirty minutes ago they had landed the plane at the nearest airstrip, then climbed into a helicopter.

Merrick was hopeful that this was going to work. Bjorn and Jacy were as close as brothers, and he intended to use that to his advantage. Even in a wheelchair Jacy was mentally up for the challenge. In fact it would be good for him—get him back into the swing of things.

The last mission had left Jacy with his knee blown to bits. Five surgeries later the prognosis wasn't outstanding, but he still had his leg.

He'd called Jacy and told him he was flying in today to see him. He'd made it sound like it was a social call—his commander checking up on one of his rat fighters.

"There, sir. I see it. Down there, in the trees."

They had just come over a mountain range of treetops covered in snow. Merrick saw Two Medicine Lake, the landmark Jacy had given him. The cabin was a hundred yards back from the frozen water. The area was surrounded by giant pine trees, and there was one lone road leading up to it. But it was the kind of road that only an all-terrain vehicle would be able to maneuver.

The cabin was bigger than he had envisioned. It wasn't anything elaborate, but it wasn't a one-room shack with a couch that converted into a bed, either. Merrick smiled over that—the six boxes were going to fit just fine. A coil of smoke drifted from a rock chimney and there was a black pickup parked not far from the back door. He motioned for the pilot to take the helicopter down—there had to be a flat piece of ground somewhere.

This is the middle of nowhere, sir," Vic said.

"Just the way Jacy likes it" was Merrick's reply.

"How's he going to take us dropping in?" Tommy asked.

"We'll know soon enough." Merrick noted the worried looks exchanged between the two men.

"Maybe you should call him and tell him not to shoot us before he knows who we are."

"He knows I'm coming," Merrick assured them.

"But what about us?" Tommy asked. "Did you mention us?"

Merrick grinned. "You're part of my surprise. You and those six boxes of equipment."

"Shit," Tommy said.

"Double shit," Vic Krandle muttered.

He might be an asshole, but Nadja was being a royal bitch, Bjorn thought. She had refused to tell him the exact location of Holic's hideout—the one she claimed she could find in the dark, drunk—her excuse being that once he knew the particulars he wouldn't need her anymore and he'd ditch her.

Not only had she refused to talk about Holic, but she had refused to talk to him altogether, saying that she was too exhausted at the moment to think clearly. That she hadn't slept well the night before and could use a nap before they landed.

She was either playing a game with him, or she'd lied through her teeth about where they would find Holic. He couldn't believe she would lie to get on this mission, but he would never underestimate a woman who carried a custom-made .45 under her skirt.

She had reclined her seat and closed her eyes soon after telling him he needed more patience. No, what he needed was to stop remembering how well they had fit together in that goddamn shower.

Bjorn contemplated his situation. He was two days behind the other agents hunting Reznik. He had a partner he didn't want, a lover he couldn't forget, and they had just landed in the middle of a freeze-your-ass-off blizzard.

"The day just keeps getting better and better," he muttered.

"Did you say something?" Nadja asked, unbuckling her seat belt.

She raised her arms and stretched, arching her back. Her breasts said hello, and the fitted black sweater moved upward high enough to expose her flat stomach and the shiny diamond stud in her belly button that winked at him.

Bjorn stared. That stud hadn't been in her navel five years ago, and that made him curious as to what else was new. Again Polax's words came to him. *She has an amazing tattoo. It's in a place I call the dead zone.*

The winter storm was still raging as they left the airplane. If it didn't subside by morning they would be forced to rent an all-terrain vehicle, and hope that the roads between Vienna and Innsbruck were open.

Bjorn spied the taxi he'd arranged to meet them. It was a van of sorts meant to accommodate six to eight people. It was only the two of them, however, and two pieces of luggage.

He said to Nadja, "That blue van over there is ours."

He saw her shiver, then pull her cape closer as a gust of wind swirled around them. It prompted another memory—the two of them on the run through the streets of Vienna. It had been snowing then, too. Damn cold as they had dodged flying bullets to stay alive.

The similarities prompted Bjorn to say, "A shower would sure feel good about now. It would warm me up, and in your case, thaw out that cold shoulder you've been giving me since we left Prague."

His words caused her to stop abruptly and turn around to glare at him. It was the only thing that saved her from being shot in the head.

The familiar *pop* from a sniper's rifle broke through the night. When the bullet whizzed past Nadja's head, she immediately shoved Bjorn to the tarmac, then joined him, making herself as flat as possible.

She pulled her Springfield and raised her head to see that Bjorn had rolled and come to his feet. In a low animal crouch, he had drawn his weapon and was now searching his surroundings.

His unflinching courage was a rare thing, a visible sign why he'd been named a rat fighter, and she wondered how she had missed that five years ago.

He remained in the crouch, as if defying the sniper to take another shot. The sniper accepted the challenge and a shot rang out, sending a powder puff of the snow six inches from her left shoulder into the air.

Nadja heard Bjorn swear, then he came out of his crouch. Yelling at her, he ordered her to get her ass up and run like hell to the van. The words were barely out of his mouth as he spun on his heels and shot out the security lights leading to and surrounding the van.

She scrambled to her feet and sprinted across the tarmac, her red cape flying around her long legs. She never doubted for a minute that Bjorn was close behind her.

Two more shots confirmed the gunman was using a night-vision scope on his rifle. The second shot shattered the back window of the taxi van.

She reached out and slid the door open, and was scrambling into the back bench seat when Bjorn tossed his duffel inside. It bounced off the other side door and landed at her feet. A second later he was diving inside on top of his bag.

The door was still open, when he yelled at the cab driver, *"Schnell! Schnell!"*

The cabby took off, as anxious to get out of the parking lot as they were. The van shot forward and made a left that caused the vehicle to career around the corner on two wheels. The vehicle rocked back, jarring Nadja almost off her seat. Then they were racing out of the lot and past the glassed-in terminal at breakneck speed.

After Bjorn pulled his legs inside the van, Nadja leaned forward and shoved the door shut.

Once they were through the airport gates and settled on a route heading toward Vienna, the taxi driver asked, "Where are you staying, Frau Larsen?"

Nadja heard the question and recognized the name. Irritated that he would use the same name he'd used five years ago, she kicked Bjorn where he sat on the floor in front of her. He grunted in pain at the force of her boot connecting with his ribs.

"*Ja*, Frau Larsen," she said in a heavy accent to mimic the driver, "where are we staying?"

"At a pension in the heart of the city," Bjorn replied. "Nossek."

"*Sehr gut*, Herr Larsen. Nossek, nice place. *Beeilen Sie sich?*"

"I think hurrying would be a good idea," Bjorn agreed. "Unless you're interested in early retirement. The permanent kind, if you get my meaning."

"*Sehr gut*, Herr Larsen."

The van picked up speed.

The pension Nossek was quiet, the rooms small but clean. The best news of all was that they had arrived in one piece.

Bjorn had had his doubts after the taxi driver had damn near rolled the van on his way out of the airport, and damn near put them in the ditch twice after that.

There had been no mention of the broken back window when the taxi driver dropped them off. He'd barely hung around long enough to collect his fare.

Bjorn had stayed at the Nossek before. When he'd called ahead and made the reservation, he'd asked for his usual room on the second floor. It offered a clear view of the street, and the second exit was less than a minute away.

Another reason he was fond of this particular pension was that each room had not only a shower, but a bathtub, as well. As soon as he checked out the place, and was satisfied it was safe to get buck naked, he intended to spend half the night in that tub thawing out his frostbitten bones—he had nearly frozen to death in the van with the back window shot out.

He felt old tonight. Far older than thirty-eight. He tugged on the collar of his coat and adjusted the duffel bag that weighed heavily on his shoulder as he followed Nadja up the stairway.

"Why didn't you pick up my bag, too? You had time to grab yours, but not mine?"

They were the first words she'd spoken to him since they had climbed out of the van and registered at the desk as Mr. and Mrs. Lars Larsen.

"I guess I was too busy chasing your ass to worry about your makeup bag."

She glared at him, swiped the key out of his hand and lengthened her stride as they cleared the landing. They were staying in room six, and he followed her inside after she unlocked the door.

He dropped his gear to the floor. "Don't get comfortable until I make sure this place is all ours." He unzipped his bag and pulled out a second gun—a Ruger target side. He attached a night-vision scope and walked to the window. Bringing the gun up, he searched the street using the scope, then the rooftops directly across from the pension. Once he was satisfied he lowered the gun, took a step back and pulled the shade, then the curtains.

He left his coat on while he checked out the room. He ransacked the place, searching for electronic bugs stuck under the corner table and behind the two scenery pictures on the walls. He checked for C-4 strapped to the bed springs. He even took the phone apart. The closet got the same treatment, as did the bathroom.

The sniper at the airport had been unexpected. He'd also been a lousy shot, but maybe that was part of his or her game, Bjorn thought. They weren't the only ones after that kill-file. The race had started two days ago— the minute Holic Reznik had escaped—and the rules were, there were no rules.

He heard her sigh heavily, then she said, "One bed. I hope you enjoy sleeping on the floor."

"I don't, and won't be."

"We'll see."

"We will."

It was going to be a long night, Bjorn decided. Nadja's mood was in the crapper, and his was no better. But his reasons were better than hers. He was back hunting Reznik, a man he'd already caught once. He never liked doing anything twice. Well, that wasn't true. There were definitely things worth doing over and over again. He glanced at Nadja's long legs, let his mind wander for a minute, then his eyes.

A minute later he was back on track, wondering who had shot at them. He'd changed their flight destination at the last minute, so no one had known they were flying into Vienna except Merrick and Polax.

He turned his head to the side and the movement reminded him that he needed to tend to his injury. He shrugged out of his coat and dropped it to the floor, then his scarf. Hefting his duffel, he walked into the bathroom, only this time he closed the door behind him.

Merrick, Tommy and Krandle made their way up the snow-packed trail leading to the cabin surrounded by mountain peaks. The helicopter pilot had set down a quarter-mile away, on the only semi-flat piece of ground they could find.

The air was crisp and the lake beyond the path was frozen and desolate looking. Winter had definitely come to the Montana mountains.

Just as they reached the steps, that famous voice that Merrick had always referred to as "the voice that could unsettle the dead" effectively stopped them in their tracks.

"That's close enough. State your business where you stand."

Merrick could vaguely make out Jacy in the fading sunlight where he sat on the deck in his wheelchair. He wore a sheepskin jacket and jeans and a beat-up cowboy hat pulled low over his eyes. He looked surly and in no mood for company. But then, that was Jacy; he always looked like he had a toothache.

"I've come to ask a favor," Merrick said as his two counterparts slipped behind him.

"I don't do favors. Never really did until Onyxx decided to play dirty. But now I'm done with that. All done."

What he was referring to was the way he had been recruited. Onyxx had made a deal to wipe his criminal slate clean if he would come on board. If not, they had been prepared to lock him up and throw away the key.

"I know that's what you said you wanted in the hospital, that it was over, you working for Onyxx. At the time I felt obliged to let you have your way. You needed some recovery time."

"You don't see me walking, do you?"

"So how is it going, the recovery?"

"Like I said, you don't see me on my feet, and if that's what you came up here for, you've seen me in this thing, and now you can leave."

"I mentioned a favor. It's not for me. It's for Bjorn. He's in the field again."

"What the hell is he doing there? I thought Onyxx set him up in a desk job running profiles."

"He took the job, that's true. And he'll go back to it once…he runs down Holic Reznik."

Jacy swore. "The son of a bitch escaped. Is that what you're telling me?"

"He escaped," Merrick confirmed.

"Who's Bjorn's partner on this one, or is everyone on it?"

"All the boys are on missions of their own. Pierce is in Hungary, and Ash is in Mexico. Bjorn has been teamed up with an agent from Quest."

"Quest? You're shittin' me."

"No. He's being backed by a female assassin."

"How did that happen?"

"It's a long story. I'll fill you in over a cup of coffee."

No invitation inside.

Merrick tried again. "I hope Bjorn doesn't do something stupid on this one. He was damn upset when he learned Holic had escaped."

"I don't blame him. I read the report. He's lucky that he walked away from that last mission. He could easily have been sitting beside me, or dead. Reznik is an elusive son of a bitch. He's an assassin with more than nine lives. He's never missed a target."

It was all true. Bjorn was going to have his hands full.

"He's gettin' too old for field duty, Merrick. You shouldn't have let him take the job."

"He knows Holic better than anyone else at the Agency. They have a history."

"You're talking about that kid he tried to save a few years back. The one Holic shot anyway."

Again, what Jacy was saying was true. Bjorn had tried to save a young boy from the assassin's bullet. He'd been there, had had the kid in his arms. Holic had shot the kid anyway, and the bullet had passed through the child's body and had gone through Bjorn as well. A piece of the bullet still remained in his spine.

"That old wound Bjorn carries around is a sour reminder that he failed that kid," Jacy pointed out. "Where Holic is concerned, Bjorn doesn't always think things through before he reacts."

A string of vulgarities followed Jacy's words. Then Merrick heard the familiar sound of a shell being injected into the chamber of the hunting rifle that had been laying across Jacy's legs.

"I ought to blow your head off, Merrick. Bjorn shouldn't be the one going after Holic. Not this time, and not with some stranger backing him. A woman, no less."

"If you feel that strongly, there's a way you can help out, if you're willing."

Jacy pointed the rifle. "If I'm willing to do what? Crawl?"

"Take it easy. This is the deal. I'm scheduled for surgery in two days. The problem is, I had planned to be Bjorn's while he's in Austria. I need you to agree to take the position while I'm laid up."

"From this chair?"

"Why not? I would be sitting at my desk, so you can sit here in your cabin. I've brought you a technician wizard, a crackerjack physical therapist to speed up your recovery, and all the equipment you'll need for both."

"And if something goes to hell, and Bjorn needs a pair of legs?"

"He has a pair of legs backing him. Long, thorough-bred legs. Did I mention she's blond?" Merrick smiled, then turned serious. "This can work, Jacy. Give it a chance. I thought you and Bjorn were friends."

"Cheap shot."

Merrick shrugged. Waited.

More profanity rolled off the deck.

Pushing Jacy was a gamble. He didn't push easy. Then again, Merrick didn't have a whole lot of choices at the moment. He needed a reliable man, and Jacy was as reliable as Maalox. Even from his wheelchair this was something he could do, and do well.

He heard the safety mechanism click on the gun. Watched Jacy relax the rifle across his lap. Then, without a word, Jacy turned his wheelchair around and pointed it toward the cabin door. He gave a sharp whistle, and a few seconds later the door swung open.

"How did he do that?" Vic asked. "I thought you said he was living up here by himself."

"He's one spooky son of a bitch," Tommy whispered. Merrick started up the stairs as Jacy disappeared inside.

He crossed the deck and reached the door, then stopped
when an animal that looked more like a wolf than a dog
blocked the entrance.

Chapter 6

Nadja hung her cape in the closet, and as she turned she saw that Bjorn had left his coat on the floor. She scooped it up along with his scarf, her intention to hang it with hers in the closet. But when her hand came away covered in blood, she stopped, examined his coat and knew immediately what had happened—Bjorn had been shot.

She replayed the scene at the airport in her mind, detailing each frame as if she'd filmed it. She accounted for each gunshot. There had been four. The first two had missed her by less than an inch. The fourth had taken out the van's rear window.

But the third...

Nadja spun around and grabbed the doorknob leading into the bathroom. She didn't bother to knock, or announce that she was on her way in. She simply barged inside, her voice clearly announcing her anger, if not her arrival.

"Why didn't you say something?"

He turned before she got the words out, a .38 aimed at her chest.

She ignored the Beretta and scanned his body looking for the hit. He'd been standing at the vanity, his torso naked, a bloody washcloth floating in the sink. There was blood matted in the hair on his chest. A trail of blood moved over his collarbone.

He said, "That kind of entrance usually buys a bullet." He laid the .38 back on the vanity and turned to face the mirror again. "You in a hurry to use the can?"

"I asked why you didn't tell me you were hit."

"I wasn't hit."

He angled his neck and that's when she saw it— blood oozing from his torn flesh.

She tossed the blood-soaked scarf at him. "Partners share everything, Odell…."

His eyes found hers in the mirror. "Everything?"

"Everything that matters involving their mission." She walked up behind him and examined the wound from behind, then she locked eyes with him in the mirror once more. "No, you weren't hit at all. I'm just seeing things, right? Your neck isn't really ripped open. And this isn't real blood." She swiped at the blood with a slender finger.

"It's blood, but—"

"But you weren't hit?"

He turned and let her get a front view of the two-inch wound. "If I'd been hit I'd still be carrying lead," he said. "Tell me I've missed it."

"You're an asshole."

"The bullet only tickled me."

"Tickled you?"

"I felt it, that's all," he explained. "It touched me."

"You're touched, all right. Are you sure it didn't touch you in the head, too?" Nadja glanced down at his open duffel. He had an extensive first-aid kit sitting on top, and a number of prescription bottles. "Do you always travel with a drugstore at your disposal?"

"It can't hurt. You never know who is hiding in an alley."

He had deliberately brought up the alley. He was going to batter her with that memory the entire trip?

She scowled at him, then squatted to rummage his medical supplies. She located a needle and thread, gauze and a scissors. One by one she took them out and placed them on the vanity.

"It's not going to stop bleeding without stitches."

"Excited about causing me more pain?"

Without looking up at him, she said, "You flatter yourself, Odell. Not much excites me these days. Certainly not spending the evening in a hotel bathroom sewing up your neck. You're supposed to avoid flying bullets, not step in front of them."

"If I hadn't stepped in front of this one, it would have taken the back of your head off."

She had been reaching for the needle and thread. She stopped and glanced up, studied his face in the mirror. Was he serious?

Suddenly a grin parted his lips. "This reminds me of another time and place. How about you? Remind you of anything?"

"Actually, no. It doesn't bring back a single memory."

"That's too bad. My memory is crystal. Should I share?"

"No, thanks." She turned away and headed for the door, determined to let him bleed all over himself the entire night.

She was almost through it when he said, "Six stitches should do it."

She stopped, looked over her shoulder. "You're Mr. Survivor. Sew up yourself."

"I would, but the angle's wrong."

"That's too bad for you, isn't it."

"Weak gut? The smell of blood make you sick? Which is it? Or is it the thought of touching me that's bothering you? I don't see why. It didn't seem to bother you five years ago. In fact—"

"Shut up."

"Come on, Nadja. Help me out. You said partners share everything. Lend a hand, for the sake of the mission."

She held his gaze for a moment, then shifted her attention to the wound. He was testing her, and if she didn't pass the test there would be more coming at her until she proved to him that she wasn't going to crumble under pressure.

She glanced at his neck. He was right. It would take six stitches minimum. Eight would be better, and there would be less scarring if she went left to right.

She wished he needed twenty stitches; his asshole smile was starting to grate on her. She wanted to wipe it off his handsome face with a hard slap.

She returned to the vanity and picked up the needle. A test indeed, she thought, one she was going to pass with flying colors.

They were going to be spending days and nights together, and she had better get used to the scent of him under her nose, as well as the sound of his voice echoing in her ear.

"Sit down, and shut up—" She pointed to the toilet seat.

When he settled, she came forward with the needle in one hand and a cotton swab moistened with rubbing alcohol in the other.

Resigned to what she had to do, she ran the threaded needle over the alcohol swab, tossed it in the garbage, then straddled his thighs.

His body was rock hard, and it regenerated a vision of them in a shower. She was conscious of her heart pounding, and his. Conscious of the fact that his expert training would key on the slightest change in her manner if she wasn't extremely careful. She willed herself to wiggle on his lap—to prove to him he wasn't the one in control.

She continued to wiggle, rock back, once…twice. The third time she felt him, felt him solid and hard between her thighs. She wet her lips, tried not to remember what he looked like naked.

She said, "Don't make any sudden moves, Odell. This needle is sharp and I don't want to hurt you…much."

He was naked, but he didn't remember being stripped and put to bed. There were several blankets covering him, and they felt good. He felt safe.

Holic blinked awake, and when he saw Pris, he smiled. "You've changed your hair, and you're even more beautiful then I ever thought possible. Your mother said so, but—"

"Never mind about me, Father. How are you feeling? Mama said you've been hurt, and I've seen your hand."

Holic fumbled with the bedding and reached out with his good hand. She took hold of it and bent her head and kissed his palm, then pressed his hand to her cheek and held it there.

"Mama said not to worry, but you've been sleeping for an entire night and one whole day."

He dismissed what she was saying and continued to stare in appreciation. It was true, there had been significant changes in Pris since he'd seen her six months ago. She had always been a pretty child, then a stunning teenager. But in the six months his beautiful daughter had grown into a regal swan.

Mady had warned him that he would be surprised, and he was. They had done well making their daughter, a child he hadn't wanted. No, not at first. But now…

Oh, yes, he wanted her now. She had Mady's gentle smile, but her dark eyes and black hair were his, as was her flawless olive complexion. He liked that, seeing himself in her. Liked having his seed so prominently displayed.

Pride filled Holic. He had never wanted to be a father. When Mady had told him she was pregnant, he had been furious with her stupidity. He had wanted to strangle her that day. Nine months later he had wanted to strangle the baby.

But he hadn't, and now Pris was his most sacred possession. His flesh and blood.

"How do you feel? Are you in pain? Your hand—"

"Will be fine. Where is your mother?"

"Mama had to go downstairs. Some problem in reservations. What do you need? I'll get it. I'm yours for the entire day."

Holic smiled. "Such a generous and obedient child."

"I'm no longer a child."

"A slip of the tongue."

"Are you hungry? I had stew sent up. And Sacher torte."

"Mady's chocolate cake is very good."

"I made it this time. I'm almost as good a cook as she is now. Can we talk?"

"About what?"

"Your accident. How it happened?"

"It was work related. That's all I can tell you."

Years ago he had told his daughter that he worked as a government assassin. He had wanted to teach Pris an appreciation for guns, and it had been a way for him to do that without explaining his work in detail. The idea had proved to be a brilliant one. They target practiced when he came home for visits, and they had built a special bond that was now unbreakable.

"My injury will keep me here a while to convalesce."

"Here at Groffen?"

"Why not?"

Prisca's smile lit up the room. "I just thought you would go somewhere warm. You do that sometimes."

"I wanted to see you."

She beamed. "How long will you stay?"

"As long as it takes for my hand to heal."

She continued to smile at him. "Do you realize that in the time we've spent together you've never told me what your favorite color is, or your favorite food. How crazy is that?"

Holic didn't have a favorite color or food. He said, "Red, I think I like the color red best. Bright red. And to warm my belly, your mother's *apfelstrudel*. Now answer a question for me."

"All right."

"Have you been still practicing?"

"I knew you were going to ask me that."

"And?"

"Every day, just like you said I should."

"Then you've improved?"

"You'll have to decide that. But not for a few days. There's a storm outside and it's shut down almost everything. But as soon as it moves off, I'll show you what I can do. Are you hungry? Do you want some stew now?"

Holic glanced down at his useless hand. There was still numbness and swelling, and he feared what that meant. A bloody curse on Bjorn Odell, he silently vowed. A bright red bloody curse.

"Don't worry. I'll feed you until your hand gets better. It will get better, won't it?"

He had fallen asleep in the bathtub drinking Sebor, the Czech version of absinthe. The famous "bad stuff" could peel paint, or put you six feet under in one damn big hurry if you drank too much of it.

He hadn't wanted to die, he'd just wanted to be put out of his misery for a while. To be transported somewhere else was what he'd needed after Nadja had finished with him on the toilet seat. She had taken great pleasure in driving that needle into his neck ten times. Or had it been a dozen?

But that hadn't bothered him nearly as much as the pain she'd caused him below the waist. That lap dance she'd done on him had been both heaven and hell.

He hadn't needed his bones warmed up after that, or anything else for that matter, but he'd climbed into the bathtub nonetheless with the Sebor.

The bottle had gone down smooth and easy. It had eventually killed the memory of her ass stroking his crotch, but only because he'd passed out. Passing out wasn't normal for him. His system was used to potent liquor, even rotgut. But he had definitely passed out.

The other thing that wasn't normal was the pounding headache he'd woken up with. It felt like someone had used his head for target practice.

What the hell had he been thinking? Someone had just tried to kill them at the airport, and he had answered back by getting stinking drunk and scrambling his brains with Sebor.

If there was serious drinking to be done you did it in a safe environment—on your own time. He knew the rules. He was the one who had written the bible.

See, this was why he should have chosen Polax's rain-or-shine brunette. Mistake number one had just been made. He reached for his pants and pulled them on. Still feeling like crap, he walked out of the bathroom and into the bedroom. The room was cast in shadows, and he remembered that he'd drawn the shade and the curtains when he and Nadja had first arrived. He focused his eyes on the bed. It was empty.

In that split second he realized that he was on a roll—mistake number two had already been made. He'd trusted Nadja to keep her ass in the room.

She should keep going, Nadja thought as she drove into Salzburg headed for Innsbruck. But the memories were too strong and they pulled her off course. Before she knew it she was heading for the river, a lump swelling her throat.

For a moment she thought she was going to cry, but

she couldn't. Numb, then. That was all there was left inside her, an empty numbness.

The snow was still coming down, so heavily that she couldn't see across the River Salzach. It had been a slow drive from Vienna, but the roads were open.

She pulled to the curb, letting the engine idle. She sat there a long fifteen minutes before she pulled back onto the road and crossed the river.

She took the principal thoroughfare, Getreidegasse on her way to Stift Nonnberg. The route was laden with memories, and with them came a deep sadness.

She parked out front and went inside to inquire at the front desk. She asked for Sister Catherine, then waited while a young woman left the desk. A few minutes later an elderly nun appeared, but it was not Sister Catherine.

"I'm sorry, *Fraulein,* but Sister Catherine left the convent."

"She left?"

"She took a position in Innsbruck a few years ago."

"Do you know which convent?"

"She didn't go to a convent. She accepted a private position. I'm sorry but I can't tell you more than that. *Verzeihung.*"

"No, wait!"

The nun turned. "I contacted her once through Father Ruger at Wilten Parish. Maybe he'll be able to help you."

"Father Ruger? Are you sure?"

"Yes."

A dozen questions followed Nadja out the door. She left the city, keeping a close watch on the weather and the rearview mirror. With any luck Bjorn was still passed out in the bathtub at the pension and fate would continue to rescue the night.

Still, Bjorn would be furious when he woke up and found her gone. More furious if he learned that she'd spiked his Sebor with a sleeping pill from his traveling pharmacy.

Nadja reached into her pocket, pulled out her phone and left Bjorn a message. He was not a man to trifle with. He was a rat fighter after all. One of Onyxx's resilient badasses.

That's why she wasn't going to fool herself into thinking that a little pill and a bottle of Sebor would slow down Bjorn Odell for long.

The smartest thing to do was plan for the worst.

The message read, "Meet me in Salzburg at the Bergland at midnight. Room six. Nadja."

The message would have been believable if she wasn't heading southwest out of the city on the main highway, Bjorn thought.

The tracking device he'd slipped into the hem of her red cape last night on their ride to the pension was steadily blinking. He glanced at his watch, then checked the map.

It was obvious she was playing a game with him. The question he needed answered was, was it her game, or an agenda assigned to her by Polax?

Bjorn flipped open his cell phone and punched in Merrick's number, but instead of hearing his commander's New England accent on the other end, Jacy Madox's rusty voice came over the line.

"Hey, bro, how's it hangin'? Or isn't it? From what I hear, the weather there can shrivel a prune."

"You heard right," Bjorn agreed. "What are you doing picking up Merrick's private phone? You're not back in D.C., are you?"

"No. I'm still in Montana."

"Where's Merrick?"

"In the hospital."

"Hospital? He and I have business going on and he's in the hospital? What happened?"

"He got a bitch headache on the flight back that knocked him on his ass. When he got here he still looked wrung out. He called his doctor and the doc told him he was out of time. That he needed the operation pronto. I know about your business with Holic. You're back hunting him. That's why Merrick came to see me. I guess I'm watching your back from here if you'll have me. You know I'll do whatever I can to help you."

Bjorn smiled as he continued to follow the route Nadja was taking as she bypassed Kufstein on E-60. "You know I'm all right with it."

"So what is it you need? This call must mean you need something."

"A cross-check on Lev Polax. I want to know who he's worked with in the past, and who, besides us, he's working with now."

"Is there a problem?

"Last night a sniper was waiting at the airport."

"I'll get on it. You all right?"

"*Ja.*"

"How about your partner, the blonde?"

Bjorn winced. He should have known Merrick would mention she was blond. "She's fine."

"Just fine? I did a little checking on her for you. Wanted to make sure she could back you up in a tight spot."

"And are you satisfied?"

"She's got dead aim, but then if she's—"

"*Ja, ja.* How can she miss at such close range," Bjorn finished.

"Something else wrong? You sound on edge."

"I'll acclimatize."

"To the blonde or the weather?"

"Both."

"Okay, so I'll see what I can find out about Polax."

"Outside of Merrick, he's the only one who knew we were flying into Vienna."

"I'll check it out."

"How's the leg?"

"It hasn't rotted off yet."

"That's a good sign. I'm glad you agreed to watch my back, Jacy. Call me when you get something."

"It's a date."

Chapter 7

Nadja waited until dark before she entered the church. She had watched people come and go for two hours at Wilten hoping to recognize one of them as Ruger. He hadn't shown yet, but maybe he was already inside.

The church was cool and the amber sconces on the walls set the tone. It was a beautiful church, stained glass scenes and candles lit.

She slipped into a pew at the back of the church waiting for her eyes to adjust to the lighting. There was a rectory behind the church, living quarters for the priests. Ruger could have entered the church from a side door and she'd missed him.

She was anxious to see him, hadn't in four years. This was the way it had to be. They had known that, after the agreement they'd made. Still, she missed him. The letters weren't enough. They said nothing, only let her know that all was well without saying it. But now the routine had been upset, and Nadja wanted to know why.

Because of the situation, she would speak to her brother here in the church. She would visit him like a repenting soul would, and that way nothing would draw attention to her.

She watched a woman leave the draped confessional and another woman go in. Minutes later a man traded places with the woman. Then a young boy.

She couldn't remember when she last had gone to confession. She must have been fourteen or fifteen. No, she was twelve. It was the day after she'd slipped out of the house to follow Mady to meet her boyfriend.

When the boy left, so did the priest, and another cloaked figure took his place, but it wasn't Ruger. This priest had a cane and walked bent over.

She waited another forty minutes as more people visited the confessional and the priest with the cane. And then he, too, left, replaced by a priest who walked up a side aisle as if he'd come from the back door. Nadja only caught a glimpse of him before he was inside the wooden confessional. But this priest was taller, walked upright, and there was something about his walk, something familiar.

A rush of relief had Nadja on her feet. It was Ruger. He was here.

She kept her pace natural and unhurried as she left the pew and headed up the side aisle. There was no one waiting, and she slipped behind the curtain, anxious to take a seat on the bench. It was dark inside, save for a single candle that glowed in a sconce on the wall.

"Father?" When there was no answer, she said again, "Father, are you there?"

"I'm here."

The voice that came through the slotted window was all wrong. Ruger had no accent—especially not a... Danish lilt.

Nadja started back up off the bench, but before she could get to her feet, the lilt froze her where she sat.

"Sit down, Nadja." Then the window slid to one side to reveal Bjorn Odell in a priest's cloak.

"You asshole."

"Shame on you. Swearing in church."

She started to stand again, but she didn't get halfway up before he raised a short-barreled gun and aimed it at her.

"Shame on you," she mimicked. "Waving a gun around in God's house.

"We're a pair, *ja.* Two peas... You have a dirty mouth and I have violence on my mind."

"Go away for an hour," she said suddenly. "Give me—"

"No."

"This is the personal business I mentioned. One hour and—"

"No."

"I need to talk to—"

"Me, right now," he cut in, "or that violence I mentioned could get out of hand."

"Later."

"Now, or..."

"Or what?"

"I'll make a scene. A bloody scene."

"You wouldn't."

"You don't know me that well to gamble, do you?"

She didn't, and so she relaxed on the hard bench. She

forced herself to look straight at him. "You were suppose to meet me in Salzburg."

"That was your plan, not mine. But then, I would have been waiting there a long time. You never did intend to meet me there, did you?"

"Eventually, yes. After I finished here. Where is it?"

"Where is what?"

"I'm obviously wearing a tracking device. That's how you followed me. Where is the bug?"

He ignored the question and asked his own. "Who are you meeting here?"

She would have to tell him something. A portion of the truth would be best, but...

"A lie wouldn't be a good idea right now. Anything less than the truth and this partnership is over. So be... careful."

"You don't understand."

"No, I don't, but I'm going to. I don't like surprises. So out with it. Why are you here?"

"I told you, personal business."

"That tells me nothing."

Nadja hesitated too long, and he swore sharply.

"I'm shipping you back."

"No! You can't do that."

"I can and intend to."

"Okay, I'll tell you the truth."

"Again I caution you to think before you speak. We're already two days off the pace. Are you aware of what's in those kill-files? If they get in the wrong hands—"

"I know what's at stake. I know where Holic is. We can be there tomorrow if everything works out here tonight. So go away for an hour."

Nadja knew the importance of the kill-file and the impact it could make on the intelligence world once the killing started. Once this was taken care of with Ruger she would be able to concentrate on the mission, and they would be successful. She had what they needed to put them well ahead of the other agents. All she needed was an hour with Ruger.

"This is bullshit. I've lost another day chasing your ass instead of Holic's. If I don't start getting the right answers soon, Nadja, I'm going to tie and gag you and send you back to Polax in a box."

He looked mad enough to do it. Mad enough to accept no less than the truth. Maybe there was a way to appease him. To offer some portion of the truth.

"I have a brother," she began. "He's a priest here. We've always kept in touch. We write to each other four times a year. But his routine changed several months ago, and I need to know why. I need to know if he's all right."

"So that's it? You're worried about a brother who's a little late answering one of your letters?"

He was such an asshole. "He's not just a little late."

"This is bullshit. You're stalling. You don't know where Reznik is, do you."

"Yes, I do. I'll take you there tomorrow. I was the right choice for this mission, Bjorn. I didn't lie."

"Let's go."

"No. Not yet. As long as we're here I want to see if Ruger's still in residence. He's got to be here."

"Didn't you check the rectory when you got here?"

"No. I didn't want anyone to—I wanted to see him here."

He gave her a skeptical look. "Need to confess something? Worried about making it through the golden arches?"

"You mean the pearly gates," she corrected. "And no, I'm not."

Quest's bedroom assassin in a confessional? Yes, she supposed it looked ridiculous. A mockery is what it was: her seated on this side and Bjorn on the other side outfitted in a priest's robe. The devil's brigade.

The truth was her soul had been lost a long time ago. She'd sold it to Kovar for a second chance at life.

"Get up. We're leaving."

His voice was gruff, and she stood slowly. When she stepped out of the confessional, he was there to take hold of her arm. He loomed over her, his surly mood evident by the jut of his unshaven jaw.

She wondered if he'd woken up with a headache, or if his stitches were too tight. Any normal man wouldn't have been able to stand after the Sebor and the pills, and would be more than a little stiff-necked after the way that bullet had torn up his flesh.

But this was Bjorn Odell, she reminded herself. He wasn't average, in any respect.

Not in or out of the shower.

"I wasn't lying," Nadja said as they left the rectory after speaking to a parishioner named Father Osip. "He couldn't look me in the eye. He knows where my brother is. He wasn't telling us the truth. He knows more, and if you would have let me—

"Let you what? Pull your .45 and threaten his life?"

He had let her go to the rectory and inquire about her brother. Why, he didn't know. They had wasted another hour, but they weren't going to waste any more. He'd appeased her and now it was over. They were going to get back on track. They had an assassin to hunt and a kill-file to recover.

"I wasn't going to shoot him, just scare him a little," she admitted.

"He wasn't going to tell us more even if you had shoved the barrel of your gun up his nose."

She ran after him, sped past him and turned, forcing him to pull up and stop. "You don't know that."

Bjorn jammed his hands on his hips beneath his pea coat. "Listen, I don't know why your brother isn't here, and I don't care. It's time to forget about this personal stuff and concentrate on the mission. Frankly, that's all I care about, that kill-file and pumping a bullet into Reznik's evil hide."

"The priest was lying. If you're any good at profile work, you saw that, right? The way he couldn't look at us when he said he didn't have Ruger's forwarding address."

Bjorn sidestepped her and started toward the SUV. "It doesn't matter."

"It doesn't matter? Of course it matters." She was close on his heels. "Ruger wouldn't have willingly left the church without a good reason. I'm worried that something has happened to him. Something terrible."

Bjorn turned back and she slammed into his chest. He reached out, grabbed her and saved her from being knocked on her butt.

She shook off his hand. "What do you want? Do you want to hear me beg?"

"It might be amusing to watch, but it won't help."

"Ruger would have written to me and told me he was moving if that was his plan."

"Maybe he was in a hurry."

"It's been over eight months."

Bjorn started toward the rented vehicle again. It had stopped snowing and there was no reason why they couldn't drive all night. He was wide awake, thanks to a gallon of coffee, and they were headed in the right direction. Otz wasn't more than three hours away.

He opened the door, looked across the hood. "Like I said, the mission is our first priority. After that's finished—"

"I can't work distracted like this."

He had climbed into the driver's seat. Now he buzzed down the passenger window. "Get undistracted, Nadja. If you can't manage that, then be prepared to be sent back to Prague."

"Asshole!"

"Okay, I'm an asshole. The truth is I don't care what you think of me. I only care about one thing right now—getting this mission started, and finished. Once we accomplish that, you can call Polax and ask him for a few weeks off to run down your brother. Who, by the way, obviously doesn't want to be found or he would have left you a forwarding address. Now, get in!"

"You have no heart. You're…"

"Really pissing me off," Bjorn warned. "You don't want to do that. Now get that cotton-candy ass of yours in the car."

She just stood there.

"Which is the fastest route to Otz?" Bjorn asked, hoping she would see how futile it was to challenge him. This game of hers was over and he'd won.

"Which way to Otz? Hmm…" She shrugged, sucked on her lower lip. "You know, I'm just not sure anymore. Like I said, when I'm distracted I can't think straight."

"Bitch."

"Asshole."

Bjorn swore and glared at her through the open window. Not even his Onyxx teammates would have dared push him when he'd clearly warned them off and given them the gutted glare. But here she was standing up to him.

"Since we're here I don't see why you can't help me break into Father Opis's office and see what he's hiding. Who knows, maybe a few answers to my questions will clear my head. It's just a thought."

Was she crazy? He had told her he was through with this bullshit and here she was trying to bargain.

"Look—"

"No, you look, Odell. Either we play this my way, or you send me back and spend the next two weeks checking out a dozen false leads. And while you're wasting time, the kill-files will probably fall into the hands of some rebel fascist group."

He could strangle her with his bare hands. His eyes must have relayed his thoughts because she angled her head to expose more of her neck.

"Go ahead."

Bjorn muttered under his breath, glanced at the church. There were three entrances, and two into the rectory. The locks were lame and the security lights poor. It would take less than five minutes to break in.

He buzzed up the passenger window and got back out of the car. "All right. Thirty minutes. That's all I'll give you once we get inside. And if you don't find anything—"

"I'll find something."

"Either way, before we go back inside, I want to hear you promise that whatever we learn in there is going to be put on hold while we refocus on the mission. Say it. Promise me we're back on the hunt for Holic in thirty minutes."

"I promise."

She was a poor liar, Bjorn thought. For a woman who was so damn good at so many things—lap dancing included—her voice lacked conviction when she lied.

So why was he still going to help her break into Father Opis's office?

Bjorn had insisted on going in first. Nadja had let him, imitating his quiet steps as they entered the church through a side door that had a burned-out security light.

They moved swiftly but quietly, and within minutes they were in the hall moving toward Father Opis's private office. The hall was pitch-black, and Bjorn suddenly produced a small flashlight from inside his coat.

They located the office and slipped inside. The bank of files stood along one wall, and together they quickly began sifting through them. But after rifling through two nine-drawer file cabinets, they had come up empty.

Bjorn whispered, "There's nothing here. If he worked here, they don't want anyone to know it."

The comment stunned Nadja. "He did work here. They can't cover that up."

"They can and have. Maybe he was renounced for during something wrong."

"Ruger didn't...wouldn't do anything wrong. He doesn't have an immoral bone in his body."

"They say that kind of behavior runs in the family. Maybe a little bit of you rubbed off on him."

"You're saying I have immoral bones?" She tried to push past him, but he deftly put her into the corner and leaned in.

"Easy, Q, your fangs are going to get in the way."

"In the way for what?"

He stared at her lips, and it was obvious what he was thinking.

"Let me go."

When he didn't, she attempted to raise her knee, but he outmaneuvered her, dodged her firing range. Then he grabbed her arm and spun her around. She ended up facing the wall with Bjorn snug against her ass.

"I did what I said I would do. I gave you thirty minutes," he whispered in her ear. "Now you're going to do what you promised. We go back to work."

"It's obvious you don't have any family or you'd understand my worry. I've sent Ruger letters for the past five years. He's been a priest here at Wilten Parish longer than that. He couldn't have done anything wrong to be asked to leave. And if he had, he would have written and told me."

A door slammed out in the corridor. Bjorn swore, then he released Nadja and doused the flashlight. Together they hurried through an open archway looking for a place to hide.

In a corner stood a private confessional lit by a lone candle. Bjorn shoved Nadja into the space, then unhooked the drapes and let them fall. He spun around as Nadja blew out the candle.

She felt him next to her, and they came together quickly. He wrapped his arm around her and face-to-face, body to body, they both listened as the office door opened. There was a glow along the edge of the drape confirming that someone had entered the outer room and had turned on the desk lamp.

A chair squeaked.

A heavy sigh.

They waited, then waited some more—another thirty minutes—both breathing in a metamorphic state to keep from being heard.

Suddenly the chair squeaked again, and then the light went out. A door opened. Closed.

More minutes ticked by, but neither Bjorn nor Nadja moved. There was no reason not to. The danger had passed, yet they remained fused together, breathing together as one until it became awkward and Nadja whispered, "He's gone."

"And so are we," Bjorn agreed. "In a minute."

Then he kissed her.

The kiss lasted longer than a minute, and left Nadja wanting more—so much more.

Finally he released her and stepped back. "Before this mission is over, I'm going to have you in the shower, Nadja. That's a promise. Now we're out of here."

He took hold of her arm and hurried her out of the office, then from the church. When they reached the SUV, he let her go and rounded the vehicle.

"Get in."

Nadja debated her next move. She didn't want to call Groffen, but what choice did she have? Nothing got past Kovar—he would know if something had happened to Ruger. She didn't want to involve him in this, but maybe if she was careful not to raise suspicion...

She couldn't shake the feeling that something was wrong.

She pulled her phone from her pocket just as Bjorn climbed into the SUV and turned over the engine. She opened the door and stuck her head inside. "I'm making a phone call. I'll be just a minute."

"Who are you calling?"

"No one you know" was all she said, then slammed the door closed and quickly dialed the number.

"Groffen Lodge. How can I help you?"

Nadja hesitated, not expecting to recognize the voice on the other end. She felt her heart slam against her chest, felt breathless and chilled at the same time. She glanced back at the SUV to make sure that Bjorn was still seated inside and hadn't buzzed the window down again.

He was there behind the wheel, but he was watching her through the window.

She turned away. "Mady, is it really you?"

"Yes, this is Mady. Who's calling, please?"

Nadja closed her eyes and took a deep breath. "Oh, Mady," she breathed, "it's so good to hear your voice. What are you doing at Groffen?"

There was silence for several long seconds. Then the woman said, "Nadja?"

"Yes, Mady. It's me. It's your sister."

Chapter 8

"You're going to have to trust me," Nadja said, not willing to give an inch.

Bjorn was out of the car, his hands on his hips, and he was furious. "Trust is earned, and you haven't come close to earning a damn thing except a quick trip back to Prague. You said Holic would be in Otz. Now you want me to believe he's in Zell am See. I don't think you know where the hell he is."

"I didn't say he was in Zell am See. I said he was near there."

He was going to strangle her. This time he would do it. He had cause.

"What kind of bullshit are you trying to feed me now? One minute you claim Holic's at his hideout in Otz, and the next minute you're saying he's somewhere in Zell am See."

"*Near* Zell am See."

"Whatever!"

"I can't explain this to you right now, Bjorn. I can only tell you that if you head to Otz it will be a mistake. It's true yesterday I thought he would be at his mountain cabin in Otz, but I was wrong. You're already mad at me for wasting precious time, but you'll be wasting a lot more if we head to Otz. Holic didn't go home. Trust me when I say that. But if you can't, then go, but I'm not going with you."

"Who did you call?"

"I can't say."

"But I should trust you anyway."

"Yes."

"Holic is near Zell am See?"

She nodded. "Enjoying the warmth and comfort of a soft bed. Once we get there, I'll find out which bed exactly. While everyone else is looking for him in Otz, we'll be back on schedule. That should make you happy."

What would make him happy was if she would keep to one story and stop disappearing on him every time he turned his back on her.

He studied her, picking up vibes. The phone call she'd made had shaken her. Which meant it had netted her information she hadn't expected. Was that information Holic's true location, or was there something else she wasn't telling him?

"If I'm lying this time you can send me back to Prague."

"And don't think I won't," Bjorn promised.

"You won't need to, because this time I know exactly where Holic is."

"This time?"

"I thought he would go home. He was ill and needed care. Care from his wife. Yesterday I believed home would be the hideout at Otz. Today I've learned that Mady and her daughter are no longer living in Otz."

Again she referred to Holic's wife with a strange kind of familiarity. Bjorn continued to wonder about that.

"They're living near Zell am See."

"Yes."

"And you know where?"

"Groffen."

"Let's go." Bjorn turned and started to round the front of the vehicle.

A second later a gunshot rocked the still night, then Bjorn, dropping him to his knees.

"The operation will take a minimum of three hours, Adolf. Is there someone you would like me to call? Someone you would like here waiting for you when you wake up from surgery?"

"No. Let's just get it over with, Paul."

Merrick turned from the window, his face pale and his head pounding. The headache he'd flown back from Prague with was back, attacking the walls inside his head like a jackhammer.

It was a good thing Jacy had agreed to walk with Bjorn. His brain was so scrambled he would never have trusted himself making coffee, let alone handle important data on a timeline.

Once Paul had left, Merrick made one phone call. Rubbing his temple, he called the corner flower shop he used and made arrangements with Sarah, the store owner.

"This is Adolf Merrick calling."

"Adolf, uh…Mr. Merrick. Are you going out of town again?"

"No, but I won't be available to deliver the rose to Johanna for a while. I was wondering if you could do it for me."

"Of course I will. For how long?"

"Maybe two weeks, but it could be longer."

"All right, I'll bring Johanna the roses for two weeks, and if you need me longer you can let me know."

"I'll do that."

"Is everything all right? You sound tired."

"I'm not, just preoccupied."

"Another headache?"

Merrick smiled through his pain. Sarah was perceptive, he would give her that. "As a matter a fact, yes, I do have a headache."

"But through it I've made you smile."

"How can you tell?"

"I can hear it in your voice."

"I've decided to have the surgery, Sarah." He had told her about the tumor. He didn't usually open up to strangers, but Sarah was easy to talk to, and she had pulled it out of him.

"That's wonderful Adolf…Mr. Merrick. That's why you want me to see to Johanna's roses."

"If there's a problem this time, I'll—"

"There won't be. Johanna will have her roses."

"If the surgery doesn't go well, and—"

"It will go fine, but if not, don't worry. I'll continue to see to the roses."

"Thank you, Sarah."

"You're welcome. Until you call me, two dozen

long-stemmed apricot Loving Touch roses will be delivered to Johanna at Pleasant View Cemetery. I'll be saying prayers for you, Mr. Merrick."

"I'll give you a number just in case."

"All right, but I won't need to use it. You're going to be fine."

Merrick gave Sarah the number of Jacy Madox's mountain cabin, and when she asked him when he was having surgery he gave her the time, then disconnected.

He'd done all he could, and seen to all that was important to him. Bjorn had his back covered by Jacy, and Johanna would have her roses. Now he could have the surgery.

To Sarah, the roses for Johanna weren't all that was important where Merrick was concerned. He needed someone at the hospital waiting for him when he woke up. Wanting to be that someone, she made arrangements to have her father come into the shop that afternoon, and arrived an hour before the scheduled surgery.

She made no fanfare as to who she was waiting for. She sat quietly in a corner chair in the surgery waiting room with her rosary in her hand, and her thoughts on the handsome gray-haired Adolf Merrick.

She sat mindful of what she'd allowed to happen—she'd fallen in love for the first time in her life. She was thirty-eight, too old to have let something like this happen, and yet unable to stop the feelings from growing each time she saw Adolf Merrick.

It was insane. She hardly knew him. Outside of his coming to the flower shop on Saturdays, she never visited him. Still, it was love that filled her, bittersweet love.

The heart never consulted the head in these matters, she reasoned. The heart loved who it loved, and she, Sarah Finny, loved a man who would forever be tied to his dead wife. A man whose love and loyalty ran deeper than an ocean.

Sarah waited six hours to learn the outcome of Merrick's surgery. Although there had been some unforeseen complications that would keep him in the hospital longer than anticipated, Dr. Paul was optimistic.

Adolf Merrick would recover.

The weather turned to shit thirty miles from Kitzbuhel. And that wasn't the worst of it. The gunshot that had torn a chunk of flesh out of Bjorn's thigh had also damaged the radiator on the SUV. The result—Bjorn and Nadja were now on foot six miles from nowhere.

Two miles into the walk Bjorn sensed something was physically wrong with Nadja. His own leg was hurting like a son of a bitch, but he'd lived through worse, and would live through this. But his partner was struggling with what looked like a nasty limp.

The temperature was minus twenty, and the snow that had dropped hours earlier was now swirling wildly. Visibility was poor, and the poor conditions were magnified by subzero temperatures that brought with them the threat of frostbite.

"So what's the problem?" he called out as they continued to follow the deserted road. "What's wrong with your leg?"

"Nothing. What's wrong with yours?"

"You know what's wrong with mine. I was shot."

"Not tickled?"

"Cute."

"You should have let me look at it before we left Wilten."

"There wasn't time." Bjorn glanced back to see Nadja tucking her cape closer to her body. She was wearing leather gloves, but she didn't have a hat. "I'm not going to bleed to death."

"No, but the chances are pretty good we could freeze to death."

She was definitely limping. He said, "What's up with the limp?"

"I'm not limping."

To prove it, she lengthened her stride and passed him by. Bjorn let her, and took the opportunity to focus on her gait for the next fifty yards. He conceded that she was no longer limping, but that didn't mean she hadn't been earlier.

He sped up and fell into step with her, his duffel slung over his shoulder. His thigh wound wasn't serious, and it was true he wasn't going to bleed to death, or need stitches, but he was damn uncomfortable. But mostly he was cold.

"How are you doing cold-wise?" he asked. "Can you feel your feet and hands?"

"Yes."

"Nose?"

"It's all good."

She took the lead again, and that's when he noticed the limp was back. This time he didn't say anything. He just kept moving, and watched her try to cover up whatever was going on with her left leg.

Polax had boasted that Nadja was the queen of pain, and if that was true, then there was something seriously wrong.

An hour and a half later they came to a sign that read, Nordzum Ski Lodge. The secluded winter retreat resembled a small village nestled into a valley surrounded by lit-up powder-perfect ski runs.

Bjorn strode past Nadja and headed for the two-story main lodge. His feet were tingling, and Nadja's limp had worsened, though he hadn't verbally acknowledged his observation. But that didn't mean he was ready to ignore it. As soon as they got settled he would contact Jacy and put him to work digging up everything that had been left out of Nadja's file at Quest. And there sure as hell had been things left out.

Again it made him suspect Polax. What was he hiding?

Nordzum Lodge was northwest of Zell am See, and had some of the best ski slopes in the Kitzbuheler Alpen. Nadja knew the place well. She'd skied there often—Kovar had insisted on it to mix up her routine at Groffen. The slopes weren't as fast or as beautiful as those she'd grown up on, but she had enjoyed the change.

The main lodge was surrounded by six small chalets. It was more spread out than Groffen, but beautiful. Few ski lodges, however, compared to the size and grandeur of the famous Groffen.

Nadja followed Bjorn into the lobby and watched as he wrangled at the front desk with a young clerk. She suspected there would be no rooms available, so when the clerk summoned someone with more authority, she wasn't surprised. After all, he was dealing with Bjorn Odell the asshole.

But what did surprise her was the man who slipped

behind the desk moments later. Rune Stein had been the owner years ago, and it looked like he still was.

She was right. There were no rooms available within the main lodge, or the surrounding chalets, Rune acknowledged.

"I'm sorry, Mr. Larsen, we're full. But I can see you need a place to stay. You came here on foot, you said?" He eyed Bjorn's bloody pant leg. "Need a doctor?"

"No. It's just a scratch."

"You say it was car trouble that put you on foot?"

"That's right," Bjorn agreed. "Our vehicle broke down between here and Innsbruck." He turned and pointed to Nadja. "My wife is exhausted. If not a room, how about a rental car to take us to the closest town?"

"The roads are closed. Should be open in the morning. I tell you what, I do have a loft above a storage site near the lift station. I've offered it before under emergency circumstances. You're welcome to it at a reasonable rate."

"We'll take it," Bjorn agreed.

Rune drove them to the site himself, and led them up a staircase inside the storage building. Once he opened the door, he stepped back, and Nadja got the first glimpse of a sparsely furnished but clean second-story room.

The good news was that the room had a double-wide bed, a fireplace, a table and two chairs, a large porcelain bathtub, a toilet and a bookshelf. The bad news was that everything, including the toilet, was in the same room—there was no divider and not an ounce of privacy. The toilet sat like a king's throne in the corner, and the deep old-fashioned claw-foot tub sat on a raised platform.

Determined to make the best of it, Nadja turned to Rune. "*Danke,* Mr. Stein."

"You're welcome, Mrs. Larsen."

Rune angled his head. "You look familiar to me. Guess it's that pale hair of yours. It reminds me of this sweet gal that used to ski here years ago. You don't see that color of hair very often. The girl was an excellent skier."

"Was? What happened to her?" Nadja asked, glancing over Rune's head to look at Bjorn.

"She had a ski accident that ended her skiing for good. Always thought her grandfather pushed too hard."

Nadja closed her eyes for a moment, suddenly back on the slopes that chilly, horrible day in Zurich, setting her skis to take the corner at sixty miles an hour. Setting them, and knowing she wasn't going to make it. She'd sailed off the course and hit the fence. When she came to, she had no idea what happened.

The memory of the pain shocked her back to the present and she blinked open her eyes. Her old life was over and she was now living a new one. And in this new life Ruger was missing, Mady and Prisca were at Groffen with Kovar, Holic was nearby, and she was going to be spending the night locked up in only one room with Bjorn.

She touched her lips, remembering the kiss he'd given her at Wilten Parish, remembering the promise he'd made her afterward.

No, she wasn't going to let Bjorn get under her skin, or under anything else, for that matter. She was going to concentrate on Mady and what she was going to say to her when they saw each other.

She hadn't seen her sister in fifteen years.

"What do you think, *Frau?* Will the room be adequate? I wish I could offer you and your husband something better, but—"

"It's lovely. Clean and quiet." She glanced at Bjorn. "We love it, don't we."

He lifted one eyebrow. Nodded. "Love it," he mimicked. "Thank you."

Nadja walked in, checking her leg before putting all her weight on it. She was not going to limp. That showed weakness, and she wasn't weak.

No never.

"Once your *herr* gets a hot fire roaring you will like it, *Frau.* There is plenty of blankets and furs." He motioned to the thick fur rug on the floor in front of the stone fireplace, and a stack of blankets folded on a wooden bench at the foot of the bed.

"The tub is *dere,* and wood outside by the door."

"I saw," Bjorn answered, making his presence known.

"If you get bored with each other…you can always read a book," Rune chuckled as he motioned to the bookcase. He backed away. "Meals are served in the main lodge, or delivered as you like. The menu is over *dere* on the table. There's a phone downstairs on the wall to place an order. *Guten Abend.*"

Bjorn nodded. "Good evening, and thanks."

Once Rune was gone, Nadja eased down on the bench to remove her boots. She heard Bjorn mumble something about firewood but she didn't look up as he left to get an armload. She rubbed her toes to circulate the blood, then went to run water into the tub. The only way she was going to get the circulation back in her leg was a hot bath. The doctors who had put her back together after the accident had clearly had their work cut out for them. The nerves had been severed in her left leg and the prognosis was that she would never walk again. But that had been unacceptable to her grandfather—after all, Kovar lived to watch her ski. To ski and win.

He had insisted they do whatever necessary for her to walk again. Walk and run, and ski—ski with the same grace and speed she once had.

Her leg felt numb now, and it hadn't felt like that in a very long time. She wasn't worried, however. No, she was healthy, and the leg was sound. She just needed to get the blood circulating again.

Bjorn came through the door and kicked it shut behind him. He crossed the room with an armload of kindling and began to build a fire while Nadja located a towel and dropped it on the floor near the deep porcelain tub.

She said, "You need to attend to your leg."

"Later. I'm hungry."

She watched him unbutton his coat and rested his hand on his hip. He looked tired, and yet as rugged and solid as a mountaintop, even with his injured leg so glaringly evident—the blood was frozen to his pants and it looked awful.

"They make deliveries," he prompted. "I'll call in something. What do you want?"

"Some soup and *mélange*. I need to warm up from the inside out."

While he went down to order the food on the phone downstairs, Nadja stripped off her clothes and slipped into the tub.

Holic didn't like the way Mady was acting. Something was wrong. If he had to ferret the truth out of her she was going to feel his anger instead of just hear it in his voice.

"What have you heard?" he demanded. "You've been as jumpy as a cat since you walked through that door. What's going on downstairs? What are you hiding?"

"I'm not hiding anything. I'm just tired. It's busy this time of year and we're always shorthanded. Prisca has been on the run all afternoon."

"That explains why she hasn't come by this afternoon. She was supposed to come back after lunch to talk."

"Talk about what?"

"Her future."

He watched as Mady's eyes turned wary.

"What do you have in mind for her future?"

"I'm not sure yet."

"I think you are sure. Tell me."

"She says she's been practicing every day. Her skills are improving."

Mady shook her head. "No. I won't let you make her into you. No!"

"Do not raise your voice at me, Mady. Pris is my daughter, and I'll do with her as I like."

"She is mine, too. Please, Holic. Please don't do this."

"My hand isn't mending like it should. It may never. I need someone I can trust. Who better than my own flesh and blood? My Pris?"

"Please, no."

"Forget about the food you brought, and come sit beside me. Come."

He watched her come to him and sit on the edge of the bed. Her eyes were wide and she looked frightened.

"Lie down beside me," he coaxed, tugging her forward.

"No, I don't want to."

"But I want you to. Lie down."

She stretched out beside him, and he rolled to his side. He raised his bad hand above her head to keep it from being bumped, then slowly drew his wife to him with his good arm. Her blond hair was pulled back from her face, and he reached up and stroked the blue vein that was pulsing at her temple. Then he brushed her cheek with the back of his hand. Trailed his knuckles over her jaw. Stroked his long fingers down her neck. Massaged each of her breasts.

Mady enjoyed his hands on her. Most women did. He knew how to trick them into thinking they were beyond special. Manipulation was one of his specialties. That, and being the best marksman in Europe.

He would say in the country, but Adolf Merrick held that title. The commander at Onyxx had been the best damn government assassin ever born. But like himself, Adolf was going to have to relinquish the spotlight before long because Pris was going to rise to the top very soon. As soon as everything was in place, and she understood what was at stake.

"Holic, about Prisca—"

"Shh…"

His hand slid back up over her left breast, over her collarbone. He curled his fingers around her neck, squeezed until it registered that he was through talking.

He said, "Hear me Mady, I say this for the last time. Pris is my daughter. I will do with her what I think is best. Whatever I like, and what I would like is my daughter taking over my business." He squeezed tighter, enough to make Mady's eyes grow even wider. "Now I want to know why you're acting so jumpy. The truth this time. Has someone come looking for me?"

She shook her head, unable to speak.

"Any inquiries by phone?"

She again shook her head, but this time she raised her hand and tried to pry his fingers away from her throat.

He released her, not in the least worried that she would scramble off the bed. She tried to speak, but nothing came out.

"Swallow," he instructed. "That's it. Again."

He massaged her throat. Kissed her lips.

Finally, she whispered, "I read in the newspaper that a man in St. Anton was found in an alley with his throat slit. There's an investigation going on to search for his killer. Are they searching for you, Holic? Did you kill that man in St. Anton?"

He should have expected as much. Mady was worried about him. He grinned. "Of course they are looking for me. I needed a disguise, the weather had turned sour, and I had a fever. Did you bring the paper so I could read the article?"

"Yes. It's on the counter."

"Good. Is that it? All that is bothering you? That useless drunk in St. Anton?"

"What if they track you to Groffen?"

"The knife I used to slit his throat is still in St. Anton, clear of any fingerprints."

"But what if—"

He pressed a kiss to her forehead. "The men hunting me expect me to crawl into a hole atop a mountain like an animal. To hide in some desolate region with miserable conditions, but I have no intention of giving up my comfort while I convalesce. No. I will eat like a king and sleep in a sweet-smelling bed. Only a fool would hide out in a crowd, or a very smart man certain of himself. I am that man, Mady."

She nodded. "If you say so."

"I do. Now, then. I need you to do something for me."

"What is it?"

"I need you to find Jakob and tell him to go to After Shock and bring me back a playmate."

Mady stiffened.

Holic touched her cheek. "Now, don't get upset. You should feel relieved that I don't expect you to play my games, Mady. They degrade a woman of your sensitivities, and as my wife and the mother of my child, I would never want to do that. I have too much respect for you. Now, go to Jakob and tell him what I said. He'll know what I expect."

"Holic, please. Not here at the lodge. Pris is only a few doors away. What if—?"

"Go now."

"I've never said anything about your appetite for variety, Holic. But please, this is where we live, and I can't—"

"Enough, Mady! Go find Jakob, and give him my message."

A half hour later Holic was visited by a smiling green-eyed long-legged blonde from After Shock, Groffen's underground pleasure club. She had pierced nipples, a talented tongue and a gift for making a man feel reborn.

Chapter 9

The food will be delivered in thirty minutes. We're lucky, the kitchen's open until midnight. We just made it, so—"

"So…" Caught naked, Nadja was just climbing out of the bathtub when Bjorn came through the door. He slowly closed it, continued to stare.

She did what any good bedroom assassin would do under the circumstances. She put her professional training into play and stood her ground.

True, this was Bjorn who had surprised her, not a would-be victim she'd been sent to seduce then kill. Nonetheless, her mastery of the game was second nature, no clutching her bosom or gasping like a caught virgin.

Virgin… Nadja pushed the word from her mind. Virginity was overrated. Sexual knowledge was power, and it wasn't exclusive to the male gender.

She towel-dried herself, then headed for the bench at the foot of the bed. There, she retrieved one of the soft blankets.

But she didn't hurry. That wasn't how it was done—a woman who knew her value, as well as the minds of men, didn't hide her assets. She embraced the power and the knowledge.

She took the blanket on the top of the pile, a soft chenille in a powder blue, and unfolded it slowly. Slipping it around her shoulders, she didn't look at him when she asked, "Did you remember to order my *mélange?*"

"We had to settle for the special, stew and dumplings, but your order for milky coffee is on its way. Like I said, it should be here in thirty minutes."

He had been gone close to that while placing the order. Nadja questioned that. It certainly didn't take that long to order stew and dumplings, and a couple of drinks.

She wrapped the blanket around her body and turned to face him. She couldn't tell by looking at him what he was thinking, if he was hiding something from her. He was too skilled to let his feelings show unless he wanted them out in the open.

He didn't trust her, that she knew for sure, and she couldn't blame him. She had given him cause to doubt her. She didn't trust him, either. They had both been in the espionage world too long to expect anyone to back them a hundred percent.

His eyes never wavered from her, hadn't since he found her standing beside the tub naked. She wanted to hold his gaze but she found herself looking past him into the fire.

It was true this man disturbed her in a way that no

man had. She had hoped it was just some bizarre once-in-a-lifetime meltdown—her surrender that night in Vienna—but it wasn't. He had what she needed. Everything she needed. Everything she craved.

He was strong and smart, but it didn't stop there. She liked his bulk, his thick shoulders and the breadth of his chest. He didn't look capable of tenderness, not at all, but he was a master at turning a woman on. Skilled beyond what was normal, and she'd known a lot of normal.

He'd known where to go first, and how long to linger. Where to go second. It was as if he had studied the female body at length, or maybe he'd been tutored in the art of seduction.

She could honestly say that night in Vienna was the first time she had really wanted a man inside her. The first time she'd wanted to surrender to the storm. The first time she had truly wanted to be taken.

If he had been tutored, the question was where and when? And by whom?

She clutched the blanket closer to her body and walked toward the fireplace, needing to distance herself from the memory he seemed to always resurrect when they were alone. Her leg was better now, but she continued to concentrate on keeping her gait even. Flawless.

You will not limp, do you hear me! Limping is for weaklings. Are you a weakling? Have you been defeated this time? No, you have not. Say it. Say, No, I have not. Say it loud. I can't hear you, Nadja. Louder. Louder!

She curled up in front of the fireplace, content to wait for the stew and her coffee. The dry wood crackled and

popped as it burned hot and warm—the smell pungent
as the charred remains turned black, then glowed red.

She turned her face to accept the heat on her cheeks,
then closed her eyes. She concentrated on the soon-to-
come hot *mélange,* and it sent her down memory lane
to the first time she'd tasted what was now her favorite
drink. She'd been thirteen, and she was sitting with her
sister at the *kaffeehaus* at Groffen. It was late afternoon, and Mady had taken her hand. She had started out
with "Don't be upset with what I'm about to tell you.
You must hear me out first. I'm planning on leaving
Groffen. I'm going to run off with someone. The handsome raven-haired skier I pointed out to you. You remember him. We were at his cabin in Otz once a year
ago. Before Grandpa moved us to Groffen. We're in
love, Nad. He's promised me an exciting life seeing the
world. You wouldn't want me to miss out, would you?
Of course you wouldn't, so you won't tell Grandpa, will
you. I'll write a letter to him after I'm far away."

And that was that. Mady had left with the raven-
haired skier. And a year later she had married him.

She'd married Holic Reznik.

His leg was hurting like a son of a bitch. Still, he'd
put off tending to it in favor of more important matters—
like calling Jacy and ordering food from the main lodge.

Once he'd gotten Jacy on the phone, Bjorn had told
his friend what he needed—everything Jacy could find
out about Nadja. He wanted to know where she'd gone
to school, who her friends were and how she'd been recruited into Quest. He'd informed Jacy about her skiing accident, explained what he knew, what was still in
question. He wanted details, and he wanted them fast.

Now, waiting for the food to arrive, Bjorn stepped out of his pants to examine the three-inch flesh wound on his thigh. Like the one on his neck, this one wasn't serious. And with its location he could stitch it up himself. He saw to it, while his belly was turning inside out with hunger.

When the food arrived, he went to the door in his sweater and underwear, then served Nadja where she sat by the fire. His own food, he carried to the window and ate looking out at the hell-storm that seemed to be getting worse by the hour. The food was tasty, and he ate it quickly, like he always did. It was hard to break old habits, and whenever his belly felt like it was touching his backbone, he was reminded of his past life and what he'd been forced to do to survive—garbage runs and moldy bread had been his diet for many years.

When he was finished with his stew he went in search of the bottle of Dutch gin he'd packed. Let Nadja have her milky coffee, he thought, he definitely needed something stronger to take the edge off.

The weather had crippled the mission, he'd been shot twice, and this room was too damn small—he couldn't escape the scent of Nadja.

"We need to talk about Holic," he said after half the gin was gone and he'd pulled on a pair of jeans from his duffel. He walked to where she sat curled up on her side. One leg peeked out, beautifully long and shapely in the glow of the fire.

"That phone call you made," he asked. "Who did you call?"

She sat up slightly, the blanket parting enough for him to glimpse her amazing cleavage. He inhaled sharply, which was a mistake. Her scent climbed inside him.

"We can talk in the morning. I don't feel like discussing it now. Did you need stitches?"

"*Ja,* I took care of it."

"What's the matter, don't you trust me even with a needle?"

"I didn't want to bother you."

"You didn't want me touching you."

"That, too. Answer me. Who did you call?"

"I can't tell you. It's for their protection."

That was bullshit, but he didn't say that. He'd try patience and skirt the issue, and if that didn't work he'd threaten to send her back to Prague...again.

"Out on the road you were limping."

"I had a catch in my knee."

"It didn't look knee related. It wasn't that kind of limp."

"An expert in everything? Is that who and what you are, Bjorn?"

"You don't want to know who I really am," he said, thinking again about the bad years when he'd felt so damn helpless and worthless. "So you agree that you were limping, at least."

"Why does it matter? Okay, yes, I was limping."

"Then why did you lie?"

"Pride, I suppose. You've already questioned my endurance."

"Let me have a look at your knee."

He set his bottle down and crouched beside her. When he reached for her leg, she tried to scoot out of his reach. He snagged the edge of the blanket and it came off one shoulder. She scrambled to rescue it and while she was preoccupied, he locked his hand around one of her ankles to keep her from escaping him.

"Let go," she ordered, her eyes flashing a warning.

"I only want to take a look."

She tried to shake him off, but he hung on, slid his free hand up her calf and squeezed. She stopped fighting him. Called him an asshole again.

"It's true Polax told me you were the wrong agent for this job. That your stamina was in question. If you're having a problem, though, I should know about it." He leaned over and forced her to fall onto her back.

He should let go of her, he thought. He was too close, and the blanket had completely fallen away now.

"Polax only told you I was questionable so that you would take a second look. Haven't you ever heard of reverse psychology?"

Her words drew his eyes to her lovely breasts. "I don't need Polax's reverse psychology to take a second look, honey, or a third or a fourth."

"If you had chosen Pasha you would both be in Otz right now," she said, ignoring her naked body. "You'd be racing a dozen other agents up the mountain to an empty cabin."

He was only half listening. Her scent had circled him, and her labored breathing was keeping his eyes fastened on her chest. She had the most extraordinary dark pink nipples he'd ever seen.

His eyes traveled to her smooth, flat stomach, then to the blond triangle between her legs. To the right, he spied the infamous tattoo, and it was such a surprise that he said, "What the hell."

She wasn't paying any attention to him, she was still trying to convince him that she was the best partner he could have chosen.

"I've saved you at least two weeks, you…"

He ignored what she was saying, his attention focused on the tattoo. It was a pair of angel wings that grew out of a small red heart. It was truly amazing, just as Polax had said. The detail in the wings sharp and feathery, colored angelic white around a delicate red heart. Amazing, but not what he'd expected from a bedroom assassin ranked number one in the country.

"We'll discuss the mission later. For now I want to look at your leg."

"Is that so? Then why are you looking everywhere else but at my leg?"

"Because a man enjoys looking at beautiful things," Bjorn admitted. "And you are a beautiful thing, Nadja."

She tried to pull away, tried to sit up and rescue the blanket. When he wouldn't let her, she kicked out at him, the easy movement dispelling the catch in her knee. She kicked again, this time aiming for his crotch.

Bjorn deflected the blow. "Careful," he said, then in a low voice that warned her he wasn't used to losing a fight on any level, he said, "I don't want to hurt you. Don't make me."

She stopped fighting him. "I'll make a deal with you."

"I don't usually make deals, but I'm listening."

"How badly would you like to know one of my secrets?"

When he didn't answer right away, she lifted her chin, then pointed to the scar on her inner thigh, two inches above her knee. "I'll tell you what's in there if you promise me something."

"In there?"

"Yes, inside my leg."

"And what's the something I would have to promise?"

"That you'll help me locate Ruger after our mission is over. I said *after*. I'll go forward with the mission without distraction. We're close now. In a few days this should be over."

Bjorn watched her eyes, checked her breathing. This time he didn't believe she was lying.

"Is it a deal? Promise me that what I tell you stays between us, and that you'll help me find Ruger once the mission is over, and my innermost secret is yours."

He released her leg, and she gathered up the blanket and stood while Bjorn remained balanced on his haunches.

"This will be our secret, Bjorn," she said, looking down at him. "Ours alone. It's worth it. Promise me, and I'll give you the inside story."

She knew what she was doing. They had a past, and she was using the memory of what they'd shared to manipulate him. He wasn't the kind to fall for such an obvious game, but he was damn curious. And it wouldn't be hard to find her brother after this was over. A week's work at the most. And maybe the inside story would shed some light on Nadja's connection to Holic.

"It's a deal," he said, shoving to his feet. "Ruger will be found after we locate Holic."

"Swear the secret will remain ours alone."

"I swear."

Nadja drew in a breath and let it out slowly. She had never imagined sharing this particular secret with Bjorn Odell.

There were only three people who shared the secret at present. Kovar had warned her never to speak of it to anyone. Polax had been included only because he had needed to cover up the truth where the files at Quest were concerned.

But if Ruger was truly missing, then she would need Bjorn's help in finding him. And for that she was willing to share her secret—at least this one.

"You read my file?"

"Polax had it in his office along with the other two candidates'. Yes, I read all three of them."

"Then you know about the accident I had in Zurich?"

"It was documented. You were nineteen. Suffered a skull fracture and concussion. Hospitalized for several months due to massive internal damage, broken bones and trauma, which led to multiple surgeries. Polax referred to you as the queen of pain. So what's your secret?"

"Broken bones heal…eventually. But some things, if the damage is too great, can't be fixed."

"What are you saying? The file didn't wave any red flags."

"Of course not. Quest's requirements and standards are quite high. No flaws are acceptable."

"Are you saying you have a flaw?"

"Oh, yes. I have a major flaw, one that Polax swept from my medical file before I was interviewed by his superiors."

"And why would he do that?"

"Money. He's always in need of money to fund his next invention. If he cleaned my file and I was accepted into Quest, then he would receive a substantial yearly allowance."

"Who bought him off? Who wanted you inside EURO-Quest?"

"I can't tell you that."

"So Polax agreed to put a double agent into his organization? And now that I know this I'm supposed to continue to work beside you, knowing that your loyalty is—"

"To the mission," Nadja promised. "I give you my word that our goal is the same."

"And I can sleep easy knowing you've given me your word, right?"

"Holic must die, Bjorn. On that we agree. And the kill-file must be recovered—otherwise our agents will die. Yours and mine."

He snorted, his face a sour mix of emotions. "I should send your ass back to Prague on the next flight."

"But you won't. We made a deal, and you agreed to it."

"Finish it."

"Are you sure?"

"I'm sure."

He was glaring at her, his blue eyes as cold as the weather outside.

"Let's hope you're a man of your word."

"Let's hope you're a woman of yours, or I might just have to kill you before this mission is over."

"Fair enough."

"It has nothing to do with being fair. It's about survival. The secret. I'm waiting."

She was going to just say it. To come out with it and then… She raised her chin. "During my accident a major nerve was severed in my leg. That's what I meant about some things can't always be fixed."

"But you're here, and from the stats in your file—"

"The doctors who put me back together told my grandfather that I would never walk again. But Kovar wouldn't accept that, so he decided that he would find an alternative."

"What does that mean, an alternative?"

"He knew a scientist in Russia who was performing experimental surgeries on laboratory rats. He was having success reattaching severed limbs."

"But your leg wasn't severed."

"No, it wasn't. Which, I was told, was better. It made the risks more manageable."

"You're saying this rat scientist operated on you?"

"He had invented a nerve chip, and used it in over a dozen operations."

"On rats."

She heard the disgust in Bjorn's voice, saw it in his eyes. "Kovar wouldn't accept me living in a wheelchair. He wanted me back on my feet. Back on the slopes."

"You could have died."

"Several times. But without the use of my leg…" She shrugged. "I was a skier, after all. That's who I was. I didn't know how to do anything else. I thought, might as well be dead if I can't ski."

"That's what he said, isn't it? Your grandfather? He used that argument to get you to agree to the surgery, didn't he?"

She had never had a choice to agree or disagree.

If you're going to exist in a wheelchair you may as well be dead. I can't look at you that way day after day. I won't. You disgust me.

She could still hear the words, the tone in his voice. She turned away from Bjorn's dead-aim gaze, the mix of emotions on his face making her more than a little uncomfortable. Why should he care what kind of surgery she'd had, or how risky it had been? She'd survived after all, so that was no longer an issue.

But he did care on some level; it was evident in the way he had flared at the very idea of having experimental surgery in a rat lab.

She turned and faced him. "My secret is I have a bionic nerve chip in my leg. It was implanted by the Russian in a research lab surrounded by caged rats. After the surgery was over, I stayed in Russia for another seven months."

"Why so long?"

"My recovery took…time."

"Meaning it took more than one surgery to get the damn chip to work?"

His tone was still the same, full of repulsion.

"Four surgeries to be exact," she admitted. "My body kept rejecting the chip. And there was a problem with regenerating nerve impulses once the chip did accept its new home. There are these microelectrodes doing something terribly complicated that trigger nerve activity. I don't understand all of the scientific jargon, or how it all works, but it doesn't matter. All that's important is that after months of therapy I was able to walk again. Then run and jump."

"And ski?"

"No. I never skied again."

"Why not? I thought that was the goal?"

"It was, but there was a problem. There had never been any research done on the chip's effectiveness in cold weather. What we learned was that it works only under controlled body temperatures. Since returning to the slopes put me in an unstable environment, temperature wise, a comeback on the ski circuit was impossible."

She watched as Bjorn's eyes singled out the leg in question. Of course he would be curious. In his shoes she would be, too. But she still resented it. A ceramic-coated chip placed in and around the nerve was what was feeding her leg, the only thing keeping her on her feet. Without it she was a cripple.

"Okay, Odell, take a good look."

She dropped the blanket to the floor, and stood naked before him. Slowly she brought her leg forward for him to examine.

Turning it outward so he could see that it was the same as the other one, with only one small difference— a two-inch thin scar on her inner thigh. She said, "Well, what do you think? The chip was there that night in Vienna. I kept up with you on the run, and later you had no complaints in the shower. My endurance matched yours. Tell me it didn't." On a roll, she said, "The question is, am I human or bionic? What do you say? Give me your expert opinion. I know you have one. A man like you has an opinion on everything."

He reached her in three steps, picked up the blanket and wrapped it back around her shoulders, tucking her inside it with the same kind of gentleness he had offered her five years ago.

She was still fighting the emotional flux from his hands on her when he pulled her close and wrapped his arms around her. She stayed there, and when he lowered his head, she angled hers back, knowing what was coming.

She let out a sigh when his lips covered her. Opened her mouth and let him taste her. Kissed him back. She felt his arm curl more firmly around her waist, bringing her forward against his hard body. He was thrusting his tongue now, sweeping her up and devouring her at the same time.

She could smell his skin, feel his body, feel his cock swelling against her.

The way he held her… Touched her…

It was too much, too potent and too full of old memories. She wrenched herself out of his arms. "You never told me what you think. How do you think of me, Bjorn? Does the nerve chip make me a bionic freak of nature?"

Bjorn let her go. He hadn't meant to let things get out of hand. That she was even letting him kiss her spoke of how vulnerable and confused she had to be. And the question she had asked confirmed that vulnerability. She shouldn't give a damn what he thought about the nerve chip. It's what she thought that was important.

"Go to bed. You need to get some sleep." He started for the door.

"You didn't answer me, Bionic or human?"

He grabbed his jacket.

"Bjorn, don't walk out."

He walked, taking the stairs two at a time once he got through the door. He needed to get some air, but the minute he stepped out into the blowing snow he wished he'd stayed. Wished he'd answered her.

Bionic or human?

The nerve chip was the reason she was on her feet. The very idea took him aback. She'd been an experiment. An experiment that had come about because Kovar Stefn couldn't abide defeat.

He wanted to hate her grandfather for that, for putting Nadja through hell, but on the heels of that thought came a very damning, selfish feeling of relief. Relief that the rat scientist had been multitalented and hadn't given up the first time or the second and third. That the result had been Nadja back on her feet. That Kovar had been arrogant and connected enough to go looking for an alternative.

Kovar is well connected.

And wealthy, Bjorn thought. Wealthy enough to buy Polax.

You're a double agent. For who?

I can't tell you that.

Bjorn leaned against the building and puffed hard on his cigarette, welcoming the nicotine into his lungs as well as the cold air.

I have a bionic chip in my leg. Bionic freak, or human? Don't walk out.

He lit up another cigarette, then had two more.

You're a double agent. For who?

He made a second call to Jacy and got him out of bed.

"I know I just called a few hours ago, but do you have anything for me?"

"I got a little. Nadja's parents are dead. A car accident that took them both at the same time. She's the youngest of two children. She's got an older brother."

"That's right. His name's Ruger."

"She and her brother moved in with the grandfather after her parents died. After that she started skiing, and got damn good at it. Kovar Stefn owned a home in Langenfeld—then he bought an old lodge near Zell am See. He tore it down and built a fancy place called—"

"Groffen?"

"That's right. Pretty plush place from what I can tell

on their Web site. Had to cost a bundle to build. Which put me on the money trail, but it turned cold right away. Something's up with that, though, because Kovar Stefn wasn't born with a silver spoon in his mouth. So that brings up the question, where did he get the money to build a multibillion-dollar ski shack?"

Bjorn tossed his cigarette. "I think Holic Reznik's at Groffen."

"At Groffen? Why would he be there? The information I have pinpoints Otz as his likely destination. He's supposed to have a wife somewhere around there. That's kind of crazy, too. We've got a name, but nothing else."

"Mady?"

"That's it," Jacy confirmed.

"She's moved to Groffen with her daughter."

"How do you know that?"

"I've got a smart partner," Bjorn said. "Anything else on Nadja?"

"She disappeared soon after the accident. I can't find any info on her during that time. It's like she vanished."

"I know where she was. What else?"

"Three years later she resurfaces. But she's no longer the sweet-faced darling who ran the ski circuit for ten years. She's packing heat and working for EURO-Quest. Her kill record is the best in her field. I tapped into Quest's computers and found out that she disappeared once more. This time for about a year. In the file it states she was captured by an anarchy group, but there's no follow-up. No information on whether she escaped or was released."

"When was that?"

"About four and a half years ago."

The first disappearance Jacy spoke of had to be when Nadja went to Russia to get the nerve chip implant. But where was she the second time? Had she been captured and held prisoner, or had she made up that story because she needed to return to Russia? Had her disappearance involved a problem with the chip? Five years ago she'd been on a mission in Vienna. That meant she'd gone missing shortly after they met.

"What did you find out about Polax?" Bjorn asked.

"He's been involved with some costly projects. He's always over budget. But as far as I can tell he's loyal to Quest."

"Check and see how Kovar Stefn and Lev Polax might know each other. And see if you can hunt down Nadja's brother. He's gone missing. She says at least eight months. He was a priest in Innsbruck at Wilten Parish. Start there."

"I'll check back with you as soon as I have something concrete."

Bjorn hung up, then headed back inside. He was exhausted and cold. He shook off a chill, or maybe it wasn't a chill at all.

Maybe it was his sixth sense working overtime.

Chapter 10

"The operation is over, Adolf. There were some surprises. I told you I wouldn't sugarcoat anything. You waited too long to have the surgery. The tumor was getting damn comfortable. Setting down roots, as they say. That's why you were in the operating room half the day. You've already been through two stages in the recovery room, and you're doing fine. You're back in your room now, and you'll be fading in and out. That's normal."

Merrick tried twice to speak but his words came out sounding ugly and unclear.

"Don't worry about your speech. That's normal, too." Paul touched Merrick's arm. "Don't worry, pal. At this point I'm not seeing anything to be alarmed about. You're in good hands. I'll check in on you in a few hours."

When Paul stepped back, Merrick saw Sarah. He didn't know why she was there, or who had called her.

Still, he was glad to see her. Maybe he had asked her to come. No, he hadn't asked. He knew what he'd asked of her. To see to Johanna's roses.

She had a tissue balled up in one hand, and her cheeks were watery. They were a deep emerald green, and he realized that he had never noticed that before now. She also had petite pink lips, a small nose and silky brown hair that reminded him of how Johanna had worn her hair over the years. Simple yet elegant is what he had always thought. Only his wife's hair had been as black as midnight and as shiny as a new penny.

Sarah wasn't Johanna, but she was beautiful. A slender woman in her mid-thirties who had never married, and had worked only in her father's flower shop.

They had never spoken beyond chatting about the weather and Johanna's roses. But now she was here and she was crying.

Crying for him.

He watched her reach for an ice chip from a cup on the portable stand next to his hospital bed. After touching his lips with the ice, she coaxed him to open his mouth and then slipped the chip inside.

"You're going to be all right, Adolf," she said softly. "I know that. Dr. Paul has an excellent reputation. He says you'll pull through because you're too stubborn not to. I know you can be very determined, and in this case that's a good thing." She touched his arm. "Enough talk from me. What you need is sleep, so close your eyes and don't worry about anything. I'll see to what's important to you. I'll see to Johanna's roses."

It was dark except for the glow of the fireplace when Bjorn returned to the loft. Nadja was in bed, and he was glad for that. He didn't want to talk anymore.

What he needed to do was think.

He stripped off his coat, then his sweater and jeans. He ached to sit in the tub, and managed without getting his thigh wound too wet. Several times he glanced over to the bed, but Nadja hadn't moved. She was exhausted, he knew, and it was best if she slept straight through till morning. Better for her and for him.

He located his duffel bag and removed his shaving kit. He pulled out his razor and a hand mirror and carried them to the fireplace. With the aid of a small table lamp, and with a towel clinging to his hips, he scraped off the stubble on his chin, then put the kit back in his duffel.

He returned to the fireplace to toss another log on the glowing hot coals, and became lost in thought after that—until he heard the mattress squeak. When he turned around he found Nadja on her back, the comforter on the floor, and the sheet draped lower along her stomach.

He let himself look, let himself remember what it was like to touch her—to feel her around him, and have her scent brand his skin.

She shifted again and the sheet moved lower. He focused on the tattoo, again questioning the feminine design. He suddenly felt her gaze on him and he locked eyes with her.

Caught in the act, he said, "Sorry."

She sat up slowly, slid her long legs off the bed. Standing with the sheet shielding her naked body, she said, "I shouldn't have told you. I thought…"

"What did you think?"

She shrugged. "I don't know. Maybe I just wanted someone else to know the truth. Someone outside my circle."

"You're no freak, Nadja. You're a beautiful woman. Sexy as hell."

"Prove it."

"What?"

"You heard me."

As much as he wanted to recreate what they'd had in Vienna it would be a mistake. "You know I want to."

"Then what's stopping you?"

She dropped the sheet.

"It would be a mistake to let this go any further."

"Would it really be a mistake? If you think so then you're not remembering Vienna in the same way I remember it."

"You were the one who left, remember?"

"Yes, I did leave. Actually, I ran. I had never—"

"Never what?"

"Felt so frightened. It was amazing…us. Frighteningly amazing."

Yes, they had been amazing together. All he had to do was close his eyes and he was there again, back in Vienna in that shower, succumbing to the power…the power of Nadja Stefn taking him someplace he'd never visited before in his life.

Every man fought against *it*, hoped that he would never feel *it*—that moment when he knew he was caught. Not just physically, but emotionally as well.

"It was too much, you know," she whispered as she came toward him. "And then…"

"Not enough," Bjorn finished.

She stopped six feet from him. "I had never made

love for the sake of making love until that night. And not since. You can believe that or not."

"Are you saying I'm the only man alive who knows what you like?"

His words sent her eyes past him to the fire, "It's true—all the others are dead."

"So I should feel lucky that you ran that night…otherwise I would be dead?"

She looked at him. "You mock me."

"No, I don't." The idea that he was the only living man who knew her intimately turned him on more than he had been already. "Honestly, I like the fact that all the other men are dead. I just can't help but wonder what would have happened if you had stayed."

"I would never have killed you."

"Because I wasn't a target."

"No, you weren't my target, but at the time I didn't know if I was yours."

That news surprised him.

Like him, she had recklessly gotten caught up in the moment. The truth was, he had been so crazy to have her that night he'd been downright stupid. Careless.

Honestly, he couldn't guarantee that he would have been quick enough to stop her if she had raised a gun to him.

"Why did you kiss me?"

"Are we talking about Vienna or tonight?"

"I'm talking about tonight, before you walked out. Don't say you don't know. A man like you always knows why he does what he does."

"I kissed you tonight because I was curious."

"Curious?"

"I wanted to make sure."

"Make sure of what?"

"That I was remembering everything clearly. Or if I'd embellished Vienna over the years in my mind."

"And?"

"And it felt good to be there again."

"You could feel better than good. Want to? We could use the bed this time."

Bjorn smiled. "I know I said I would have you before this mission was over, but I've rethought that. I think one too many times could be the death of me."

She moved back to the bed, swept up a blanket and wrapped it around her. "Then it bothers you?"

"Bothers me? What are you talking about?"

"What I am. You didn't know what business I was in that night, but you do now. Having trouble rising to the challenge?" She looked over her shoulder, lowered her eyes to the towel wrapped around his waist. "No, it doesn't appear to be a problem. You're physically aroused, but in here—" she tapped the side of her head "—are you disgusted by what I am? Or is it the leg?"

"I'm not disgusted, and I don't have a problem with the chip being the reason you're on your feet."

She didn't look like she believed him. It was important that she did. Bjorn closed the distance and turned her to face him. "This isn't why I chose you for this mission."

"I chose the mission," she reminded him. "I forced your hand, remember?"

She took one of his hands and slipped it inside the blanket. Bjorn moaned and pulled her to him. She went willingly, let go of the blanket and fused herself to him, crushing her full naked breasts to the warm wall of his bare chest.

He bent and covered her mouth, kissed her slow and deep. Then deeper still. She opened her mouth. He used his tongue.

He felt her nipples like hot stones where they touched him. He heard himself groan low in his throat, and with his surrender, she in turn surrendered.

It was happening again, so much heat and pent-up need that neither could break the force that claimed them.

"Don't stop," she sighed, shuddering violently when he backed off to catch his breath. "Please don't question this. Don't make me beg. Touch me."

It would be his pleasure to touch her. In touching her, she touched him. She didn't realize that, but it was the way it worked with her. She had the power.

He had the power to make her lose control. One kiss. A single stroke of his hand. It had worked that way in Vienna, and it was the same here. There was just too much going on between them, underneath the surface, to back away.

He dipped his head and sent a dozen kisses along her jaw and down her neck, and Nadja felt weak in his arms. Weak and strong at the same time. How did he do that?

She snuggled closer, tugged off his towel and worked her body against his cock, gyrating her hips. Making him moan, and catch his breath.

"We're going too fast," he said, then lifted her.

Nadja curled her legs around his waist, and he slid inside of her. He was pumping hard and fast before they reached the bed.

"Let it come," she sighed as he began to climax after a solid thrust.

"Can't stop."

"Don't try." Nadja curled herself around him and drew him in deeper. Holding him there.

But it was only the beginning. They both knew it.

Both knew they needed sleep, but they needed each other more.

Besides, there would be time to sleep. The storm that had caused Bjorn and Nadja to seek shelter at Nordzum was about to stall over the Kitzbuheler Alpen.

But for now the storm was the last thing on Nadja's mind. She lay watching Bjorn sleep, putting to memory all they had shared throughout the night. Enjoying a chance to stare at his handsome face and study his rugged features.

She liked his hair. Liked that it was longer than that of most men she knew. She decided that his looks fit his lovemaking. It was edgy and challenging. Addicting. It's what set him apart from all the other men. No man touched her like Bjorn. He knew every spot on her body that wanted to be touched.

To speak of love was foolish, so she wouldn't. But she had never felt anything remotely close to the way she felt in this man's arms. So if love was real, then, yes, maybe this was love that she was feeling. But she wasn't going to examine it any more than that. It was too fragile. Too dangerous.

She sat up and straddled him. He stirred and as he began to grow aroused, she angled her body to envelop him. When he felt her and opened his eyes, saw her astride him, he arched his hips, seating her deeper.

"You're not afraid I have a gun under the pillow?" she whispered.

"No. But if you do, and you plan on using it, wait a bit. This feels too good to be cut short."

He smiled and she saw no fear in his eyes. No need to check beneath the pillow.

"How's your leg?" she asked.

"Fine. How's yours?"

"The circulation has definitely improved. Thank you."

"You're welcome." He fastened his eyes on her breasts. "You look good riding."

"Men like to see jiggling breasts, and enthusiasm."

"And am I about to see both?"

She began to move on him. "Yes."

"Lucky me."

"We shouldn't be able to do this again. It's unnatural."

"Who says it's unnatural?"

"Three times in three hours?"

"With the right partner anything is possible. Didn't you know that?"

Nadja had never believed in destiny. She had always believed that a person made their own fate. But if it was true, if people came into your life for a specific reason, then she knew why Bjorn had entered hers.

His hands slid over her thighs and she came out of her musing.

"Where did you go, honey?"

"Nowhere."

"You sure?" He gripped her hips, pulled her forward. Back.

Nadja didn't answer, she couldn't. Bjorn was touching her again, and she simply couldn't think past that.

"You were born in Copenhagen?" Nadja asked the next evening.

"I think so, but I'm not sure."

They were seated in front of the fireplace on the fur rug, wrapped in blankets. Outside the snow continued to fall, and there was no way they were going to be able to leave Nordzum until it let up. Bjorn had been listening to the weather reports, and it sounded like the storm was expected to stall out for another twenty-four hours.

"You're not sure where you were born?"

"I don't remember much growing up except that I hated the orphanage I was in. Later, once I was on my own, I was preoccupied with trying to stay warm and fed."

"I'm sorry."

Bjorn studied her. They had been breathing each other's air, cooped up in this room for two days straight. He knew her body inside and out, and she knew his just as well. They were connected now, in a way that he'd never been connected with anyone. And yet it felt too new to be comfortable. In many ways they were still strangers.

"You must have been lonely."

He didn't answer her, though it was true, he had been lonely as a boy, and as a man, too. It was a kind of comfort zone for him—what he knew.

"How did you survive it?"

"Eventually someone took me in."

"How old were you?"

"About twelve. I ran away from the orphanage at seven. With two other kids. They were a little older. We lived on the streets together. Looked out for one another."

He didn't like talking about how he'd existed in Copenhagen. It had been hell on the streets, but it hadn't been much better at Anna's place. He'd seen more and done more in her whorehouse than any kid ever should. And that's why he would never judge Nadja and what she'd done to stay on her feet. At least she had a cause behind who and what she'd become. For him it had been totally self-serving.

"Unwanted kids," he mused. "They would be better off dead. Our mothers should have disposed of us before we were born."

"That's horrible. You can't really believe that. Look at you. Who you are."

"Who am I?"

"An Onyxx rat fighter. You help people. Fix the world's problems."

Bjorn chuckled. "A regular superhero, that's me. What else do I do…to you?"

She paused, then said, "You feed my soul."

He reached out and stroked her cheek with the back of his hand. "So tell me how you came to be at Quest."

The question brought immediate tension to the lines in her lovely face. She pulled back from his hand and drew her blanket more securely around herself. "You know how. Once Kovar realized that I wasn't going to make a comeback on the slopes, he wanted revenge."

"On you?"

"Yes. He thought I threw the race that day. That I deliberately lost control."

"Why would he think that?"

"I had asked him to give me some time off. My life with Kovar was simple and single-minded. He lived to see me ski. It's all I did from the time I was eight until I had the accident at nineteen. I skied for my grandfather's pleasure, not my own. I was tired. After the accident when the use of my leg was gone, he wanted to punish me for taking it all away from him. And he found a way to do it."

"How?"

"He gave me back the use of my leg, let me get comfortable living again, then gave me a choice. Become his pawn in the intelligence world, or give back the bionic chip and return to a wheelchair. To this day he likes to threaten me with the promise that he'll have it removed if I don't do what he says. Of course life… walking and feeling whole can become an addiction. I won't lie, I'm hooked on the alternative. I can't ever go back no matter what, and Kovar knows it."

Bjorn swore.

"I feel like a prisoner sometimes just waiting to be set free. But it will never happen. I—"

"Shh…"

Bjorn shrugged off his blanket. Naked, he pulled her onto his lap. He kissed her and stroked her, shoved her blanket off her shoulders.

It started out with just a taste, but soon they were sprawled on the fur in front of the fire making another memory.

It didn't have to be this way. You could have been the best, Nadja. We worked so hard, you and I. You know how I feel about human weakness. And so we will forget about the skiing because we must, and focus on another passion close to my heart. You will have a choice. You can remain on your feet by agreeing to support my cause, or you can decline the offer. The choice is yours. Life or death. It makes no difference to me. You see I no longer love you. I can't after what you've done. But I

*can and will punish you, over and over again. Make
your choice.*

She had no idea why she was remembering that
awful night, or why she'd told Bjorn the intimate details of her sorry life. Maybe it was being stuck in this
small space that was making her feel so vulnerable, or
maybe it had been the physical intimacy they had shared
that had loosened her tongue.

For three days it had snowed nonstop, and for three
days she and Bjorn had hardly left their bed. They ordered room service, and it was delivered by a young
man named Gil who came on a snowmobile wearing an
insulated parka and a knowing grin. They talked for
hours, played cards, and caught up on their sleep
spooned together as one.

It was now the fourth day, and the weather was
changing. Standing at the window, looking out over the
snow-covered mountains, Nadja knew her time with
Bjorn had come to an end.

She left the window and returned to the bed, slipping
beneath the comforter to snuggle close to the length of his
body. She listened to his even breathing, all the while enjoying the feel of him next to her. He was lightly dusted
with hair, and she'd noticed a number of scars on his
body. She'd asked about them and he'd told her stories
about his escapades as a young boy on the docks in Copenhagen. Some were funny, and they had laughed together.

She drew the sheet back and looked at the length of
his muscle-hard legs, then his firm butt and smooth
back. She had never slept with a man all night long. Had
never woken up in a pair of strong arms, or made love
all afternoon. Until three days ago. She would remember, she vowed—all of it.

Snuggled in their room away from the complications of the world, she'd almost allowed herself to believe that anything was possible. But she knew better. It seemed appropriate, however, that she have this time with him. The guilt had lifted, and she was prepared to face whatever she must, once she found Ruger. She was no longer going to question why things happened.

Ruger was right, it had all been part of God's plan. What that meant was that she and Bjorn had been destined to meet that night in Vienna. And what had happened afterward had been destiny, too.

At dawn, with a heavy heart, Nadja slipped away from Bjorn's warm body. She made two phone calls, then left him sleeping on his stomach, the sheet riding low, exposing his memorable ass.

The storm had finally blown itself out. The roads were being plowed open, and although the air was crisp, the sun was out.

It was a perfect morning for a little target practice.

Holic watched his daughter hit the bull's-eye dead center, then pump seven more shots into the chest of the paper target. He gauged her balanced stance. The way she extended her arm and gripped the SIG. The way she squeezed off the rounds with meticulous precision, breathing only between shots.

Her shoulders were relaxed, the angle of her head perfect as she looked through the gun's sights. It was all there—she had inherited his style as well as his black hair and dark eyes.

Holic smiled, unable to hide his elation.

Soon, then, very soon.

His pride soared as she turned and smiled at him.

PLAY THE
Lucky Key Game
and you can get

Do You Have the LUCKY KEY?

FREE BOOKS
and a FREE GIFT!

Scratch the gold areas with a coin. Then check below to see the books and gift you can get!

YES!
I have scratched off the gold areas. Please send me the **2 FREE BOOKS** and **GIFT** for which I qualify. I understand I am under no obligation to purchase any books, as explained on the back of this card.

300 SDL D39X   200 SDL D4AF

FIRST NAME   LAST NAME

ADDRESS

APT.#   CITY

STATE/ PROV.   ZIP/POSTAL CODE

2 free books plus a free gift   1 free book

2 free books   Try Again!

DETACH AND MAIL CARD TODAY!

"Will I ever be as good as you?"

The question brought more pride.

"Tell me what you think," she pressed. "I can take it. What do I need to work on to get better? My stance, or do you think—"

"Change nothing. Just keep practicing. There can never be too much practice." Grinning, he raised an imaginary bottle to salute his daughter. "*Prost!* To perfection."

She tossed her head and let a peal of laughter touch the cold morning air. She laid down the gun and hugged him, careful not to bump his hand. She kissed one cheek, then the other.

"I love you," she whispered. "I'm so happy you're home, Father."

It was time, Holic decided—when her spirits were high and her eyes full of love for him. Time to have a heart-to-heart with his daughter. He'd never wanted her to know the ugly truth behind his business, and if he was careful, she wouldn't have to. He'd tell her only what would motivate her and bring her to his side.

Yes, loyalty was the gift that could move mountains, and make a rich man even richer.

"Are you cold?"

"A little." He faked a shiver. "Let's go back inside and I'll help you make hot cocoa."

"You're going to make cocoa? I thought I made the best you ever tasted," she teased.

"It's true. You do."

"Then I'll make the cocoa while you watch. And we'll talk. I never tire of talking to you." She tucked her arm around his waist. "You're stronger today. How's the hand?"

It was stiff, and unchanged. Worrisome. He'd been using some effective drugs to combat the pain, but he didn't want her to know any of that.

"It feels better," he lied. "It's going to take some time, though. Longer than I had first thought. That's one of the things I wanted to talk to you about."

They began to walk back to the lodge.

"Will that be a problem? Are you feeling pressured to return to work?"

"I was given time to recover, but the work is important."

"What will happen if you can't work for a while?"

This was where he would start. She'd opened the door for him and that was all he needed.

"You know my work is very important. World affairs often are. They've asked me to recommend someone while I'm healing."

"A replacement?"

"It would just be temporary, but there is a schedule to keep. A very important schedule."

"And do you have a recommendation for them?"

He stopped walking, looked down at her. "I didn't, not until today." He smiled when her eyes widened. "But only if you feel comfortable, Pris."

"Me?"

"You're perfect. Your shots are clean and on target every time."

"But—"

"I saw with my own eyes. You could be my replacement until my gun hand mends. You have the gift. Will you at least consider it?"

"I would need to know more."

"Of course, and I'll tell you everything. It's very

confidential work. Top secret. You'd be required to travel."

"Travel?" She was smiling back at him now. "I've always wanted to travel."

"I know. Your mother told me. The question I need to ask you is this. Could you kill someone? Could you shoot someone evil? Could you pull the trigger on a man or woman targeted for assassination in the name of government security? Could you, Pris? It's such important work, but it's not for everyone."

She thought a moment, then nodded. "Yes, I think I could pull the trigger for the right reason, Father."

"How it works is, you get a file with a name and a location, and you go. You hunt, pull the trigger and disappear. No reservations. Could you do it?"

"I would be like you?"

Holic shook his head. "No, you would *be* me, Pris."

Again she hugged him. "Thank you, Father. I won't disappoint you. I promise."

"I'll make a phone call."

Holic kissed his daughter's forehead, knowing he didn't need to call anyone. He alone controlled his destiny, and now he controlled his daughter's, as well.

Chapter 11

The ski runs made Groffen famous, but the lodge it-self was as breathtaking as the snow-covered mountain peaks that surrounded it. Towering like a castle made of glass, the ten-story architectural wonder was truly a skier's paradise. With sixty lifts, and ninety miles of piste, the world-famous resort offered world-class entertainment on and off the slopes.

Nadja walked into the lodge filled with a mix of emotions. It didn't matter if she was eight, eighteen, or now thirty, her life had always been, and would forever be, controlled by Kovar.

She pushed thoughts of her grandfather aside for now. She didn't want to see him yet. She hadn't had to deal with him directly for several months, and that had been just fine with her. She didn't know why he'd been avoiding her—he'd canceled two meetings with her in

Prague in the past six months—but she wasn't complaining.

She could live a lifetime without seeing him. But that wouldn't be possible on this trip. She'd entered the lion's den, and eventually she would have to face him.

But first she would meet with Mady at the *kaffeehaus*. It seemed appropriate. That's where they had last seen each other years ago when Mady had confessed her intention to run off with Holic.

She had an hour before they were to meet at nine-thirty, and since she hadn't been back to Groffen for three years, she decided to reacquaint herself.

As she strolled the corridors, she was reminded of the games she used to play as a child. Solitary games because she had never had any friends to play with— Kovar had called them "unwanted distractions."

To combat the loneliness, she had become her own best friend and escaped into a pretend world. She'd imagined that she lived in a palace. Which wasn't far from the truth—Groffen was as grand as any storybook castle. But as in most fairy tales, there was a dark cloud. That cloud had been Gerda, Kovar's assistant.

Gerda had been a real-life storybook witch. A cruel woman with a bitter disposition, man-size hands and bad breath.

With any luck the witch was dead, Nadja thought as she found the stairs that led to the fourth floor and a block of rooms where she had lived with Kovar. She didn't go up; instead her gaze shifted to the stairway leading down to the lower level. If she followed it she would come to a locked door with a sign on it that read Private. It was Kovar's own personal entrance to After Shock, the exotic pleasure den and gaming hall he'd designed for those vacationers with the right credentials who wanted a little extra fun and were willing to pay for it.

The secret door bypassed the Two Winters nightclub, and was used primarily for Kovar and his personal friends. It was the kind of place a man like Holic Reznik would like, Nadja thought suddenly. Yes, it was exactly the kind of place for a man with a certain taste.

And if he wasn't staying somewhere at the lodge, then he might be up on Tulay Pass in a private chalet or in one of the cabins higher up on Glass Mountain.

Nadja headed back through the grand lobby and entered the viewing room where guests could watch skiers coming down the mountain. There was nothing to compare to it—Groffen's room of glass with its plush seating and high-powered telescopes.

Her grandfather had designed the room specifically with her in mind so he could watch her practice on the slopes. Day after day, he would sit there and make notes—then they would discuss her mistakes at mealtime. There were lectures and critiques, a schedule to keep, and discipline. After all, they were striving for perfection in all things.

She scanned the room, surprised when she saw Kovar with his wild gray hair seated at a table near a bank of windows. She skirted the room, curious as to why he would be there. He'd retired from teaching years ago.

She had no wish to speak to him, but she kept moving closer anyway. Feigning interest in the skiers who were enjoying the two feet of fresh powder that had fallen during the storm, she acted like a vacationer.

She strolled behind him, and as she moved past she

decided he had lost weight. She glanced over his shoulder to the computer screen in front of him, not expecting to see herself on the screen. She was fifteen, there was a trophy in her hand and she recognized the surroundings—Zurich, a few years before the accident.

Mistakes number three through nine had all been made in a matter of seventy-two hours. Royally fucked was the term that best described what Nadja had done to him…again.

Bjorn swore, then glanced at the clock. It read seven-thirty, the fire was out and Nadja was gone.

He pulled on his clothes, packed his duffel and left the loft with the scent of Alpine heather on his skin and his ill mood out in front of him a good ten feet. Ten minutes later he entered the main lodge and went straight to the desk where Rune Stein was bidding a pleasant good-day to a group of skiers.

"Say, Stein," Bjorn began, "you seen my wife?"

"Your wife…uh, yes, I did. Fixed her up with a car. Should be *dere* by now."

"And where would that be?"

"She was going to Zell am See. I told her she should wait a few hours but it seemed important that she leave as soon as possible. I sent her behind a plow at six-thirty. It was the best I could do."

"Is the road open to Groffen?"

"Groffen? She didn't mention going to Groffen. But I imagine it is. Busy place, Groffen."

"How far is it from here?"

"Forty miles to Groffen. But your wife's driving to Zell am See. That's about thirty miles from here. On a good day you could get *dere* in a long half hour. But today, I'd say closer to an hour. Following the plow would slow her down some, but it was the safest way to travel. That's what I told her. I asked her if she didn't think she ought to wait for you, but she said you weren't feeling well. Are you feeling better now?"

"Better, *ja.*" Bjorn forced the words from his mouth. Damn her to hell, he thought. "Do you have another rental car available?"

"I've got two, besides the one your wife took. One's already gone, but the other one is scheduled to leave in…" He checked the daybook. "Twenty minutes. The good news is it's headed that way, and there's available seating. Maybe the women wouldn't mind giving you a lift."

The women didn't mind, and Bjorn volunteered to drive. After pacing the lobby for thirty-nine minutes— two of the women were late—they made it to Zell am See in under an hour.

From there Bjorn rented a Jeep and sped north to Groffen Lodge, cursing Nadja the entire way.

Lost in thought, Nadja jumped when a hand touched her shoulder. She was standing at a window gazing out over the snowy mountain slopes, and she spun around.

It was Mady who stood in front of her. She hadn't seen her sister in a number of years, but she had no trouble recognizing her. She was still beautiful, her blond hair long and simply styled the way she had worn it years ago.

But there was one change that Nadja noticed—the night Mady had left she had been brimming with excitement, her eyes sparkling with desire for the man who had swept her off her feet. But there was no longer the glow of newfound love dancing in her doe-brown eyes.

"I thought, no, that can't be Nadja. But of course it's you. Kovar has a picture of you by his bed, and an album on his coffee table." Mady stepped forward and openly hugged Nadja. "You look wonderful."

"So do you," Nadja said, although she was concerned with how thin her sister was.

"I expected you sooner. But then—"

"You were expecting me?"

"It's been five months since Kovar's heart attack. I just thought—"

Nadja glanced across the room at her grandfather. He'd had a heart attack? When?

Suddenly it all made sense. Kovar's canceled trips to Prague the past six months. His brief conversations on the telephone.

"I know you're busy. Still, I was surprised that you didn't answer any of my messages. When I mentioned it to Kovar, he said you represent an international insurance agency and that you're required to travel a lot."

Nadja went along with the lie. "I'm rarely home," she said.

"That's why I started leaving those updates."

"The updates… Uh…yes, the updates. Thank you."

"I hope I didn't get too carried away. But I was sure you would want to know the details, as well as his prognosis."

There had been no messages on her phone. No details or prognosis reports. Or if there had been, someone had seen to it that they were erased. Had Polax been that someone? Or had Kovar taken it upon himself to hire someone to keep his illness a secret from her? Kovar, she believed. He had the manpower. But why? Why hadn't he wanted her to know he'd had a heart attack?

Nadja slipped into the game. Actually it was perfect—she'd use Kovar's heart attack as her reason for coming home.

"I wanted to come sooner," she said. "I really did, Mady."

"I know. You and Kovar were always so close. It must have been hard to stay away. But your cards and flowers were appreciated. Kovar looked forward to them."

She hadn't sent flowers, or any cards, but Nadja never contradicted her sister. She just listened.

"I imagine it'll be hard for you to see him like this. But let me assure you that he's doing much better, and the doctor expects a full recovery." She motioned to where he sat. "Have you seen him, yet?"

"No, I—"

"He's had a recent setback. Blood clots in his legs. That's why he's in the wheelchair."

Nadja looked at Kovar. How had she missed the wheelchair?

She stepped around Mady, having no choice now but to face him. She crossed the room as if eager to see him, coming to stand on the other side of the small table, then waiting until her grandfather looked up from the computer.

When he did, his eyes widened. "Nadja, what an unexpected surprise."

She studied his face, noted his pale complexion, his sunken cheeks. He spun the chair away from the table, and that's when she saw his swollen ankles and the slippers on his feet.

Before Mady joined them, Nadja quickly rounded the table and bent down so that when she spoke, only he would hear her. He angled his face, lifted his cheek, expecting the kiss he had always required of her. But she never put her lips on him.

Instead, for his ears only, she whispered, "I just learned that you suffered a heart attack months ago. Of course Mady believes that I knew about it. Don't worry, I'll play your game, whatever the hell it is, but I *will* have answers." She straightened. "Nonetheless, I speak from my heart when I say, it's good to see you Kovar... doing so poorly."

"Ruger moved to Italy, Nadja. I'm surprised he didn't write you and tell you that," Mady said.

"Where in Italy?"

"Somewhere near Verona."

"Do you have his address?"

"Kovar does."

They were sitting at a table in the *kaffeehaus*, and Kovar was back upstairs resting. He had suddenly complained of being exhausted, and although Mady had no idea what had prompted the lie and put him in such a sour mood, Nadja had enjoyed seeing his lips thin and his knuckles turn white in his lap.

Now sipping *melange,* she listened to Mady as she talked about their brother.

"He's been terribly distraught since the scandal. Kovar suggested that distance would help, and he pulled some strings to get Ruger a new position in Italy."

"The scandal?"

"You didn't know about the child?"

Nadja felt a lump swell her throat. "The child?"

"Ruger's daughter. He had an affair a few years ago. He managed to hide the child with the help of a nun, but then eight months ago someone at the parish found out and…well, when the scandal surfaced, Ruger was faced with excommunication from the church. That's when Kovar stepped in and fixed things."

"Fixed things?"

"He went to Innsbruck, paid off the church to keep the scandal quiet, then found work for Ruger in Italy."

"And the child?"

"Kovar brought Alzbet here."

"Alzbet? The child is here?"

"And doing very well, though she does miss Ruger. Don't feel bad about being kept in the dark. I didn't know about any of this until Kovar had his heart attack a few months ago and he called me in Otz to come to Groffen to help out."

"You've been living in Otz?"

"Part of the time. We remodeled the mountain cabin and made it more of a home. You remember the cabin, don't you? I took you there with me once before Holic and I went away together? Anyway, that's how we came to be here—Kovar's heart attack and Ruger's daughter. But now that we are, I'm hoping we can stay. Kovar's asked me if I will. He'd like me to take over managing the lodge. And of course there's Alzbet to think about. She needs a female influence in her life."

"When did you say he brought her here?"

"She's been at Groffen since Ruger left for Italy. It must be seven months now."

The time frame fit, Nadja thought. "So you've been taking care of her."

"I have help. Mrs. Enders is still here. You remember Gerda, don't you?"

Nadja's stomach knotted. The witch was still alive.

"I spend as much time as I can with Alzbet, but it's not enough. But my daughter's here. She and Alzbet have become close."

"Prisca is here, too?"

"Oh, yes. She loves it here almost as much as I do."

"And Holic? Does he like it here?"

"He thinks—uh…he's not here at the moment. Off on business. I'm so anxious for you to meet my daughter. I've told her about you, and she's seen Kovar's pictures of you. Prisca is nineteen now, and she looks so much like Holic that I told him—"

He was there…somewhere. If not at the lodge, then somewhere in the mountains.

Nadja wasn't sure just how much of his deadly business Holic had shared with his wife. He had shared something, though; otherwise her sister wouldn't be talking in broken sentences and fidgeting in her chair.

"Aunt Mady, help! Don't let her catch me."

At the sound of a child's voice Nadja turned her head to see a little girl with silky white-blond hair running through the *kaffeehaus* toward the table where they sat. The minute the child reached them she dove beneath the table.

Out of the corner of her eye Nadja saw a body enter the *kaffeehaus*. She focused, recognized Gerda and watched as the woman hurried to their table. She had put on weight, and her gray hair had thinned and turned drab, but there was no mistaking her—it was the witch.

And she still had the leather strap attached to her belt.

The woman jerked to a halt, but when she attempted to speak, Mady held up her hand. "It's all right, Gerda. I'll bring Alzbet up for her nap. But first I want her to meet someone."

Gerda huffed loudly, then turned to look at Nadja. When recognition dawned, she took two complete steps back. "Well, finally the queen decides to show her face. I'll tell your grandfather you're here."

"There's no need," Nadja said. "I've already seen him."

Gerda snorted, then with a curt nod she looked at Mady. "A spoilt child is a weak child. And weak children are disappointments." Her cold eyes found Nadja and she offered a smug grin before addressing Mady again. "Alzbet needs discipline. Your interference will only cause her pain in the end."

The last was said with Gerda's eyes fastening back on Nadja, and the image of herself in Gerda's iron grasp being struck with the leather strap flashed behind Nadja's eyes. The witch had loved hearing her scream.

She drew in a heavy breath, checked herself and watched as the elderly woman turned and walked away. Nadja could still feel the sting of the leather strap on the back of her thighs, still feel the old woman pinching her butt. Pinching so hard that she would be bruised for weeks at a time and each time she sat she was reminded of it.

"She's gone, Alzbet." Mady bent over to speak to the child tucked beneath the table. "Now come out so you can meet your other aunt. Nadja is here, the one in all the pictures in Grandpa Stefn's bedroom."

Slowly the child crawled out from under the table. "Auntie Nad is here?" the sweet voice asked. "The one who can ski faster than the wind?"

Her eyes were huge when she turned and looked at Nadja, and in that moment Nadja's world tilted. She had always wondered what her daughter looked like, but she had never asked Ruger to send a picture. And now... now she was here. Her daughter was at Groffen.

So the truth was, Ruger had never adopted out the baby as he had told her he would do. He had kept Alzbet with him. She recalled what the nun had told her in Salzburg, and then the priest in Innsbruck.

Everyone believed the child was Ruger's. Thus the scandal, a scandal that had put him out of the church, and Alzbet into the hands of Kovar.

As calmly as she could manage, Nadja said, "Hello Alzbet. I'm Nadja."

Her girl nodded, her eyes still huge. "I know. I've seen your pictures. Grandpa tells stories about you all the time. You're pretty."

Nadja looked into the child's eyes. Unable to help herself, she said exactly what she was thinking, "You're pretty, too, and you have beautiful eyes, Alzbet. Sky-blue eyes."

Your father's eyes, she thought.

Nadja reached down and lifted the little miracle onto her lap. She had to touch her. It would be the first time, and the need to put her hands on what she'd been forced to give away was too much. She couldn't resist.

She caught Mady staring, and she checked herself again. This wasn't the time or place to reveal feelings that no one would understand. Feelings that would give birth to a dozen questions if she slipped up. Still, she felt tears sting her eyes, and she blinked them back.

"I ski, too. Grandpa's teaching me. He says you didn't start soon enough. That's why he's starting me now, and if I do everything he tells me I'm going to be the best there ever was. Even better than you."

Oh God, he knew? Somehow Kovar had found out

that Alzbet was her daughter. She had tried to prevent it, had given her child up to protect her. Only it hadn't kept her sweet baby out of Kovar's long reach. The only thing it had accomplished was to make her a stranger in her child's eyes.

Bjorn took Groffen apart a floor at a time, and by the time he was finished he had decided that he and Nadja had grown up in two completely different worlds. He had been invisible most of his life—living in back alleys eating garbage, while she had lived in a cut-glass fishbowl, fed from a silver spoon.

He'd been in contact with Jacy again, and he had confirmed that Kovar Stefn had connections in high and low places. That it wouldn't have been hard for him financially to buy his way in or out of any situation. Groffen was a testimony to his staggering wealth. But there was more to Kovar Stefn than money and a few connections.

While Bjorn continued to familiarize himself with the lodge, Jacy funneled information to him as he uncovered it. One of those pieces of information was the existence of a secret club in the underbelly of the lodge designed specifically for a select group of guests—an exclusive club appropriately named After Shock.

Jacy had pointed out that it was the kind of club meant for the bold and beautiful, and that to get inside you needed to look rich and required a sponsor.

"I'll see what I can do about getting you that sponsor," Jacy had said. "One name is all you need."

Bjorn wasn't surprised when an hour later Jacy called back with a name that would guarantee him entrance to the club.

It was as he was moving from one floor to another that Bjorn caught sight of Nadja walking down a corridor with a slight blond woman and a small child. He followed at a discreet distance and watched them get into an elevator.

Chapter 12

The doctors who put her back together after the accident in Zurich had told her it would take a miracle for her to be able to conceive a child. That the ability to get pregnant was nonexistent due to the extent of internal damage that had been done.

And yet, after one night with Bjorn Odell, she'd been given the gift of motherhood, and then nine months later the miracle had been born—a beautiful baby girl Ruger had aptly named Alzbet—"consecrated to God."

The child had weighed six pounds, seven ounces, and had been nineteen and a half inches long. She'd been mostly bald and had all ten toes and fingers. This had all come from Ruger. Nadja had refused to see her baby for fear she wouldn't be able to give her up once she laid eyes on her.

The fact that she had given her baby away knotted

Nadja's stomach once more and she ran back into the bathroom for a second time to vomit—oh God, Kovar had found out she had a child, and now he owned her little girl, too.

Alzbet…

It was a pretty name. A perfect name for a cherub-faced baby with dreamy blue eyes and an angelic smile.

Nadja's fingers stroked over the tattoo she'd gotten after she'd given her child away. With a keening noise akin to that of a dying animal, she dropped to her knees, tears streaming.

The guilt that had started to lift over the years was back, and with it a sickening kind of resignation. She stood and went to the sink and splashed water on her face, then looked into the mirror.

"Pull yourself together," she chastised as the tears continued to fall. "She needs you now, and you will not desert her a second time."

Against her better judgment Nadja left her room. She needed to see her daughter again.

She slipped into the room down the hall where Mady had ushered Alzbet for her nap. The room was dark, the shades drawn. She entered with the skill of a master spy, her steps soundless and her ears attuned to anything unusual. She didn't expect to hear muffled crying, but when she did her body stiffened. She followed the sound of weeping through another set of doors. This room was even darker, and she stood for a moment to let her eyes adjust. When they did, she made out a small shape curled up on the bed. She knew it was her daughter, and somehow Alzbet sensed that someone was there and sat up.

It was then that Nadja knew the degree of her daughter's suffering, the same suffering she had been forced to endure at the hands of the witch.

Gerda…the bitch from hell was at it again.

"Auntie Nad?"

"Yes, baby, it's me."

Alzbet sniffled.

Nadja entered the room and moved to the bed. She turned on the small light on the nightstand, then eased down beside her daughter.

"Are you hurt?"

"Nein."

Nadja wasn't convinced. "Come here, baby."

She reached for her daughter and lifted her onto her lap. When Alzbet's bottom made contact she sucked in her breath.

"Was Gerda here?" she asked, in as calm a voice as she could manage.

Alzbet nodded.

"I promise she won't hurt you again," Nadja assured her.

"Don't say anything. I can't tell. If I tell, she'll—"

"Shh… It's okay." Then she stood, careful not to cause her daughter more pain. It felt wonderful to hold her, and she had the urge to pull her close and squeeze.

Instead, she said, "You're safe now, angel eyes."

"But Gerda—"

"Believe me when I say, Gerda isn't going to hurt you ever again."

She slipped into the hall and carried Alzbet back to her suite. Inside her daughter said, "Grandpa won't like that I'm here. He has rules and I'm supposed to take a nap after lunch." She pushed Nadja's hair away from her ear, then leaned in and whispered, "I shouldn't have run from Gerda this morning. I know better."

"It doesn't take much to make the witch mad," Nadja said, remembering.

Her comment pulled a small smile from her daughter. "I call her that sometimes," she admitted.

Nadja studied her daughter's face. There were no marks on it, no scars, only red eyes and tear-marked cheeks. But that was no surprise. Gerda's abuse was never visible; she had always been careful where she laid her strap. Not even Kovar knew the extent of Gerda's discipline, because the marks were always hidden beneath a layer of clothes.

She said, "A nap can be taken anywhere, and this one is going to be taken here, in my suite."

She sat Alzbet in a soft chair and heard her suck in her breath again as her little bottom met with the cushion. "Would you like a cookie?"

"The witch says no sugar." Alzbet wrinkled up her nose. "She says it'll make me fat and sluggish on the slopes. Grandpa agrees."

Nadja went to her bag and rummaged through it until she found the chocolate-mint cookies she'd bought before leaving the lobby at Nordzum. Cookies in hand, she settled in the chair opposite her daughter. She couldn't stop staring—staring at the beautiful little girl she and Bjorn had created five years ago.

She handed a cookie to Alzbet. "I don't think you have to worry about getting fat, it's not in your genes."

"Really? Did you know my mother? No one talks about her. I've never seen any pictures either."

Yes, you have, Nadja wanted to say. *Yes, you have,*

sweet baby. But she couldn't. Her daughter would never understand why her mother had given her away.

"Take a bite of the cookie," she urged. "It tastes yummy."

"Yummy. That's a funny word." She nibbled the corner of the cookie.

The second a burst of chocolate mint exploded in her mouth her eyes widened. Nadja sat mesmerized, watching. She was aware that she was sharing a first-time experience with her daughter—a chocolate-mint cookie.

"I think Kovar Stefn is working with the KGB," Jacy Madox said the minute Bjorn put his cell phone to his ear.

"Do you have any proof?"

"No. Just a lot of coincidences. And you know me and coincidences."

Bjorn listened, recalling what Nadja had told him about her bionic chip, and the Russian scientist.

"What else?" he asked.

"Remember when you told me Holic Reznik was a skier?"

"*Ja.*"

"Guess who his coach was."

"Kovar Stefn," Bjorn said.

"That's right. How does that fit in, do you think?"

"I don't know. But I suppose you'll need to run this by someone at Onyxx.

"I'm thinking the Agency is going to see this as a breakthrough. They may want to reevaluate this can of worms."

Bjorn could hear the energy in Jacy's voice. He was pumped.

"You're not going to like to hear this, bro, but in my opinion Holic is worth more to us alive than dead if some of this stuff checks out."

"You're right, I don't want to hear that."

"Any closer to locating him?"

"Not yet. Put a call in and give the Agency what you've got. If you can talk to Merrick, tell him I still want the son of a bitch dead, but I'll reconsider if the money doubles and I get a two-month vacation once this is all over."

"A vacation? You? You don't take vacations."

"I'm going to need one this time."

Bjorn caught sight of the thin blonde heading up the stairs. The woman who had been in the hall with Nadja. "I see someone I need to have a conversation with. Call Merrick, then let me know what he's decided. I'll do dead or alive. But dead with more enthusiasm."

He was on the move before his phone was in his pocket. Dressed gangster rich, wearing glasses and a Rolex he'd bought in one of Groffen's exclusive shops, Bjorn caught up with the slight blonde just as she stepped into the elevator.

Once the door closed, leaving them alone, he said, "You don't work here by any chance, do you?"

"Actually I'm a granddaughter to the lodge owner. Is there something I can do to make your stay more enjoyable? Or is there a problem?"

The lodge owner's granddaughter? As far as Bjorn knew, Kovar Stefn only had two grandchildren, Nadja and Ruger.

Stashing the information, he said, "I have a friend who recommended Groffen to me. He mentioned there was more here by way of entertainment than just great skiing."

He flashed her a playboy smile. Waited.

His hint of something more gave her pause, and for a moment he wondered if she was going to deny that there was more action available than Two Winters nightclub.

He hoped he hadn't come on too strong. But then, maybe she'd been kept blind to what other entertainment was offered at Groffen. No, she didn't look stupid. Too thin, but not stupid.

She slipped her hand into her pocket and pulled out a notepad. "Your sponsor's name is?"

Bjorn didn't hesitate. Jacy had already done an extensive amount of digging, and knew what it would take to get into Groffen's gaming den.

"Cornell Peters."

She wrote the name on the paper, then slid the pad and pen back into her pocket. "If the name checks out, Mr...."

"Larsen."

"Mr. Larsen. Then you can expect an invitation delivered to your door by this evening. You are a guest, *da?*"

"Yes. Room 609."

She pulled the pad out and wrote the number next to his name, and when the elevator stopped, she stepped out. "Enjoy your stay, Mr. Larsen."

The elevator had stopped on the fourth floor. Bjorn didn't follow her out, since his room was two floors up. It took a moment for the door to close again, and in that space of time his attention was directed halfway down the hall to where a door had opened up.

When Nadja stepped out into the hall, he made no sudden movement, hoping her eyes wouldn't wander to the elevator. He hadn't wanted her to know he was at Groffen just yet—but it was too late for that. She raised her head past the woman he'd ridden up the elevator with and locked eyes with him.

She gave no reaction, offered no expression. On the other hand he pulled his businessman's glasses to the end of his nose as if in appreciation of a beautiful woman. Then, so that she knew they would be seeing each other soon, he acknowledged her with an upward jerk of his head.

The elevator doors were starting to close when he heard Nadja say, "Mady, there's something we have to discuss."

The name caught Bjorn's attention. If the woman he'd shared the elevator with was Mady Reznik as well as Kovar Stefn's granddaughter, then that meant she was also Nadja's sister.

The very idea that Nadja was Holic's sister-in-law sent his head spinning. "Son of a bitch," he muttered, realizing that the can of worms had just started to stink.

"I'm going to visit Kovar. Can you stay here? Alzbet is asleep in the bedroom."

"She's here? Why?"

Nadja turned back to her sister. "Because Gerda has been using a leather strap on her."

"A leather strap? That's impossible. I would know if she—"

"You didn't know she was using it on me when I was younger."

Her confession took Mady aback. "On you? Why didn't you tell me?"

"For the same reason Alzbet has been keeping silent.

Fear it would get worse. But what happened years ago doesn't matter now. What matters is that Gerda is up to her old tricks and she's abusing my…Alzbet."

"I'll talk to Kovar."

"No, *I'll* talk to Kovar. In the meantime, keep Gerda away from her."

"I can't believe this. How could I not have seen what was going on?"

"Because Gerda is very good at what she does. She keeps the bruises hidden."

Nadja caught a glimpse of a bruise on the back of Mady's arm. "It doesn't look like Alzbet is the only one around here wearing bruises. What is yours from?"

Nadja's question had Mady looking terribly uncomfortable. She slipped her hand over the bruise high on the back of her arm, and said, "This was my fault. Sometimes I get clumsy."

Nadja knew a lie when she heard one. If the bruise was inflicted—and that's what it looked like—then someone had squeezed until they had managed to break several small blood vessels. And if that someone was Holic, then that meant he was here—the bruise wasn't two days old.

Mady reached out and touched Nadja's arm. "Don't worry about me. This is nothing. But you…I'm sorry I wasn't there for you when Gerda—"

"It's in the past, Mady. What's important now is Alzbet." Nadja reached out and took Mady's hand. "And if you need my help, I'll help you, too."

Her sister pulled her hand away. "I told you. I get clumsy sometimes. What do you think, that Holic beats me? I assure you he doesn't."

But he had. Nadja could see it in Mady's eyes. The

pain and the sadness. This was just more proof that Holic was a monster, she thought. She was experienced with his kind, knew how they operated, what got them off. It was all about power and control. She was a connoisseur of evil men—men who lived to feed off the weak.

Suddenly she said, "I don't mean to judge you, Mady. Never. I only want you safe." Nadja stepped back then. "I'll go speak to Kovar now. You'll stay with Alzbet—"

"I have a few important matters to see to downstairs, but I'll call Prisca. She'll come up and watch Alzbet." She pulled a notepad from her pocket and glanced at it, then addressed Nadja once more. "My errand list isn't too long. I can be back in a couple of hours. Then, if it works out, we'll all go to dinner later."

Nadja glanced at Mady's errand list, surprised when she saw *Mr. Larsen* written at the bottom, along with another name and a suite number.

She had no idea why Mady would have Bjorn's alias on her list, but she would find out now that she knew he was in suite 609.

But first she would speak to Kovar about Gerda.

Chapter 13

Kovar was asleep when Nadja broke in to his suite and then slipped into his bedroom. She stood by the door and stared across the room at him, thinking it would be so easy to take one of the pillows off the bed and place it over his face. A little pressure and it would be all over.

Or would it?

Never think you've seen the worst. There's always another far more sinister.

She had read that once, and she believed it was true. She walked past the bed and went to the mirror. There was a button on the right, hidden behind a picture of her. She was maybe ten in it, and she wore a pink ski outfit. She was holding her skis, and she was smiling. But then, she had had no reason not to smile.

It wasn't until age fourteen that she'd begun to realize that Kovar's obsession with her was unnatural. No, it wasn't sexual or kinky in any way—it was simply all-consuming. He owned her mind, body and soul.

She pressed the button and the floor-length mirror became a door that she opened and walked through. Inside her eyes went straight to the swivel chair that sat in the middle of the room, then to the surrounding walls cluttered with pictures—and the shelves lined with trophies she'd won over the years.

Kovar referred to the room as the T-room—time-out to trophy count. It was where he sent her when he hadn't been pleased with her performance on the slopes. Where he sent her when she needed to reflect on what was most important.

Had Alzbet been placed in that chair?

No, not yet, she thought. Not until Kovar had brainwashed her into thinking that skiing and pleasing him was, above all else, the most important goal in her life.

At the far end of the room was another door, and she opened it and stepped inside. This was where Kovar kept his secret files and his impressive stash of weapons.

Kovar had been a mole for the KGB for years. It's how she'd come to work for them after the accident. "I knew you wouldn't be able to stay away."

She heard the words clearly and she turned to see no one there. She backtracked and found Kovar sitting in his wheelchair in the T-room.

"I came to ask you a question," she said softly, but with the promise that she would have an answer.

"I know what you came for. You saw her, didn't you." The grin he offered was victorious. "You've seen my beautiful Bethy, haven't you."

My Bethy...

Nadja felt the hair on the back of her neck stand up.

"Whatever made you think you could hide her from me?"

He knew the truth. Nadja raised her chin. "Desperation, and the need to protect what is mine."

"You are mine and therefore anything that you've made is mine. I wish I could have seen your face when you learned you were pregnant."

She said nothing.

"I retraced your steps. Five years ago you were in Vienna. You were sent there to kill Raywolf. What a messy outcome. Blow your target's brains out, then realize that you're pregnant. Messy, indeed."

Kovar thought Alzbet was the child of Raywolf Cain, one of the Russian mafia's hit men. Nadja felt herself relax. Good, let him think that Alzbet's father was dead. It was better that way. Safer.

Yes, she had canceled Raywolf in Vienna the night before she had met Bjorn. But the child was not Raywolf's child. She knew that without a doubt, because she had killed that monster before he'd dropped his pants. He had been a vile beast. And the thought of letting him touch her had made her sick.

"It's good he's dead," Kovar said, "or I would have seen to it myself. No sense borrowing trouble. Men in high places can be unpredictable when they learn they've fathered a child. Any man, for that matter."

Again Nadja kept quiet.

"Your daughter…my great-granddaughter is perfect. I thank you for that. I never thought I would be able to say that, but she is wonderful. Above average in height just like you were at that age. Perfect for the slopes. She has your magnificent long legs and balance, but as you know, it takes more than that to be a winner. The bones are the secret ingredient. They can't be too bulky, or too fragile. Bethy's bones, like Mommy's bones, are special."

"How did you find out about her?"

"I went to see Ruger…unexpectedly. But fate…ah, fate, it can be a grand thing, don't you think? Imagine my surprise when I saw her in his home. It was a gift I had never imagined. I must tell you it nearly brought me to tears."

Kovar in tears would have been rich. Nadja said, "Ruger lives at Wilten and they—"

"He did live there, but he moved into his own place. A woman met me at the door. I believe her name was Sister, uh…what was it?"

"Catherine?"

"Yes, Catherine. She was the one who delivered my Bethy. She admitted that to me—under duress of course."

"Where is Sister Catherine now?"

"She had an accident. Clumsy women don't live long."

"You killed her?"

"In a matter of speaking, I suppose you can lay the blame at my feet. I didn't actually pull the trigger, but I did give the order."

"I hate you."

"Yes, I know. And I love…to hate you. Since that day in Zurich when you ripped out my heart and shredded my soul."

"It was an accident. How many times do I have to say it was an error that pulled me off course?"

"You do not make errors. Errors cause accidents, and accidents are not acceptable. You knew that. You knew what I expected. What I wanted. What we needed that day to win." He drew in a breath, calmed his voice. "Getting back to Ruger. He really does have grit. I always saw him as weak, but he told the perfect lie that day about Bethy. He said someone had left the little girl abandoned on his doorstep, and he was temporarily caring for her.

"Still, a priest lying," Kovar tisked, "such a terrible sin. I didn't confront him that day. Instead I went home and began making plans. I researched those months after you'd been in Vienna. You went missing, remember? It was about four months later. You told Polax that some anarchy group had captured you and held you prisoner.

"It was a perfect lie. It bought you time while your belly swelled, isn't that right? Ruger took care of you during that time. Made arrangements for you to stay at the convent, Stift Nonnberg. And once the child was born you left her with him and went back to work. After escaping the anarchy group that had captured you, of course."

"Does anyone at the KGB know I have a child?"

"I thought it best to keep it our secret. Ours and Ruger's, of course. I couldn't very well kill him, my own grandson, though I did entertain the idea."

"Where is he? Where is my brother?"

"His decision to aid you and lie to me has been costly. But he is alive, and I imagine in prayer daily for his abominable sin."

"Where?"

"In Italy. And he will remain there. Do not cross me on that, Nadja. Do not think you can attempt to rescue him. I assure you he is alive, and that should be good enough."

She looked at his swollen ankles. At how weak he appeared.

"Don't let my appearance fool you. My mind is sound, and my power is still superior to yours. One phone call and your beautiful leg will become a lifeless club once more. I can do it and I will."

It was always there, the threat that he would take away what he'd given her—a life of his choosing in another prison with him as the jailer.

His eyes drifted over her from head to toe. She was dressed in a black sweater dress that molded and hugged her hips and brought attention to her long legs.

"They are beautiful, you know. Your legs are to die for, as I believe the American expression goes."

"Alzbet is mine. I won't let you have her."

"She was never yours. And how are you going to stop me? Kill me? You could, you know. But then what about Ruger? He could be lost forever. You know how it works. I never leave anything to chance. I own you, and you will do as I say from now until forever. Even after I die there will be no escape. I've left instructions behind, and I have no doubt they will be carried out—you are of value to the cause."

"Why can't you forgive me and give me back my life?"

"Because I don't want to. Because it still hurts, what you destroyed. What you threw away. Tell me, how is the chip doing these days? Any worries or concerns I should relay to Velich? He asks about you often. I think he's in love with you. Of course you were his first real experiment success. Human, that is."

"The chip is doing fine."

"Very good, and the current mission you're on? Is it progressing? Have you located Holic yet?"

"You know I haven't."

"True, I do know that. However, because he is of no interest to the KGB, I haven't kept up on the details. Enlighten me. Did you come here to see if Mady could tell you where he is? Is that what brought you here? I'm not fool enough to think you missed me."

"Do you know if Holic is here?"

"Why would he be here? This is a busy place."

"Busy enough to be overlooked."

"I suppose so, but I think not. Nonetheless, I haven't seen him."

That meant nothing. Kovar was in a wheelchair most of the time. His outings were limited.

"Tell me. Will you kill your sister's husband when you find him? Will you be able to do it?"

"You know I have no trouble following orders."

"That's been true so far, but can you break Mady's heart? She loves him still, even though he isn't worth loving. And Prisca, can you take her father from her?"

"Holic is a monster," Nadja said, reminded of how many innocent people had been killed by her brother-in-law. Women, as well as men—even children—had died at his hands.

"Then killing has gotten easier? I remember the first time you pulled the trigger and splattered brains everywhere. I believe you were sick for a week."

"Why didn't you tell me about your heart attack?"

"I didn't want to give you false hope. I'm not going anywhere and neither are you. Besides I wanted to spend some uninterrupted time getting to know my Bethy." Each time he said "my Bethy" he sneered. "Tell me about your partner, this Onyxx agent. Odell, right?"

"There's nothing to tell."

"That means there is a lot to tell."

"He's a rat fighter. What more is there to say?"

"Yes, I know of Onyxx and the men they employ. Tough men. Survivors beyond the grave."

Nadja turned to leave, then stopped and looked back. "Before I go, there's one thing I need from you. Get rid of Gerda."

"No."

"Do it."

"She has been in my employment forever. She is loyal."

"She is a witch. She used to strike me with that leather strap on her belt. Did you know? Do you know she's doing the same thing to Alzbet?"

His eyes narrowed, revealing that he didn't.

"I don't want her near my daughter another minute. Get rid of her. Do it today, or tomorrow you'll find her dead in one of the linen closets."

Merrick hung up the phone after talking to Jacy. He was getting stronger and his speech was better—a little slow, but he was beginning to sound like himself again. He eased off the hospital bed, stood on weak legs.

There was a storm about to hit Austria, and it wasn't weather related. He'd just received a vital piece of information. Information that needed his full attention. But he couldn't return to Onyxx yet. He wasn't strong enough to leave the hospital. Not for at least another week.

He dialed headquarters, delivered Jacy's information to a trusted colleague, then hung up and dialed Polax on his private line.

When Quest's commander picked up, Adolf said,

"This is Merrick. I've just learned that Holic Reznik's wife is Nadja Stefn's sister. Did you know?"

For a moment Polax said nothing, then, "That's impossible."

"My source is reliable. And there's something else, too. Q's a double agent."

Silence.

"Polax, did you hear me?"

"Are you sure."

"Yes."

"Then we need to talk."

"Yes, we do, but not over that phone."

"I agree."

"I can't leave D.C. right now. You'll have to come to me," Merrick said. "I'll give you the address."

"I'll clear my calendar for the next seventy-two hours and be on the next flight."

Ten hours later, Merrick watched Lev Polax pull off his hat as he entered his hospital room at seven o'clock in the morning. "You must have hopped the first plane out of Prague to get here so quickly."

"I didn't like what I heard. I don't believe that Nadja's sister is Holic's wife." He shook his head. "And a double agent? How can that be?"

Merrick climbed out of the chair next to his hospital bed. He wore black pants and a black sweater. It had taken a lot to convince Paul to let him dress in street clothes, but he'd won the battle. He no longer looked like he was hovering at death's door, but he didn't look like he was going to win a race to the bathroom, either. He'd had major surgery after all, and the evidence was visible from the size of the bandage that covered his head.

"My source says you and Kovar Stefn were school chums. Is that true?"

"Yes."

"And is that how Nadja came to work at Quest?"

"Yes. I was presented with an opportunity. Kovar is quite wealthy. He was interested in investing some of it in my inventions."

"And in turn you made it possible for Nadja to join Quest?"

"That's correct. It was a bit unorthodox, but I knew him, and I trusted him. To this day I have trusted him and he's given me no cause to regret what I did. I simply saw no harm in—"

"Allowing a double agent into your midst."

"I wouldn't have had I known. I believe in Quest and our work there. If you think I would deliberately sabotage—"

"I don't."

"This other agency. Who does Q serve other than Quest?"

"We're not sure yet. She didn't offer that information, but we have it straight from her that she is a double agent."

Polax groaned, then walked to the hospital window on the third floor and looked out. "This is going to ruin me. Unless we can turn it around in some positive way I—"

"I've been thinking about that. There might be a way." Merrick started pacing slowly around the room; he needed to get his strength back and get out of there. But that wasn't going to happen if they kept feeding him watered-down soup and pureed fruit.

Polax turned from the window. "What do you mean, there might be a way?"

Merrick motioned to a file on the foot of the bed. "I've been going over the files. And I have an idea. We could turn this thing around."

"I don't see how. I've withheld information about Nadja to the board at Quest. When I return home and call a meeting…" Again he shook his head. "How in the hell am I going to tell them she's a double agent? Or that she's got a… Never mind. I just don't think there is any way to repair the damage."

"Don't call a meeting. Don't tell them."

"I'll be imprisoned if I don't."

"Only if they find out." Merrick rubbed his jaw, considering just how much of his plan to share with Polax.

"Then you have a plan?"

"Oh, yes, I have a plan, but it's going to take an act of faith on your part. An act of faith in me. Could you do that, Polax? Could you put yourself and Quest in my hands?"

Before Polax could answer, Merrick's private phone rang. Merrick picked it up and turned his back. "Yes."

"Sorry to bother you again," Jacy said. "There's something else I need to run by you."

"Okay, shoot."

"I've been doing some more digging for Bjorn. I've learned that Kovar Stefn used to be Holic Reznik's ski instructor. And since Kovar is Nadja's grandfather, and her sister is married to Holic…well, you can see where I'm going with this. Patterns and matches. You know me. I don't—"

"Believe in coincidences."

"No, I don't. Odd matches and triangles wave red flags. I'm beginning to think Holic is more valuable alive than dead. What do you say?"

"When we had him incarcerated last time we couldn't get anything out of him."

"Things change. Maybe we didn't offer him a sweet enough deal."

"You may be right. But I can't make that decision. I'll call the person who can, though, and see what he says. Did Bjorn act surprised by the news when you gave it to him?"

"Not really."

Merrick thought back to that day in Polax's office with Bjorn. He had sensed something was different the moment Nadja Stefn had entered the elevator. He didn't like surprises and he didn't like his agents holding out on him, either.

"Tell Bjorn to sit tight until I can make our case to the right pair of ears. I'll have an answer within the hour. Maybe you're right, maybe Holic would be more useful to us alive."

When he hung up the phone, Merrick said to Polax, "It just keeps getting better. I've learned that there's a connection between Holic Reznik and Kovar Stefn. It could be just a coincidence but—"

"I may be confused at the moment, but one thing I do know is that there is no such thing as coincidence."

Merrick grunted. "I was afraid you were going to say that. Then I'm back to my question. Do you have faith in my ability to handle this?"

"It looks like I don't have much choice."

"Then I need to know what else you're hiding. There's something, isn't there?"

"There is."

"Have a seat, and I'll order us breakfast. Would you like your applesauce with a bottle of water or without?"

* * *

Nadja needed to check out the chalets on Tulay Pass, but the current weather conditions weren't conducive to a ski trip. Not for a person with a nerve chip in her leg. To make the trip, she was going to have to wait until tomorrow, when a warming trend was supposed to push the temperatures up into the high thirties.

But she wasn't so sure that she would find him there. Not when the nightclub scene was so close.

Then it was settled—Tulay Pass tomorrow, and tonight she would visit the Two Winters nightclub and see if she got lucky. She had already picked up a few pieces of clothing at an exclusive dress shop in the lobby, but not anything naughty enough for After Shock.

An hour later, two shopping bags in hand, Nadja returned to her suite. As she closed the door, she saw a dark-haired young woman seated on the couch next to Alzbet. "Aunt Nad! Mom said you were here. I can't believe it. Finally I get to meet you. I'm Pris, your niece."

The dark-haired beauty left Alzbet on the sofa and hurried forward. She looked so much like Holic that Nadja stood speechless for a moment before setting down her shopping bags to accept her niece's open embrace.

Prisca's hair was as shiny and black as Holic's raven locks, and she had the same dramatic dark amber eyes, too. She also had her father's slender shape and long legs. If Mady had given her daughter anything, it was her feminine voice, sleek, well-shaped nose and shy smile. But truly she was Holic's daughter.

"I want to sit for hours and visit with you, but I need to get Alzbet to her ski lesson. Can we talk later? Mom said something about dinner."

Dinner would disrupt Nadja's evening plans. She

said, "I'm tired from the trip. How about lunch tomorrow, instead?"

"That's perfect. I'll tell Mom."

Nadja glanced at her darling daughter. Alzbet had come off the sofa. She was rubbing her left eye.

"What's wrong?" she asked.

"I have something in my eye."

Nadja squatted and lifted her daughter into her arms. "Let's have a look. We'll go into the bathroom where the light is better." She said to Prisca, "We'll be right back."

In the bathroom, she set her daughter on the vanity near the sink. "Okay, look up, and try not to blink."

Alzbet did as she was told, and Nadja examined her eye. There was an eyelash irritating the corner. As gently as possible she touched the corner with a tissue and collected the eyelash.

"It's all gone," she said. "Feel better?"

Alzbet blinked her blue eyes twice. Smiled, then reached out and hugged Nadja.

Nadja froze for a moment, then gathered her daughter into her arms. Her heart pounding, she hugged the child back. "I'm so sorry, baby. About everything."

Alzbet looked up at Nadja. "It's okay. My eye doesn't hurt anymore. See." She blinked and blinked.

Nadja laughed, then touched her daughter's adorable nose. "That's good."

Alzbet put her tiny hands on Nadja's cheeks and pushed them together, forcing her lips to pucker. Then she leaned forward and kissed her.

"You did good, Auntie Nud. Don't tell anyone, but I love you best."

Chapter 14

Bjorn's invitation came by messenger—an Alpine giant who stood four inches taller than Bjorn's six-three. His name was Jakob, and he was a bull of a man sporting a bald head, a uni-brow and scarred knuckles—all of them. A serious head cracker who lived for the sight of blood and the sound of bones breaking.

When the messenger left, Bjorn opened the invitation. It simply said he would be welcome at After Shock this evening, then listed the entertainment for the next three days.

He still wasn't sure if Holic was at Groffen, but if he was, then After Shock would be on his entertainment list. It was worth checking out.

Bjorn dressed in the rich man's suit that he'd purchased down in the lobby, then tied his hair back at the nape of his neck. He was just leaving his room when his phone rang. It was Jacy again.

"I spoke to Merrick a few hours ago, and he just called me back. Sorry, bro, but they want Holic back in Washington alive. Your agenda has changed. I know that's not what you wanted to hear, but—"

"It's not, but I figured it was going to come down to that."

Seven years with Onyxx had taught Bjorn to expect the unexpected. He wasn't surprised by any of what Jacy had told him. In fact, it cleared up a number of unanswered questions. And as much as he didn't like how the puzzle pieces were coming together, things were starting to make sense. Most of them, anyway.

"This sure is a twisted mess. So now what are you going to do?"

"I still don't have a definite location on Holic. He's here somewhere. I feel it in my gut."

"Go with your gut. It's never been wrong yet. Is there something else I can do?" Jacy asked.

"Not now. But I'll stay in touch." Bjorn thanked his friend for the information, then headed out the door.

In the elevator he turned his thoughts to Nadja. He had wanted to hunt her down all day, but he had resisted because he knew that his motives weren't entirely based on the mission.

Time, that's what he needed to clear his head, and so he had busied himself all day checking out every closet and storage room Groffen owned. He'd even found a body—an elderly woman in a closet up on the seventh floor. She'd been shot once between the eyes.

But now, hours later, he was back thinking about Nadja and how good it had been between them at Nordzum. So good that he couldn't let it go. That meant he was in big trouble.

See, that's why you never mix business with pleasure. It screws with your head and makes you want things that you knew you shouldn't want.

No, it makes you want what you can't have.

The tiny strapped dress was electric red—its design and purpose to give every healthy man at the nightclub a hard-on. But Nadja was only interested in one man looking at her twice—if Holic Reznik was there, she intended to be the feast for his insatiable appetite.

She'd twisted her hair up to show off her slender neck, and she had bought the lowest cut shimmering shift in the dress shop. And no bedroom assassin would be completely dressed without a pair of scarlet-red ankle-strap fuck-me heels.

The garnets that dangled from fine silver chains at her ears were delicate and expensive, her lips glossy and outlined to perfection. She had sprayed her shoulders with the sweet scent of Alpine heather, and sprinkled diamond dust across her chest.

I love you best.

Her daughter's voice came again, the memory so sweet that her heart constricted. She nearly tripped as she entered the club, and realized the danger of not staying focused. She redirected her thoughts and glanced around, noting that the dress was a hit—a number of eyes were already following her as she strolled through the crowd.

There were elegant black leather half-circle booths tucked into the outer walls. Hoping to spot Holic, she took her time scanning them one by one, and when she didn't find him there, or at the bar, she searched the dance floor. But she held out little hope that he would be there—not in his condition.

She made her way to a polished twenty-foot bar and perched on one of a dozen gold leather stools. "A dirty martini, please. Extra dry."

The bartender nodded, and as he mixed her drink, she turned and watched another dozen people walk through the black-and-gold door. None of the people were Holic, but she wasn't giving up. She continued to browse the room for Holic's flawless face and unforgettable long raven-black hair.

It was during her second run through the crowd that she spied the "memorable ass." Like before, at Quest a week ago, she recognized the tight tush immediately. He was, however, memorable in other ways tonight. His suit was expensive, his hair smoothed out, and she marveled at how he could go from rugged to refined so easily.

She felt a sense of pride looking at him. He was, after all, Alzbet's father.

As much as she liked looking at him, she didn't want to talk to him tonight. She left her martini on the bar, slid off her stool and started toward the door.

She refused to look back, or think about the laughter coming from the boobalicious brunette entertaining Bjorn and hanging on his arm and his every word. She almost made it through the door, but she stopped when she saw a head of long raven hair. The man had his back to her and he was talking to a blonde wearing a skirt that barely covered her gender.

She lingered near the door, and when he turned she saw, with disappointment, that it wasn't Holic. She started out the door, but this time she was stopped by a hand that caught her arm from behind. She didn't have to look back to know who it was. The touch was dangerously familiar.

Bjorn had spotted her before she could escape.

Not only spotted her, but caught her.

"Running away again?"

Nadja faced him. "No," she said easily. "There's just no reason to stay. What I'm looking for isn't here."

"You're right, he's not. I've already checked in every corner and under every table."

"So thorough."

"You know I am."

The comment was meant to remind her just how thorough he had been over the past three days. What followed was a knowing look, and the sexual content in it was as potent as his words.

A butterfly took flight in her stomach.

Nadja had never experienced butterflies until Bjorn Odell had come into her life five years ago. She had heard women talk about them, but she'd always thought they were an exaggeration—wishful feeling that was pure fiction. But they weren't fiction. Butterflies were real.

Bjorn had made them real.

He handed her the martini she'd ordered at the bar. "You forgot this."

"You saw me?"

"Who didn't see you when you came through that door? That's quite a dress."

She reached out and patted the lapel on his expensive jacket. She followed it up with "I see you've attracted at least one admirer tonight yourself."

"Then you saw me, too?"

She wished she'd held her tongue. But the memory of the woman clinging to Bjorn's arm had irritated her more than she would have liked.

He stepped closer, his eyes going straight to her mouth. "You left your partner this morning without saying goodbye and without wheels."

"But you're here. Which means you're as resourceful as you are thorough."

"Then you intended me to follow."

"I thought it best that we arrive separately."

"Why not just say so?"

"I'm not sure. Maybe I just needed to leave."

"We need to talk."

"About the mission."

"That and a few other things."

"We don't need to talk about anything other than the mission. Nordzum was nice. Let's leave it at that."

"Nice? It was...nice?"

"We can go back to the bar and talk strategy if you want, but I really don't have anything new to discuss at this time. Do you?"

"Not much." His eyes drifted to her cleavage. "This dress is making it hard to keep my mind on the mission, I mean. Maybe you and I should get out of here so you can take it off."

"I don't think so."

"It was just a thought."

Because she needed to distance herself from the way he continued to look at her, she took a step back and finished her drink. When she lowered the glass, she saw that he had lowered his gaze further, and was studying her curves crammed into the tight shift. Then her shoes.

"Can you dance in those heels?" he asked, studying her feet.

"Yes."

He brought his eyes back up and smiled. "Good, because they're playing our song."

That was ridiculous. They didn't have a song, but suddenly he had slipped his arm around her and was guiding her toward the dance floor. He took the empty glass from her, and as they passed by the bar, he set it down.

He drew her to him when they reached the lit circle, and she put one hand in his and the other on his shoulder. She would never have guessed that he could dance, but when he started to move to the music with sure feet—a slow romantic classic—she was stunned by how experienced he was in that…too.

He was her partner.

Her daughter's father.

Bjorn Odell, partner, father, lover.

Butterfly maker.

"If I wanted to wake up next to you tomorrow, what would it take? Will I have to tie you up?"

They kept moving in time to the music. "That would never happen," she said. "It's not a part of my game, but if you'd like me to tie you up, I'll indulge you."

"And what would you do to me after you tied me up?"

She leaned in and whispered next to his ear. "I would keep you my love slave for days on end."

"And where would this happen?"

"In a quiet beach house somewhere far away from here. On an island in the middle of the ocean."

Her bold answer had him pulling her closer. "When do we leave?"

Instead of continuing the game, she changed the subject. "Aren't you afraid that if Holic is here he'll recognize you?"

"I told you, he's not here."

He seemed so sure—sure of Holic and himself. "What have you learned?" she asked, knowing he had been busy all day.

"I learned you were quite a good skier years ago. There's a large picture of you at maybe fifteen in the lobby. You won some race in Zurich."

"One of many. I'm talking about the mission. Did you search every floor? Get into any rooms?"

"Yes." He shrugged, turned her in his arms and brought her back to him. His hand again palmed her ass with familiarity. "I found a dead body."

"What?"

"An old woman in her sixties. She was shot with a .45 between the eyes."

Nadja stiffened. "Where?"

"I found her stuffed in a closet up on seven."

It had to be Gerda. But who had shot her? Kovar must have followed through with her threat. Then he really hadn't known that the woman had been abusing Alzbet, or her years ago.

"What else? I'm your partner," Nadja said, matching his footsteps around the dance floor. "We're suppose to share everything."

"We have been." He kissed her neck.

"Tell me. Do you know where Holic is right now?"

"I know where he isn't. He's not here, or at After Shock."

"You know about After Shock? How? The club is by private invitation only. And—" She stopped herself, re-

membering that Mady had Bjorn's alias on her notepad.
He must have approached her. Did he know that they
were sisters?

"At what age did you become aware of After Shock's
existence?" he asked, dancing her toward the cove that
led to the exotic club.

She had been seventeen when she'd actually been allowed inside, and that had only been because she'd told
the doorman that it was an emergency, and she needed
to speak to her grandfather. But before that, she'd followed her grandfather one night, and when the guard
had left the door for a moment, she'd slipped inside. She
must have been thirteen, and she'd gotten caught. But
not before she'd realized what kind of place it was.

"Nineteen," she lied, because she didn't want to explain the other two times.

"We'll have to go...together sometime."

Or not, Nadja thought, pushing the image of Bjorn
with the laughing brunette out of her mind. The women
at After Shock would be all over him.

"Where did you learn to dance?"

"In Copenhagen. I stayed with a woman for a while
who liked to dance."

"Stayed?"

"I worked for her."

"And she taught you to dance?"

"*Ja,* to dance and other stuff."

It was the word *stuff* that caught Nadja's attention, and
she was suddenly curious as to what kind of *stuff* the
woman he had worked for had taught him. There was no
disputing that Bjorn's dancing skills ranked as high as
his talent in the bedroom and the shower. That he had
nice manners when he ate, and an uncanny ability to

survive. All these attributes were not typical of a street orphan.

Was the woman who had taught him *stuff* responsible for molding him into this confident overachiever? Had she been a mother figure to him, or something more intimate?

"How old were you when she took you in?"

"Fourteen."

"And you stayed how long?"

"Too long."

"Meaning?"

"It's not important."

When people used that line it meant it was very important, just not something they felt comfortable discussing. Nadja respected that. She was, however, still curious. But then, how could she not be—this was her daughter's father, and she suddenly wanted to know everything there was to know about him.

"We need to go somewhere," he offered close to her ear just as the music was ending.

"We shouldn't leave together."

"You're not planning on running away from me if I let you leave first, are you?"

She pulled back and looked at him so that he could see her face when she answered. See that she wasn't lying when she said, "There is no reason to run any longer. I've come to the end of the road, as they say. He's here somewhere."

They ended up at her suite. Bjorn insisted, following four minutes behind her and knocking only once. She knew why he'd wanted to visit her suite once she let him in—he cased the place like he was expecting to find Holic stashed in her closet.

Irritated, she said, "I would have told you if I'd found him, and if I had, I wouldn't have needed to go shopping to find something to wear tonight."

The mention of her clothes sent his eyes to her exposed shoulders, then to her breasts where they rose high above the contour of the sexy dress. From there, his gaze drifted to her narrow waist, then over her curvy hips. He studied her long legs last, then her naughty red-strapped high heels.

"Is this how you dress for work?" he asked.

"Sometimes. It depends."

"On what?"

He kept looking. Kept telling her with his eyes that he liked what he was seeing.

"Please stop looking at me like that. This really isn't who I am."

"Then who are you, Nadja...really? Tell me about the girl in that picture in the lobby. Then tell me about the tattoo."

"The tattoo is just a silly design. A heart with wings," she simplified, knowing that its meaning was far more than that. It was symbolic, and she'd used it to keep her sanity. When she touched it she felt close to her baby, and she'd needed to feel a connection. But Bjorn would never know the story behind it. He couldn't know.

"How is Mady?"

The question brought her out of her musing. "You already know, so why ask?"

"Tell me why your sister isn't listed anywhere in your file."

"Because she's my half sister and my father never claimed her. It was Kovar who cared for her growing up."

"And when did your sister marry Holic?"

"He followed her to Groffen and became one of Kovar's students for a while. She was seventeen when she ran off with him. They married a year later when she became pregnant."

"What is your plan, Nadja? Are you here to interfere in the mission? Where do you stand?"

"I stand beside you, Bjorn. You're my partner. And I'm prepared to follow through with our assignment. Killing Holic won't be a problem for me."

"We're not going to kill him."

"Excuse me?"

"The mission's been changed. We're suppose to capture him alive."

"No. That's impossible."

"My contact back in the States assures me that Quest is in agreement with Onyxx. We retrieve the kill-file, and apprehend Holic. Check with Polax if you don't believe me."

"Don't worry, I will."

Nadja had left her phone in the pocket of her wool cape when she had gone downstairs. She walked to the closet, retrieved it and dialed her commander.

Looking straight at Bjorn, she said to Polax the minute she heard his voice, "Is it true? Have our orders been changed?"

"Q, it's good to hear from you. I was going to call. Listen, Merrick has told me something disturbing. He claims you're a double agent. And he also says you're the sister to Holic's wife. Hell, Nadja, do you have any idea what you've done?"

She glared at Bjorn. "I could tell you that it isn't true."

"But it is true, isn't it?"

"Who gave Merrick the information?"

"Who do you think? Odell and that computer-whiz friend of his in Montana, Jacy Madox. I wish they had been wrong about you."

"They are."

"Merrick said you confessed to Odell."

She turned away so Bjorn couldn't hear. "I would never put Quest at risk. I know that the words 'trust me' sound ludicrous knowing what you know, but if you could do it just for—"

"My superiors will hang me for this if they find out how you came to Quest. What I've overlooked. And if I'm hung, so will you be."

"Give me some time."

"The only way you could possibly redeem yourself would be to make this mission a success and come back a winner. But even then…"

She looked over her shoulder at Bjorn. "To do that Holic must live?"

"Yes. We need him alive."

"Need him for what? Onyxx already interrogated him. He wouldn't talk."

"It's out of my hands, Q. Bring him back breathing. You have your orders."

"I've got to go."

"Q, wait! About this double agent business—"

"It never interfered with Quest. I kept the two jobs separate."

She hung up and laid the phone down on the coffee table. "Why did you tell your commander I was a double agent? We made a deal."

"Our deal was to keep the chip in your leg a secret, and I have. It's ours, just like I promised."

* * *

"Let's call it a night," he said, thinking that if he got her off her feet and into bed, then afterward she might tell him what she was still keeping from him.

There was something. He could see it in her eyes. Even more now that they were here at Groffen.

"Yes, let's call it a night. I'm exhausted."

She started to the door to see him out, but he pulled her back. Before she could protest, he slid his arm around her. "I'm staying here, with you."

"On the sofa?"

"You don't want that." He brought his hand up and palmed the back of her head. Holding her so she couldn't get away, he moved in to kiss her. She tried to avoid his lips, but he stayed with it. Caught her mouth. She let out a faint cry, then surrendered.

He kept the kiss going as he peeled the tiny strap off her shoulder and sent his lips down her throat, moving slowly past her collarbone.

"You smell good," he murmured. "Feel good."

He slid his hand over her ass, worked her against his crotch, then started to back up down the hall, taking her with him.

They moved in unison, and when her hands found the buttons on his shirt, he smiled and crossed the threshold into the bedroom, sliding the zipper down the back of her sexy dress.

Hard and aching, he didn't pay any attention to who had turned on the light next to the bed until a voice said, "Auntie Nad, who is that man?"

Chapter 15

It was amazing how things worked out. How the future could be reshaped in the blink of an eye. Holic smiled, feeling empowered by the plan he'd hatched.

"Do you know if Kovar's will is in order, Jakob?"

His henchman shrugged. "I don't know, but with so much at stake and his recent heart attack, I'm guessing it's up to date."

"Don't guess, find out. And find out how his billions will be split. Who gets what."

"Right away," Jakob promised. "Is there anything else?"

Holic's mind was suddenly working overtime. He could thank the drugs for that. His pain wasn't gone, but he couldn't feel it, and that was allowing him to think again. Think and make plans.

And what he was thinking was that Groffen was

worth a fortune, and although he had millions of his own, the idea of owning the lodge suddenly suited him. A man could never have too much money or too many women.

He had met Kovar years ago when his dream of becoming a professional skier had led him to train with one of the best instructors in the country. But few people have the makings of a champion, so Kovar had said, and Holic had fallen short. He would always remember how bitter he felt about that. But he supposed that he owed Kovar a thank-you anyway. He'd found his true talent after that— shooting guns and watching whatever he'd hit die.

Within a year, with the right connections, he'd become a busy freelance assassin. And over the years he'd been hired by some very rich, powerful men.

Yes, his idea was perfect. He would see to it that Mady was the sole heir to Groffen, and while she operated the lodge, Pris would take over his legacy, while he retired in style.

He'd invest, vacation, visit his many mistresses and enjoy a life surrounded by all that he loved.

"I'm guessing that the estate would be split among his three grandchildren," Jakob said.

"Unless of course there was an accident. Find out where Ruger and Nadja are these days. Do it immediately." He stroked his growing erection, courtesy of thoughts of his distant mistresses. "But before you get to work, run down to After Shock and bring me back a pair of long legs. Make sure she's just as sweet as the one you brought me after lunch, and just as talented with her tongue."

Jakob made a joke about being blown away, and Holic's laughter followed his henchman out the door.

He was still laughing a minute later when Mady walked in with a coffee tray and a sweet pastry.

"I've brought you something," she said, setting the tray on the table. She kissed him on the cheek.

He eyed the two cups. "Are you joining me?"

"I'd planned on it, but now I can't. There's a problem in the kitchen. I'm sorry, I have to go straight back."

"Don't be sorry. Groffen is important to you."

"I do love it here, Holic."

"Then maybe we should make plans to stay indefinitely."

"Could we?"

"I've been thinking about retiring here."

"Oh, Holic. That would be so wonderful."

He kissed her and she kissed him back, her smile making her look younger.

She checked her watch. "I wish I didn't have to go, but I do."

"Go, and don't think about me. I'm going to bed early. Thank you for bringing me the coffee and sweets, but lately I've been thirsty for champagne. Can you have a bottle sent up?"

"Of course."

"And a bowl of strawberries with whipped cream."

Bjorn spun around searching the room for the voice. He still had his hand on Nadja's zipper. It was halfway down her lovely spine, and he sent it back up.

"Alzbet," Nadja whispered. "What are you doing here, sweetheart?"

"I had a bad dream. The witch was chasing me."

Bjorn watched Nadja hurry to the bed and scoop up the child who sat in the middle. The kid looked maybe five. It was the little girl he'd seen with Mady earlier in the day. "The witch is going to find me and—"

"No, she won't, Alzbet. I told you she's not going to hurt you anymore. I've taken care of it."

Bjorn cleared his throat and Nadja glanced over her shoulder. "You're going to have to leave."

"Leave?"

"Now."

"Now?"

"Are you having a hearing problem?"

He glanced at the kid, then back to Nadja. She had her arms around the girl like she thought he was going to steal her. He wasn't. He didn't share the same sentiments about children that most people did. He felt sorry for them, that was about it. Life sucked, and if you were a kid it sucked even more.

So who was this kid? And who had brought her into this messed-up world? he wondered. Was she Mady's and Holic's child. He knew they had a daughter named Prisca, but she was older.

He stepped closer to get a better look and Nadja went ballistic. She shot off the bed. "I said leave, Bjorn. I mean it. Now!"

"Is he a bad man, Auntie Nad?"

The kid had pulled back to get a breath of air. That made sense; Nadja was squeezing the girl so damn tight he was surprised she wasn't turning blue.

"He's not bad," she said, "it's just late and you need to sleep now."

The last word was punctuated with a solid get-your-ass-gone glare directed at Bjorn.

"I'm not tired. Aunt Mady says if I'm not tired I can read. Did you know that I can read?"

"No, I didn't. That's wonderful. But I'm afraid there aren't any books in here that would interest you, and it's very late. You should have been asleep hours ago."

Bjorn listened to the conversation. Nadja was all soft words and gentle tones with the kid. He watched her tuck the girl back into bed and kiss her forehead.

"You can sleep here tonight. I'll settle it with your grandpa. Close your eyes, I'll be back in a few minutes." She turned out the light, before Bjorn got a good look at the kid, then grabbed his arm and tugged him out of the room and closed the door.

He let her lead him into the living room, and once they were there she let go of his arm and turned and faced him. Her sweet disposition—the one she'd tailored for the kid—was gone now. Her jaw was set and she looked ready for a fight.

"So who is—"

"Shut up, Bjorn. I don't want to answer any questions right now. I just want you to go back to your room and we'll talk in the morning."

"Tell me about the kid first. Whose brat?"

"She's not a brat. She's…"

He saw her hands fist at her sides and her nostrils flare. He gauged the signs, said, "What is it, Nadja? What don't you want me to know? At Nordzum we made a deal, remember?"

"Okay, then I'll tell you what you want to know."

"Good. I'm waiting."

A rap on the door interrupted them, and Nadja spun around just as her niece said, "Aunt Nad, it's Prisca. Can I come in? It's important."

Nadja glanced at Bjorn, and he quickly nodded. "Ask her in."

"Not dressed like this."

He tossed her the black sweater dress that had been draped across the back of the couch, motioned for her to get rid of her shoes and the pins in her hair, then started to back out of the room and head for the hall.

"Bjorn, get back here," she warned as she held the black dress in one hand and began to pull pins out of her hair with the other. "Bjorn, not the bedroom."

"Are you awake, Aunt Nad?"

Two hours later Nadja opened the door to her bedroom wearing the black sweater dress and bare feet to find Bjorn asleep on the bed, their daughter curled against him. She was so taken aback by what she saw that her heart nearly stopped.

She couldn't move, and yet she needed to. Needed to get Bjorn out of there. No, it would be better if she took Alzbet back to Kovar's suite.

They were sharing a pillow, and the light beside the bed lit up their faces. Alzbet was a mix of both of them, but she could see her daughter had Bjorn's sleek nose and his skin tone. Her mouth and heart-shaped face were her mother's.

Nadja touched her own cheek, followed the contour down to her chin. She was again struck by the miracle of her daughter. The miracle of Alzbet here. Her baby. Her daughter asleep next to her father.

Quietly she walked to the bed and scooped up Alzbet in her arms. She stayed sleeping, and Nadja left her suite with her daughter's head resting on her shoulder. She had expected Kovar's door to be locked, but it wasn't. She stepped inside, her intention to put Alzbet to bed, then leave.

But Kovar was sitting in the living room at his desk. He wore a black robe and his gray hair hung to his shoulders. The desk lamp was turned down low, but she could make out that he was again at his computer.

She walked up behind him and saw that he was again watching a skier on the slopes. But this time it was her daughter's little form, and like her mother, it appeared Alzbet wasn't afraid of speed.

"She reminds me of you." He turned, glanced at Alzbet on Nadja's shoulder. "Is she all right?"

"Yes. I found her in my bed."

He raised an eyebrow. "You didn't tell her—"

"No. She was having a bad dream. She was being chased by Gerda."

"That bitch... I never knew that she was hurting you for all those years. You never said anything, but you should have. Anyway, she won't be hurting Bethy any longer. Put her to bed, then we'll talk."

Nadja did as he asked, tucked her child into her bed, then returned to the living room. Kovar had turned off the computer and switched on a lamp in the corner. He wasn't using his wheelchair but it was close by in case his ankles gave out. He'd poured himself a glass of wine.

"Sit," he said, and pointed to the chair backlit by the lamp. "Would you like something to drink?"

"No."

She did sit, however, though she was anxious to return to Bjorn. She didn't want him waking up and finding her gone again. She wasn't sure what he would do if that happened.

There were several minutes of dead silence, then he said, "I wanted to tell you that I called Velich and told him that the chip is holding up and so are you. He appreciated the call and told me to tell you that he's at your disposal anytime, and reminds you that your checkup is next month. You need to go this time."

"I will."

More silence.

"About my heart. I told you today that I was fine, but the truth is I'm not as well as I would like. But death…it comes to all of us. Some of those bastards you've blown away weren't thirty."

"True."

"Anyway—" he eased down on the red velvet couch and lifted each leg onto the cushions "—I want you to know that I've provided for Bethy's future. She'll be cared for regardless."

This was an odd conversation.

Nadja pushed her hair away from her face. "I can provide for my daughter."

"No, my Bethy will have what she needs, and it will come from me."

"Why? Why can't you just let me have her? Why can't you change how you think? Why can't you alter the future? You have the power."

"Because we can never shed our true skin, Nadja. Our past shapes who we are. The lessons learned serve the future. Remember that. If you're smart you will own who we've become, and embrace it. I embrace who I am, and what I own I will never surrender—not my property nor my creed. Not even in death."

Holic was livid. Jakob had just given him the bad news.

"Tell me again."

"I said the kid gets everything. The whole damn estate."

Holic couldn't believe it. Something was wrong. Why would Kovar change his will and give his entire estate and all his billions to Ruger's four-year-old kid?

"You're sure she gets everything, Jakob?"

"I'm sure, Holic, but here…look at this. I made a copy of the will for you. The kid's not Ruger's."

"What?"

"She's Nadja's child."

"She can't be. Mady wouldn't have lied about that."

"Well, that's what it says here."

Jakob laid the paper on the table and flipped through it so Holic could see the proof of his words.

"Kovar's no fool," Holic said. "In order for the will to be valid he needs proof. A birth certificate."

"I haven't found that yet, but I'm working on it. Look at this." Jakob dug into his pocket once more, pulled two pictures out and laid them on the table. One was of Nadja at age seven or eight, and the other a current picture of Alzbet. "They look a lot alike. Especially their hair color."

"Ruger's blond," Holic pointed out. But there was a certain likeness between Nadja and the girl, aside from the hair.

"And here's Nadja a few years ago, I think." Jakob pulled out another picture. "I got this out of Kovar's bedroom."

Holic stared at the second picture of Mady's sister. A fairly current picture, he imagined. He frowned suddenly, realizing that he'd seen her somewhere recently. And then it dawned on him where.

"Leave me, Jakob," Holic said in a dead calm. "I have some work to do."

In the dark, in front of his computer, Holic brought up the kill-file and sifted through the many faces. He rarely scanned ahead and read profiles on his victims until he was actually on the hunt for them, but he did enjoy looking at their faces from time to time.

"Ah, there she is," he said, studying a similar picture to the one Jakob had filched from Kovar. She was number twenty-six on the Chameleon's list. He selected the picture, hit Enter and pulled up her file. And as he read he opened his drawer and reached for the bottle of pills he'd come to depend on over the past week.

"Interesting," he muttered. "She's been an agent for EURO-Quest for six years. She goes by the nickname Q, and she's considered the best bedroom assassin in the intelligence business."

Holic smiled at the last, his mind working overtime now that he was again high. He began to plot his next move, a little disappointed that such a lovely creature would have to die. But in death games such as this there could be only one winner.

Chapter 16

Nadja slipped back into her suite and headed for the bedroom. She was guiding herself through the dark, sidestepping the furniture from memory, when a light next to the sofa switched on.

"I thought you weren't going to run."

"I returned Alzbet to her own bed."

"Whose kid is she, Nadja?"

She hesitated, then followed through with her plan. "She's Ruger's little girl. My brother's child."

"The priest had a kid?"

"Yes. And I don't need to hear any crude comments, so keep them to yourself if you have any."

He stood and came toward her. He was in the suit pants he'd worn to Two Winters, but he'd taken off his jacket, unbuttoned his shirt and pulled it loose. His hair was again down and made him ruggedly handsome.

"You've been his confidante through this, haven't you?"

"Yes.

"That's why when he stopped writing those letters you got so worried."

"Yes. But I don't want to talk about any of that now."

"What do you want to talk about?"

Nadja wet her lips with the tip of her tongue. "I don't want to talk at all," she said in a soft seductive voice.

He kept moving forward, and it forced Nadja to either stand her ground or back up. She took a few steps back and, when she felt the wall against her spine, she said, "Now what? What are you going to do to me? Will I like it?"

"You have before."

"I can't deny it." And she wouldn't, not tonight. "You want to kiss me?"

"You know I want to kiss you."

"While I touch you."

"That would be...nice."

She smiled. "Nice?"

"I've decided I like your word for us."

Us. Nadja steeled herself against reading too much into that word. If Bjorn ever learned the truth about Alzbet he would...

He would what? Hate her? Punish her? Take the child? Or maybe all of it and more. Maybe he would want her dead.

"What's wrong?"

"Nothing's wrong. The mission has had delays and setbacks, but now I think we're on the right track. Holic's here, we just have to—"

"We'll strategize tomorrow. You were right, the other

agents hunting Holic are combing the mountains of Otz. We're at least two days ahead of them now. We have time."

"And the shooter, who do you think that is?"

"I don't know. That's been a concern, but since there hasn't been an incident for five days, I'm thinking we might have lost him in that snowstorm."

"And the wounds…" Nadja reached out and lightly touched the small bandage on Bjorn's neck. "How is this?"

"Almost ready for the stitches to come out."

"And your thigh?"

"Good. But I do have a growing pain a few inches to the left."

Nadja arched an eyebrow, feigned worry. "Oh? Would you like me to take a look?"

He came closer, crowded her space. "I'd like you to do more than look. You mentioned something about touching me while I kiss you."

She let him kiss her then, as she slid her hands inside his open shirt and to the back of him. He was such a strong sturdy man, so solid. That had been one of the attractions. She'd never been able to lean on anyone, but somehow she knew it would be different with Bjorn.

No, it could have been different if they had met in another lifetime.

She let him coax her mouth open. His tongue was so very…nice. His hands moved over her hips, drew the sweater dress up an inch at a time. The heat from his mouth was potent, and his hands on her body were making her hot.

Each time he touched her it was new and exciting, and she marveled at that.

She forced him to step back as she worked his belt loose, then unzipped him. When he broke the kiss, she sent her mouth over his jaw. Then to the bandage, lightly touching it with her lips, as she slid her hand into his pants to touch him there.

She heard him exhale heavily, and she smiled. He was already hard and stretched. She brought her eyes up to his face, and that's when he said, "You really are amazing, you know. And I'm not just talking about this. The sex."

She wasn't going to buy into that line. She knew from past experience that men said anything when their pants were on the way to the floor. Men were all about getting off—it was at the front and at the back of everything they said and did when they were in a woman's company.

She said, "That's what they all say, baby, but thanks anyway. At least I know I'm not slipping."

She had said the wrong things, and she knew it the minute the words came out of her mouth. He pushed her away and stepped back, but then suddenly he was back, pushing her against the wall hard and fast.

"You know, honey, that isn't what I wanted to hear right now. You..."

"Bjorn, you're hurting me. Let go."

He didn't let go, but he loosened his grip. "No more talking. You didn't want to talk so we won't. We'll just fuck, since that's what you're used to."

"No!" She tried to shove him away, but he held her against the wall and kissed her roughly. Suddenly he stopped, swore and stepped back.

"Bjorn..."

"I'm out of here."

"No, please…"

He turned back. "Please what?"

She stepped forward, put her hands on his smooth warm chest. "I'm sorry. It was a defensive thing. What I said. I—" She broke off and lowered her head.

He reached out and cupped her chin, lifted. "Look at me." When she did, he said, "Tell me what you want. It's that simple."

It wasn't simple at all. "You're the profiler," she said. "You tell me."

"I want to hear it from you."

"I want…heaven. I want the butterflies."

"Butterflies?"

"The butterflies I didn't believe existed until that night in Vienna. Release the butterflies, Bjorn. Consume me."

She didn't give him time to answer. She slipped away from him and wiggled out of her dress, leaving her in black panties and nothing else. Her gaze found his and she knew in that moment that she had him, had him all the way.

And that was the plan, Nadja told herself. She was on top of the game as always, doing what she'd been trained to do. At least that's the way she had to play out tonight. The only way she could play it.

Life wasn't fair, but she'd learned that by the age of ten. Her heart's desire didn't enter into this game. There was no room for luxuries such as love and wishful thinking. She would make another memory, and that would have to be good enough.

Nadja savored the taste of Bjorn all night and then again in the shower the next morning. And by evening she was again dressed to kill and on the hunt for Holic Reznik, in the most likely place he'd be if he was at Groffen.

Nadja took the back stairs, whispered a single word to the lean-faced guard, then watched as he opened the door into the decadent underground club. She swept her red shawl from her shoulders, handed it to him, then smiled as his eyes widened and his cock stiffened.

"I guess I wore the right outfit," she said, then strolled into the club dressed in a naughty red see-through fishnet dress.

She felt anxious. After last night she realized that she couldn't continue to play such a dangerous game with Bjorn. He was too smart to deceive for very long, and that meant they needed to get this mission in the bag and get out of Austria. Once he was far away from Groffen, she would decide what to do about Alzbet. With Gerda gone, she had time to make plans for her daughter.

Inside After Shock she saw that nothing had changed. The lights in this first room were the same dif fused purple that she remembered, with the same fa-mous smoky mist rising off the floor. The atmosphere was what had made the club famous. It was all about the mood—and that had been created with an unusual colored mist that changed from room to room.

Soft erotic music floated on the air as Nadja walked deeper into the room. Her steps were as seductive as her appearance, and she fit in easily. The people inside were beautiful, and smiling.

This particular room was the warm-up room, where introductions were made and the nature of your desire and expectations were explored. There was a full bar and intimate tables. Plush couches and a dance floor. The furniture was soft on color and expensive on comfort, inviting you to relax and stay...all night. And beyond the purple room, a dozen other rooms existed, designed to fulfill your every shocking fantasy.

She hadn't spoken to Bjorn since that morning when he'd left her suite saying he was going to check out the chalets up on Tulay Pass. It had been too cold for her to go with him, and he'd mentioned it before she had. She wasn't worried that he hadn't returned yet. There were several chalets along the pass and it was a job that would take more than one day, though he had told her he would be back tonight. When she didn't find Holic in the first room, she moved on to the next. It was circular with a built-in plush butter-cream-colored sofa that outlined the continuous wall. Lap dancers were hard at play everywhere, their practiced moves slow and grinding. Potent and infectious. She scanned the crowd to see if Holic was among the guests seated on the sofa. Searched the shadowed faces.

The dim lighting and the smoky mist—a murky yellow in this room—hung heavy in and around the moving, moaning bodies, making it hard to identify the players.

If Holic was one of them, she couldn't tell.

Not giving up yet, she moved through the mist. She was sure he wouldn't recognize her; they hadn't seen each other in eons. She doubted that he had ever thought about what had become of Mady's shy little sister after he stole Mady away from Groffen.

She had met Mady and Prisca at noon for lunch. They had brought Alzbet with them and she had sat beside her daughter. During the meal they had laughed and talked about nothing important. Finally Mady had asked how long Nadja planned to stay.

Alzbet had piped up and said, "Forever, pleeease, Auntie Nad. Stay forever."

Nadja's heart had broken then. She'd wanted to scoop up her daughter and hug her, then run, run as fast and as far away as she could. But running wasn't the answer. Kovar would never stop hunting her if she ran with her daughter—not without a perfect plan of escape.

She turned down two men who stopped to invite her to join them for some fun. She had expected the attention. After all, she was dressed for the kind of fun men liked best. But she wasn't interested in playing with just anyone tonight.

If Holic was here, in one of the rooms, she would find him. And once she did, she intended to feed the monster a deadly dose of Nadja Stefn.

The yellow mist swirled around him, and Holic closed his eyes. He was high again and liking it, as well as the woman with the skilled hands and the gyrating hips. She made him feel invincible.

Or was that the drugs making him feel so damn horny?

He'd been confined on the tenth floor too many days. The short hour he had been out on the firing range with Pris hadn't helped his restlessness.

His hand was still as useless as the day he arrived—useless and so painful that he'd been forced to use the drugs regularly to get through his waking hours. He knew that the drugs weren't the answer, but he would worry about that later.

"You stupid bitch! Watch out for my hand."

"I'm sorry," the blonde purred. "So sorry…"

"Prove it. Get off my lap and on your knees."

Holic waited for her to do as he asked, and when she did, he closed his eyes. She slid her hands down the inside of his legs, her thumbs extended wide to catch and tease his erection. His head fell back and he let the music and her skilled hands take him. He really shouldn't have doubled the dose on those painkillers, he thought. He felt like the room was spinning.

He blinked open his eyes in time to see a beautiful blond vision stroll past him. She had hair past her shoulders and her body was crammed into a see-through shift. Under it she wore a red leather bra and thong.

She was amazing.

The sight of the blonde turned him on more than did the bitch between his legs. He swore, tried to push the redhead away and stand up, but the room spun again and he slumped back on the sofa.

The beauty glanced his way, and he thought she looked familiar. Then the thought vanished as the woman between his legs lowered her head.

He moaned when she swallowed him up in a bath of hot wet heat and began to suck.

"Ahh…that's good," he said on the end of a long groan. "Go after it, bitch. Get it good."

When she saw him she was ready to move on to the next room. But there he was, sprawled on a sofa with the yellow mist hiding all but his face and raven-black hair.

His forehead was damp with sweat, but it wasn't entirely pleasure related. He looked pale, his cheeks thinner than in the picture in his file. She wondered about his injured hand. It was hidden in the mist, and she was curious to see what it looked like. Still bandaged? Still useless? Or was he back one hundred percent and more dangerous than ever?

He didn't look a hundred percent. What he looked was high. That wasn't in his profile—that he had an addiction to anything other than killing and women.

Nadja stopped, and their eyes met. Holic's were a rich shade of brown—she remembered that from the pictures in his file—but they were as empty as a bottomless hole. Yes, it was all in the eyes. Eyes were the window to your soul, and what she saw in Holic's eyes was a very black soul.

He deserved to die, and yet the mission had been changed. His life would be spared—that was Polax's orders. But…accidents happened.

It would be so easy to kill him here and now. She could join the party—his party—then silence him with a kiss. But she wouldn't kill him tonight. She needed to locate the kill-file, and if he'd been clever in hiding it, she would need his cooperation, willing or not, in uncovering it.

Nadja was so focused on Holic and what her next move would be, she never noticed the man who had been watching her from across the room. The same man who now slipped up behind her and whispered in her ear.

She had no time to react to his words before he swept her up in his arms. In a matter of seconds he had her on the leather sofa, swallowed up in the mist.

She inhaled sharply as something stung her eyes and burned her throat. She blinked, fought the yellow mist. But it wasn't the mist that was smothering her.

She slumped on the sofa, vulnerable to whatever game her companion wished to play, as the odd smell overtook her.

"I saw her," Holic insisted. "She's here, Jakob, so find her."

"Are you sure it wasn't someone who looked—"

"Don't question my eyesight. It was Nadja. She was at After Shock. Start there, and search the entire lodge if you have to."

That was an hour ago. Now in his room, the drugs wearing off a little, Holic was able to collect his thoughts as well as the images he'd seen at the club. The woman in red was Nadja Stefn.

"Why would she be here?" he muttered more to himself than Jakob. "Unless she's here searching for me." The idea put a new slant on Holic's plans. He said, "Do some legwork, Jakob, and do it quickly. Make some phone calls. Narrow down which agencies are gunning for me. And then find her...find Nadja."

"If she's here, Mady would know what room she's staying in," Jakob pointed out.

"Check the registry, but be careful not to alarm my wife. If her sister is here, she's probably aware of it."

But was she aware that Nadja was here looking for him?

The question needed an answer, and Holic was determined to get it. If Mady knew that the brat was Nadja's and she had lied about it, then she could also be aware of her sister's affiliation with Quest and why she'd come to Groffen.

No, his wife would have told him if that was the case.

Mady loved him above all else. Her loyalty was unconditional.

He would always be her first priority.

Holic waited to hear from Jakob. Two hours passed, and then another, before his henchman knocked on his door. But he didn't have good news to report where Nadja was concerned. She was no longer at After Shock, or Two Winters, or in the suite she was staying in on the fourth floor.

But he did have a piece of good news. It looked like Holic would have his revenge on the past after all. Jakob had learned that Quest had teamed up with Onyxx a week ago to hunt him down. That the man who was Q's partner was none other than Bjorn Odell, his old enemy—and the man responsible for crushing his hand was here as well.

"Find out which room Bjorn Odell is in," Holic ordered. "Quietly, Jakob. I don't want to spook Odell until I'm ready to make my move."

Chapter 17

Nadja woke up with Mace Kimball in her line of vision. He was twirling a six-inch knife in one hand, with the dexterity of a circus performer, while holding a phone to his ear with the other.

"Tell him I have her. Tell the bossman she's as good as dead, just like he ordered. And tell him Odell will be next. I've already set the trap."

Nadja listened as she glanced around. She was tied to a bed, her arms stretched out over her head and lashed to the iron headboard. Her legs had been shackled to the bed as well. Her fishnet dress had been removed.

"What the hell, Kimball," Nadja said the minute he disconnected and slipped his phone into his pocket. What's all this? Why am I tied up?"

"You know my name? I'm surprised. In the past five years at Quest I've never heard you use it."

Of course she knew his name. He was one of the "butlers" at Quest, one of the elevator guys who also ran the halls, juggling files and coffee between boardrooms. Kimball was the long-bodied, short-legged one with a receding hairline, and bad gums.

"I don't really work for Quest, you know."

"So who do you work for?"

He grinned. "Wouldn't you like to know."

Nadja decided she had just found the shooter. She said, "The shot at the Vienna airport was hurried, Kimball. Bjorn and I both would have been dead if you had eased the trigger instead of jerked it."

"It wasn't me, it was the snow conditions."

"And what was your excuse at Wilten Parish?"

He didn't like her bringing up his shortcomings. He stepped forward and backhanded her across the face, driving her teeth into her inner cheek. She tasted blood.

"Odell will die today. Within the hour, while you watch. And then..." He slid his hand up her thigh, over her narrow red leather thong, then down her other thigh. "Then you and I are going to get to know each other better—before I kill you, too." He licked his full lips. "My orders said nothing about not enjoying my job."

"I had no idea you were such a party boy, Kimball."

"I like to party," he acknowledged, "and we will. But not right now. We'll wait for Odell to show up. I've invited him to join us."

Nadja again checked out her surroundings. If they were in a gaming room at the club that meant it was soundproof, and Kimball had the only key. And by the plush interior and smoky blue paint on the wall, it looked like that's where they were.

The best she could hope for was that Kimball would

grow anxious, or her taunts would get him so over-
heated that he would alter his master plan.

"Come on, baby." She blew him a kiss, concentrated on making her nipples hard beneath her leather
bra. "What are you made of, Kimball? I've seen all
kinds. Long, short, thick, skinny. Which one are you?
Come on, big guy, show me your party animal and
let's play."

Nadja must have struck a nerve. Mace Kimball obviously didn't have a sense of humor.

She said, "Being overly sensitive isn't a good sign.
Or do I have it all wrong, Kimball? From experience I
know what's hidden in a man's pants is attached to his
ego. And I can well understand that, because I'm a
woman and I know what I like. What every woman
likes if they're honest. Here's a tip, Mace, we like our
fun-sticks two ways. Big and…bigger. Which one are
you? Or is there a reason for that sober, *limp* look on
your face?"

"You're a bitch, Q. I never did like you," he said, then
he reached for the chloroform rag he'd used on her earlier and shut her up.

Bjorn pulled out of his pocket the note—the one that
he'd found under his door when he returned from Tulay
Pass. Examining it again, he wondered why Nadja
wanted him to meet her in a private room at After
Shock? Why not just call him and leave a message on
his phone?

His gut told him that something was wrong. That the
note wasn't from Nadja. That's why he had ignored the
time and decided to show up early.

He located game room three, the room designated on

the note, but he didn't knock on the door; he walked past it and found an alcove. He pulled his phone from his pocket and made a call to Jacy.

When his friend picked up, he said, "Do you remember me asking if you could get a floor plan of Groffen? How did you do?"

"I got it."

"Take a look at it and tell me if the rooms in the underbelly are self-contained and can only be accessed through the front door, or if there's another entrance and exit."

"Hang on. Let me pull up the blueprint on the computer." A few seconds later, Jacy said, "Some of the rooms have false walls that enable the rooms to double in size, and some have secondary entrances."

"Does room three have a false wall?"

"It does," Jacy offered.

"Does it join with room four or two, or both?"

"Just two."

"Thanks. I'll catch you later."

Bjorn hung up, then tried door number two. He found it locked and cursed his luck. He backed up and tried room three, turning the knob as gently as he could. It was unlocked, but then he had known it would be. Whoever was inside—and he doubted that it was Nadja—wanted him walking into a trap.

He didn't go in. He backed off and checked his watch. He was thirty minutes early—that was the only advantage he would have, and it wasn't much. If whoever was inside was paying attention, he would have seen that doorknob turn.

He pulled his .38 from his shoulder holster and then made his move. He went in fast, and luck was on his side. The man was definitely not expecting him yet. The guy spun away from the bed with his pants down around his ankles. It gave Bjorn an open view of the bed where Nadja lay on her back, tied up. He saw the blood on her lips, saw her breasts uncovered.

By the time he looked back to the man with the short-changed dick, he was staring down the iron sights of a SIG-Sauer.

Bjorn fired, but only after he saw the flash of fire from his adversary's gun. He felt the sting of the bullet, and that, he knew, was a good sign. Even though he was getting sick of being shot on this mission, feeling the burn meant he was still alive.

The man across the room, however, wasn't so lucky. He was dead as he hit the floor.

"You killed him. Dammit, Bjorn, now we'll never know who Kimball was working for."

"Kimball? You know this guy?"

"He works for Quest. At least I thought he did. But he's a double agent."

"There are a lot of them floating around," Bjorn said as he cut through the ropes that held Nadja prisoner.

She gave him a pissed-off look. "Cute. You can go now," she said.

She remained on the bed for a moment. Her bruised shoulder hurt and the red marks on her breasts from Kimball's sick torture made her cringe, but she pushed it aside. This was no different from the other times.

She saw Bjorn staring at the corpse and she wondered what he was thinking. Kimball lay on the floor with a bullet hole between his eyes and his pants down around his brown loafers, his genitals exposed.

On shaky legs, she stood. She felt dizzy from the chloroform, and she locked her knees.

"We needed him alive, Bjorn. A dead man tells no tales, and right now I'd like to hear his," she said. "I'd like him to sit up and spill. Not more blood, or any other body fluids, just who the hell he was working for."

"He fired first."

The words sent Nadja's eyes toward Bjorn and she saw that he'd been shot, again. Blood was oozing from his arm.

"He shot you."

"Oh, is that what's wrong? I've been getting creased so damn many times this past week that the color red is starting to look as good on me as it does on you."

He was staring at her red leather thong, frowning.

"Where the hell were you, or do I have to ask? Where did Kimball get the drop on you?"

"I was here looking for Holic, and guess what. I found him. He's here."

She felt good saying that. It made all this worth while.

"Still," Nadja said, "couldn't you have just wounded him? He was hired to kill us, and I'd like to know by who."

"Did he admit he's the one who's been tailing us since the airport?"

"Yes." She gave him another annoyed look. "What are we going to do with the body?"

He stepped forward and gently touched her bruised shoulder. "That looks like it hurts."

"The body, Bjorn? Where are we going to put it?"

"I don't like you doing this."

"Doing what?"

"What you do."

"The body? How are we—?"

"I'll take care of it later." He pulled the blanket off the bed and wrapped it around her shoulders, then crouched and riffled through Kimball's pockets for the key. When he stood, he jerked the sheet off the bed and tossed it over the half-naked dead body.

"Come on. I'll lock him in and be back later."

As they left the room, Bjorn put his arm around her. "You need some ice on your jaw."

"I need a shower worse," she said.

"Done. And I'll order you a *mélange*."

Again Bjorn ignored his gunshot wound to see to Nadja's needs first. She'd protested when he insisted that they go to his room instead of hers. But he'd held fast to his decision. In the end he swept her into his room and locked the door behind them.

"I have no clothes," she said. "I—"

"You don't need clothes. There's a robe behind the door in the bathroom. I'll get you some clothes from your room later."

He walked past her and headed for the bathroom. He turned on the shower, laid out a white towel, and when he came back into the room he saw that she hadn't moved.

"What's wrong?"

"Let me see how bad Kimball's bullet 'creased' you."

"It's not any worse than the others," he assured her.

She examined the wound after he slipped off his shirt. "Kimball must be a lousy shot. You're right, flesh wounds all three of them."

"Lucky for me."

He wrapped his arms around her and pulled her close.

She angled her head and he pressed for contact. When she inched closer and let go of the blanket he hugged her.

She whispered, "Are you going to make me say it?"

"Not if you can't."

She looked up at him. "You have the power to make me forget my name, Bjorn, when you're touching me. You have a way of making me forget everything ugly in my life when we're together. Make Kimball disappear from my mind. Make me forget my name and all the ugliness."

He studied her face, and it must have made her uncomfortable because she broke eye contact, then wiggled out of his arms and walked into the bathroom.

He called room service for the *mélange,* then followed, stripping off his clothes as he went. His arm was still oozing blood, but he ignored it. The red thong was on the floor, and he stepped over it to enter the shower.

She had arched her body and tipped her head back to catch the shower spray. He watched her, waited, and then, with one taste, it was happening again—time stood still and nothing else mattered but being a part of Nadja.

Two hours later Bjorn stood by the window with his pants riding low on his hips and his chest bare. He puffed on a cigarette while his eyes followed the lights that covered the mountain. It was almost midnight and there were still skiers on the slopes.

Nadja had bandaged his arm after they left the shower. Like his previous wounds it was more of an annoyance than actually painful. Hardly of any significance except to prove that Mace Kimball was a bad shot under pressure.

Nadja was right; he should have shot off Kimball's kneecap instead of planting his bullet between his eyes. Now it would be damn hard, maybe impossible, to find out who he had been working for. But at the time he hadn't been thinking about the Agency, or what he'd rehearsed time and again in his training years. In that instant all he'd had on his mind was killing that sorry bastard for what he had done and was about to do to the woman he loved.

Yes, the woman he loved. He loved Nadja, and…

"Bjorn…"

He turned from the window and saw her standing naked in the amber light by the bed. Her eyes told him she wanted him again, and there was no question that he wanted her…all the time.

This was why emotional baggage on a mission was deadly. At the moment he didn't give a damn about Mace Kimball or where Holic was. All he wanted was to take Nadja in his arms, and hear her moan when he was inside her again.

"What are you thinking?"

"I'm thinking you look cold." Then he put out his cigarette and made his move.

"He's going by the name Lars Larsen. But it's him. He's in 609. And I found out something else I think you'll find amusing."

Holic turned back from the window in his suite to see his henchman grinning. The sight irritated him. If he wasn't feeling happy, he really didn't want to see anyone else happy. And he wasn't happy. His hand was throbbing again and he needed another hit, but it was too soon.

"I'm not in the mood to play Twenty Questions, Jakob. Get on with it."

"What I know is that Odell and Nadja might be partners, but that's not all they are to each other. Odell is screwing her."

"How do you know that?"

"I paid off the boy on a room service call to Odell's room. He says Bjorn Odell came to the door fresh out of the shower with a towel around his waist, and that Nadja came out a minute later wrapped up in a robe. He said her hair was wet and she looked flushed, like she'd just gotten out of the shower, too. Or maybe she was glowing for another reason, you suppose?"

Holic didn't find the situation a bit amusing. Odell and Nadja? No, he didn't like that, not one bit. After seeing her at After Shock he'd been fantasizing about her, and he didn't want anyone else stealing his fantasy, especially not Odell.

"What would you like me to do now? I can bring Odell to you if that's what you want, or I can bring him and the woman."

"No. In good time, but not yet. Keep your phone close, I'll be calling you soon."

Holic departed his suite five hours after Jakob left. He wore a ski jacket and stocking cap, his raven locks tucked underneath. He looked like any other skier headed for an early morning run on the slopes. But he never left the lodge. He rode the elevator down to the fourth floor and entered the suite at the end of the hall using the skills of a master thief.

Inside, thirty minutes later, he made a call. Jakob answered promptly, and in similar attire, Holic's henchman joined him on the fourth floor.

Chapter 18

Nadja woke up to her phone ringing from inside her boot. She sat up quickly and looked around. She was still in Bjorn's room. He, however, was nowhere in sight. She saw her boots where she'd left them the night before in the middle of the floor. She climbed out of bed and slipped her hand into the inside pocket and snatched up the phone.

"Hello," she said as soon as she'd brought the mini-compact invention to her ear.

"Nadja, it's Mady. Where are you? Do you have Alzbet with you?"

"I'm… Never mind where I am. What about Alzbet? No, she's not with me. Why?"

"Because I can't find her. She wasn't in her bed this morning, so I thought maybe she was with you. You're all she can talk about, and after yesterday I thought…

So I went to your suite. When I didn't get an answer, I let myself in. I see you didn't spend the night there, so where are you?"

Nadja ignored the question and went straight to the heart of her concern. "What do you mean you can't find my dau—find Alzbet?"

"This is strange. She never runs off." Mady's voice was flat. "I've got staff checking all the floors but no one has found her yet. Prisca is out looking, too."

Nadja was starting to feel a mix of panic and fear. "Maybe she's on the slopes having an early ski lesson."

"No, she's not."

"How long have you been searching?"

"Over two hours. Nadja…it's like she's just disappeared. To make matters worse, this morning the wind-chill is below zero. If she's out there without proper clothes…I don't know, I'm really scared something bad has happened to her."

Mady's fears were also Nadja's. "I'll check with Kovar and see what he thinks. I'm on my way."

"All right. I'll run down Prisca and see if she's had any luck. I'll meet you at Kovar's suite as soon as I can."

Nadja was frantically looking for something to wear when Bjorn came through the door. "What's up?"

"Mady called. Alzbet is missing. Where have you been?"

"Taking care of Kimball, getting you something to wear and to eat."

She spied the black pants and sweater draped over his arm. He was also carrying a pastry bag and two coffees. She ignored the food and nearly knocked him over to collect the clothes he'd brought her.

"I stuffed the goods inside the sweater," he said.

"The goods."

He smiled. "You know, underwear."

"Oh." She shook out the sweater. A pair of black panties and a black bra fell to the floor. She scooped them up and dressed quickly.

"The cup marked M is yours. How you can drink brown milk is beyond me, but—"

"Did you hear what I said? My Alzbet is missing. I'm going to talk to Kovar. She couldn't have just disappeared. Something's wrong."

"Want me to go with you? You seem rattled."

"Rattled?"

"*Ja,* rattled. Don't worry, kids run off. It's what they do. She's probably in a closet somewhere with a flashlight, playing I Spy."

"I can only hope, but something tells me that's not the case."

"Want me to do something?"

Nadja jammed her hands on her hips. "Yes, as a matter a fact I do. You can be a damn bit more worried."

"She's not my kid, so why would I? Besides, kids aren't my thing. Don't get me wrong. The other night she was cute enough. From what I saw of her in the dark, but—"

"Just shut up." Nadja grabbed her boots and plopped down on the couch to pull them on. "You don't think Holic found out we're here, do you?"

"No. Why?"

"Because if he did and he learned that— Never mind." She shoved her foot into the first boot and ran the zipper. As she reached for the next, she saw Bjorn set the cups on the coffee table, then he sat down beside her and relaxed on the sofa as if to take a nap.

"Nadja, listen. Calm down and give it some time—she's all right."

She blew him off, and finished zipping up her second boot. But when she attempted to stand, he grabbed her arm, pushed her back and leaned into her space. With his free hand he reached across and braced it on the arm of the sofa to pin her in. He was no longer nonchalant, and she suddenly realized that he'd been playing a game with her.

"Now then, just what the hell is going on? Talk to me, honey. What are you hiding? What's this kid got to do with Holic?"

"She doesn't. I'm just worried, is all. She's small and vulnerable, and from your experience on the streets, you should know what it's like to be cold and alone." She shoved him hard and scrambled off the couch. "I have to go see Kovar. I'll call you if I need you, so don't go anywhere."

Kovar was dead when Nadja entered his bedroom. She knew it without touching him, without even searching for a pulse. She stared down at her grandfather where he sat slumped in his wheelchair. Although it appeared that another heart attack was the cause of his death, she suspected otherwise. That became fact when she examined him and found his neck broken and all the fingers on both of his hands broken as well.

She knew then who had killed him. It had to be Holic. He usually used a single bullet to the right temple, but in this case he had entered the suite not as an assassin, Nadja decided, but to harvest information.

Had he gotten what he had come for?

She hadn't ever thought that her grandfather's death would bother her—she had only envisioned relief and freedom—but she was suddenly struggling for air. She forced herself to take a deep breath, then to move. She began to search the room for clues, but after ten minutes she had found nothing. Not even the secret room had been touched.

There had been no struggle on Kovar's part, which meant either that he had been expecting Holic, or that someone else had accompanied her brother-in-law into the suite to force Kovar to cooperate.

She was confident that Holic didn't know she worked for Quest, so if he had learned that she was there at the lodge it shouldn't have raised suspicion. Not unless...

Unless she was on the kill-file. Polax had told her there was a possibility that a number of Quest agents had made the Chameleon's roster. If she was one of them, then last night at After Shock, when she'd locked eyes with Holic, he could have identified her.

The broken bones in Kovar's hands, and the manner in which it had been done, guaranteed that he'd been tortured mercilessly. There were signs that he'd been gagged. No doubt to muffle his cries of pain.

The question that came back to her time and time again was, had he died guarding their secrets, or had he crumbled and eventually divulged that Alzbet was her daughter? If he had, then that would explain why Alzbet was missing.

Nadja called Bjorn. "Get over here. Fourth floor, end of the hall."

As she hung up, the door opened and closed, and she rushed into the living room. It was Mady.

"What did Kovar say? Does he know where she is? I've been thinking about Gerda—maybe she— What's wrong, Nadja? You look so pale."

"It's Kovar. He's dead."

"What? No!" Mady hurried past Nadja and entered Kovar's bedroom.

Nadja followed. "I found him like that. He—"

"Had another heart attack."

"No. It wasn't his heart."

"Not his heart?"

"His neck's been broken, and his hands."

Mady's eyes went wide. "His hands?"

"Every finger on both hands." Nadja watched Mady's behavior for a moment, then asked, "Mady, what do you know?

"What are you asking?"

"I think you know what I'm asking."

"I don't. Why would I?"

"Stop it, Mady. Holic was here. He's been here this past week. Don't say no—I saw him at After Shock. He did this."

"Are you crazy? He wouldn't do this. He has no reason."

"Your tone is defensive, and the words spoken too fast. Both incriminate you."

Nadja and Mady turned to see Bjorn standing in the bedroom doorway.

"Who are you?" Mady asked.

"Ask your sister who I am."

Mady addressed her sister. "Nad?"

Nadja glared at Bjorn, then said to Mady, "He's my partner."

"Partner? What kind of partner?"

I work for an intelligence agency, Mady. I'm not in insurance. Bjorn and I are—"

"You didn't come to visit Kovar, you're here to hurt my husband."

"He's a killer, Mady. Powerful people pay him to kill their enemies. He's a hired assassin, and he's very good at it. He's wanted by every government agency in the country."

"He kills only bad people," Mady reasoned.

"Then you knew?"

"Not in the beginning."

"Why did he kill Kovar?"

"I tell you he didn't do this. He wouldn't."

Bjorn moved through the door and crouched in front of Kovar's still body.

"Let's ask Holic," Nadja suggested. "Where is he now?"

"I'm not going to tell you that. I'm not going to help you hunt down my husband. You said you were an agent. What kind of agent?"

Nadja glanced at Bjorn. "I…"

"We're in Special Operations."

"And do *you* kill people?"

Again Bjorn answered. "Sometimes."

"You, Nad? You've killed people? Honestly, what happened to the sweet Naddy I remember?"

"What happened, Mady, is I had my eyes opened at the end of a leather strap, and Kovar's iron will, while you were away pretending that love could turn poison into wine. But it can't be done. Not where Holic is concerned."

"You kill people, too, and yet you judge him."

"And you, you support him even though he killed Kovar."

"He didn't!"

"And I believe he's taken Alzbet."

"I tell you he didn't do this." Mady shook her head wildly. "And why would he take Alzbet? For what reason?"

"Where's Prisca?"

"I'm not sure. I've looked but she wasn't where I thought she'd be. She's not answering her cell phone, either, so I've asked a few of the maids to search for her."

"You're as worried as I am, Mady."

"I'm not worried."

"Yes you are, and I know why. Holic has taken both of them."

"Don't be ridiculous. He wouldn't kidnap his own child. He wouldn't need to."

"No, unless he's on the run, and wanted to make sure she went along. The other night when Pris stopped by she mentioned him. She's very taken by her father. She loves him very much. What would she do for him, Mady? Would she break the law? Lie? Steal?"

Her words seemed to alarm Mady even more. "No, he wouldn't take her from me. He wouldn't make her do those things." She started rubbing her arms while she paced. "He wouldn't leave without telling me. He just wouldn't."

"Mady, talk to me before he gets too far away. Tell me what you know."

She glared at Nadja. "Stop it, Nad. I'm not going to help you, so just stop it! Now get out of here. Both of you."

"We're not going anywhere." She asked again, "Where would Holic take Prisca and Alzbet?"

"He would never hurt Prisca. And I told you, he has no reason to take Alzbet, just like he has no reason to kill Kovar."

"Tell me this. Has he been acting differently the past day or two? Anything unusual?"

"He asked to see Alzbet."

"And why is that odd?"

"Holic isn't fond of children. He didn't even like Pris until she was older."

"When was this?"

"Last night. He asked me to bring her for a visit."

"And did you?"

"Prisca took her up."

"Up?"

"He's been staying on the tenth floor."

Nadja thought about the helipad on the rooftop. "If the helicopter is gone, then he has Alzbet and he knows."

"Knows what?"

It was Bjorn who had asked the question. Nadja turned to him in time to see him set his jaw. It was as if he was waiting to hear what he already knew. But he didn't know. How could he?

"He knows *what*, Nadja?"

"That we're here."

"Maybe."

He was still looking at her as if he knew. If he did, then why hadn't he said something? She had to tell him the rest. It was the only way to spur him into action. Alzbet needed to be found.

She said, "If he took Alzbet there's a good chance he knows who her mother is."

"And that's important because…?" Again it was Bjorn asking the question.

Nadja raised her chin. "She's my daughter, not Ruger's."

"Bingo. Why did I already know that?"

"If you did, then why—?"

"Make you say it? Because, honey, you promised me days ago no more bullshit."

"She's not yours," Mady interrupted. "Kovar said—"

"What you needed to hear so you wouldn't ask too many questions. She's mine, Mady," Nadja confessed, "and I think Holic knows it and intends to use her to lure me into a trap so he can kill me. Me and Bjorn."

Mady's eyes shifted from Bjorn to Nadja, then back to Bjorn. She studied him for a moment, then said, "I knew there was something about you that looked familiar in the elevator the other day, Mr. Larsen. It was the eyes. They're Alzbet's eyes. You're her father." She looked back at Nadja. "It's true, isn't it? He's your child's father?"

Jakob directed the helicopter pilot toward Glass Mountain. They had left the helipad on the rooftop at six sharp.

While Prisca held Alzbet, Holic considered his next move. Nadja would soon find Kovar dead and her brat missing, and then... Then after a few hours of painfully waiting to hear something, he would give her a call, and an ultimatum. His plan was perfect, and in the end he would have what he needed to move forward.

The use of his hand was gone; he no longer entertained hopes that it would heal. He would never return to the life he loved, but he would survive. He was a wealthy man, and he knew how to get what he wanted. And right now he wanted two things. He wanted revenge on Bjorn Odell and his daughter's loyalty. He would have both shortly.

He still wasn't sure about Mady. It looked as though she'd been lying to him for days. Maybe years.

Loyalty was everything.

If there was none, then what good was she?

If Mady's love was false, he'd been a fool.

He looked to Prisca and realized that if that was the case, the only person he had left in his life—that he wanted in his life—was his beautiful daughter.

She must have sensed him looking at her, because she turned around and smiled. He smiled back as if nothing was wrong. As if their sudden flight with Nadja's brat was nothing to be alarmed about.

Nothing would stop him now, he decided. Revenge was in sight. Revenge as well as the pleasure of seeing Mady and Nadja racing up the mountain to save their children.

Of course it would do neither of them any good to plead with him. He already knew who would live and who would die. Still, it was always entertaining to see a beautiful woman on her knees pleading for mercy.

"Jakob, I have a question to ask you. Did you say Otto was near by?"

"Graz. Why?"

"Contact him. I need a favor. It involves Pris."

Jakob grinned where he sat opposite Holic. "You know anything that involves your daughter would be Otto's pleasure. He's always had an eye for Prisca, and he'd hoped one day the feeling would be mutual."

Not in my lifetime, Holic thought. Otto Breit was resourceful and smart, good bodyguard material, but nothing more. He didn't voice his thoughts, however.

He said, "We'll discuss Otto's future once we get to the cabin."

Chapter 19

He would have strangled her if he hadn't walked out. And two hours later he still wanted to.

He had a child. A little girl. And Nadja had kept it from him.

Bjorn stood facing Glass Mountain, the cold wind whipping at his hair and clothes, but for the first time in his life he didn't feel it. He didn't feel anything. He was numb.

He had a child. A little girl with blue eyes like his— if what Mady said was true. And it was. He'd seen it in Nadja's face.

He had been with the girl last night, and because there had been no books to read he had told her a story about a boy in Copenhagen who had lived on the docks. He'd made his life into a fairy tale, when it had been far from one. The irony was that he'd been telling *his* story to *his* kid.

It had been dark, and the low-watt night-light on the table next to the bed had given everything in the room a muted amber glow. He hadn't paid much attention to his daughter's face.

His daughter.

Bjorn drew hard on his cigarette, ignoring the phone in his pocket going off again. It was her. Nadja had been ringing him for the past hour.

When he'd walked out, she had called him back, but he couldn't do it, he couldn't look at her.

Her face when Mady had said Alzbet was his... He would never forget it.

Damn her to hell, he thought. She'd had plenty of opportunities to tell him about his daughter. She could have said something in Prague. And if not Prague, why not Nordzum? They'd been snowed in for three days together. She'd admitted she was a double agent, and that she had a bionic nerve chip in her leg. Hell...why had she stopped there?

Last night she'd looked him straight in the eyes and lied again. Then she'd made love with him—made love like she had truly wanted him. Cared for him. But that was her specialty, making men believe in the magic.

After all, she was the best in the business. The stats at Quest proved it.

If Holic hadn't made his move and killed Kovar, then what? If he hadn't kidnapped their little girl, would she ever have told him?

No, he didn't believe she would have, and that was why he could never forgive her. Not ever.

It was just a good thing he hadn't told her how he felt last night. How he'd been feeling since he'd laid eyes on her in Prague.

Bjorn remembered the tattoo. A heart with angel wings. At least she had cared about their child. He knew she had, because when she'd learned that Alzbet was missing she had been in a panic. He had keyed in on that, and that's when he'd begun to rethink her actions since they'd arrived at Groffen. Why would she be so upset about Ruger's child? A little worry was normal, but she'd been shaky and close to irrational. An agent of her caliber irrational?

No, it didn't fit.

He swore again, then checked his watch. He'd better get back. Nadja was right—Holic had their daughter and he was going to use her as bait. Soon they would get a message detailing the conditions of their daughter's release. Only Holic would never let the child live. Not *his* child.

The last time they had faced off and a child had been involved it hadn't gone well, and he knew that men like Holic wouldn't stop where revenge was concerned. After Cupata the assassin would want blood.

The game this time was death, and at the moment Holic held all the cards.

When Bjorn returned to Kovar's suite, what he found was Mady seated on the bed, her eyes red and face puffy from crying. Kovar was still slumped in the chair.

"Where is she?" Bjorn asked.

"I've called the police," she said. "They'll be here soon. You better go or they'll want to speak to you."

"I asked you—where's Nadja?"

"I begged her not to go up there but she wouldn't listen. She went in there, and when she came back out, she was carrying a backpack." Mady pointed to the mirror. "I told her to wait for you but she wouldn't listen."

Bjorn walked to the mirror and found that it camouflaged a hidden room. He slipped inside and looked around. The entire room was wall-to-wall pictures of Nadja in all stages of her life—Nadja and hundreds of trophies. A lone chair sat in the middle of the room, and he could only guess what it was used for.

He moved through the next open door, and when he saw the guns and the Russian flag on the wall he knew Jacy was right—Kovar Stefn had been working with the KGB.

Back in the bedroom, he asked Mady, "Tell me what happened after I left."

"Holic called. The girls are with him, just like Nadja said."

"With him where?"

"At the cabin. Why didn't you answer your phone? Nadja called you, but…"

Bjorn felt like someone had just stuck him in the gut with a knife. She'd been trying to call him and tell him about Holic's message, but he'd been so angry, and struggling with the news that he was a father that he'd ignored his own rule—never let your emotions overtake sound judgment.

"Don't tell me she went to the cabin alone."

"I couldn't stop her. I tried."

"How long ago?"

"About an hour."

"What did Holic say?"

"Nadja was right, he used the helicopter. He's sending it back at six tomorrow morning. He's instructed both of you to be on the roof. Me, too. The pilot will fly us to the cabin. You're to come unarmed. He warned Nadja that if anything goes wrong he'll kill Alzbet. I can't believe he would do that, but…"

"But you believe he killed Kovar, don't you?"

"Yes." She started crying again. "I told Nadja to ask about Prisca. When she did, Holic said that my daughter was going to be leaving the country tonight. That means she'll be gone before I get there."

"Do you know which cabin?"

"Yes. I had supplies dropped there two days before I went to pick Holic up in St. Anton ten days ago."

"How was Nadja traveling when she left?"

"There are no roads leading to the cabin. It sits in the valley beyond Glass Mountain. A helicopter can land and take off from there, but there's only one way to get there if you're not flying. Nadja's on skis."

Polax's mission was to break Merrick out of the hospital. Dr. Paul had been too stubborn to listen to reason when Merrick told him that something urgent had come up. It had forced him to take matters into his own hands. Not trusting Sarah to be his accomplice, he'd turned to Lev Polax.

He now sat in the wheelchair as Polax, dressed in a white orderly's uniform, pushed him down the hall toward the elevator.

"If we get caught, you better hope we don't find ourselves on the front page of the morning newspaper, Merrick, or I'll have some explaining to do to my superiors."

"Just tell them you stepped back in the field to reconnect and appreciate what your agents go through every day. That should gain you a few points upstairs, and maybe a bigger budget."

"A bigger budget I could always use, but points... I'm going to need more than points if this idea of yours blows up in our faces."

"Trust me."

"I'm working on it."

"Work harder—there's Paul. Get us the hell out of here."

Polax spun the wheelchair around and nearly pitched Merrick out on his ass. They ducked into an alcove, and once Dr. Paul had walked past, Polax swung Merrick around and sprinted the wheelchair to the elevator as if they were in a race.

"You know this wheelchair could use a few electronic improvements to make it more efficient," Polax said once they were inside the elevator. "I should send this place a blueprint of my office chair."

Bjorn hung up from talking with Jacy. He'd just asked his friend to create a miracle, and to do it in less than fourteen hours.

He wouldn't think on it any further; he would just trust that it could and would be done—he had ground to cover and the clock was ticking.

His focus now shifted to Nadja. She was at least two hours ahead of him.

He'd gotten what he needed from Kovar's back room, enlisted Mady's help in obtaining directions to the cabin, warm clothes and supplies. A pair of skis.

He'd left Groffen by three o'clock, knowing it would be after dark by the time he reached the cabin. He could only hope that Nadja's leg held up and that, if she made it, she wouldn't do something stupid—like sacrifice herself to save Alzbet. He knew from experience that Holic had no conscience when it came to killing children or women. He didn't discriminate. Bjorn traversed the trail with the proficiency and agility of a man half his age. Merrick's men had been trained to do it all. Not even the fresh arm wound from Kimball's gun the night before altered the breakneck pace he'd set for himself.

As he maneuvered the trails and dealt with the weather, his thoughts returned to Nadja. After seeing the room full of trophies and pictures, he realized that her actions had to do with Kovar and his obvious obsession.

Five years ago she'd done the only thing she could do to protect what must have suddenly become the most important thing in her life. The only thing that was truly hers. The child growing inside her.

He only hoped that his lapse in judgment earlier hadn't cost him more than time. He shouldn't have walked out on her. He needed to tell her that, and that he understood why she'd guarded the secret. Even why she'd played the game the way she'd done once they were reunited in Prague.

Once he'd told her that he understood, together they would face Holic. And then they would salvage the mission, after they rescued their daughter.

Chapter 20

Nadja sat in the snow, the backpack and gear she'd assembled from Kovar's back room beside her. She took out a heat pack and wrapped it around her bionic leg. Already she could feel it beginning to give her problems.

Damn the cold.

She'd skied six miles, and there was at least another sixteen to go. It would take her longer to reach the cabin stopping like this, but it was crucial that she keep the blood circulating in her leg.

She wouldn't rely on luck, or the weather turning warmer. It was late afternoon now and that meant the temperature would be dropping soon—dropping and causing more problems for her leg.

No, she couldn't rely on luck, the weather, or Bjorn—too much of a coward to answer his phone.

And he wondered why she hadn't told him he had a daughter?

He hadn't been able to handle the truth. The look he'd given her had proven it. That betrayed glare had burned clean to her soul. And then he'd just turned and walked away.

She'd called him back, but he'd kept going. He hadn't even slowed his pace. Well, he could just keep on going as far as she was concerned.

Yes, she'd lied, and had kept the lie going. But it was to protect her baby. He should have understood that, and when she came face-to-face with him again, she would remind him how things were in the intelligence business. A spy's feeling and needs came last, if at all.

Truthfully her child had been in danger of never being born five years ago. If she had told Polax she was pregnant, she'd have been forced to terminate it. So she'd made the only choice she could make at the time. She'd wanted her baby to have a life, even if she couldn't share it with her. And, yes, her decision had been magnified by the fact that the baby was Bjorn's.

She'd tried so hard to protect her, and now Alzbet was in the hands of a monster. If there was a God in heaven—and Ruger promised that there was—he would not let her beautiful baby suffer for the evil that some men do for power and greed.

Nadja stopped three more times to attend to her leg before the trail divided and she saw the cabin nestled in the valley, a swirl of smoke coming out of its chimney. In the distance sat Groffen's rescue helicopter. She dropped her gear behind a stand of snow-covered pine trees and removed her skies. She was no speed skier

these days, but Kovar was right—the lessons learned in
the past had served her well this day.

The sun was gone now, and the plan was to wait until
dark to make her move. The wind had picked up and
the temperatures were bitter. She'd used up her last heat
pack. How long could she withstand the severe cold and
remain on her feet?

While she was contemplating that very bone chilling reality, the cabin door opened and out walked Prisca
and Holic. Nadja immediately reached for her backpack
and took out the compact case that held Kovar's 223
semiautomatic AR M-4 Sniper. She pulled back the
collapsible stock, attached the ten-round magazine and
clipped the scope into place. It was at her shoulder
within thirty seconds.

Holic walked Pris to the helicopter, his arm around
her. Nadja watched through the scope. She could have
picked off Holic so easily. But where was Alzbet? The
question came to her as she was curling her finger
around the trigger—and she immediately backed off.

Holic wouldn't leave her daughter alone, and with
that thought she lowered the rifle. Someone else was inside the cabin with Alzbet.

She watched as Holic kissed Pris, then helped her
into the helicopter. It took off minutes later.

Holic's henchman was outside taking a piss underneath the stars when Bjorn dropped down beside Nadja
and put his hand over her mouth to keep her from
screaming out her surprise.

He had been watching her from a distance for the
past twenty minutes and he could see that the cold
weather was giving her some problems. She wasn't hy-

pothermic yet, but her reactions were sluggish—that's what had allowed him to sneak up on her.

She hadn't built a fire, and that was good. His strategy was contingent on Holic's orders that they arrive in the morning.

He whispered next to her ear, "I've got something that will warm you up. I'll be right back."

He left her there and went to retrieve his gear where he'd stashed it a few yards away. When he returned, she was sitting with her knees drawn up to her chest and her stocking cap low over her ears.

He opened his bag and pulled out a flask. "Here, take a sip of this."

"What is it?"

"Brandy. It'll help warm you up."

She unscrewed the cap and took a swallow.

"Another one."

She did, then handed the flask back. He took a few swallows himself, then capped it.

"So, Odell, what brings you up here? A conscience, or don't you like a woman getting one up on you?"

He supposed he deserved that for not answering his phone. "I've never disputed your talents in or out of bed, Nadja. You're a damn good agent, just too involved in this assignment for your own good."

"But you're not, are you. You're just a detached father."

"Because you wanted it that way."

"No, because it had to be that way. You still don't understand that I had no choice."

"I'll buy that until a week ago. You've had seven days to get it out of that pretty mouth of yours. You could have chosen any one of those damn days, honey."

"I chose today, and you couldn't handle it."

"Mady chose today, not you. And I handled it. Just not the way you had expected."

"No, I never expected you would be a coward and walk—but it's good to know for the future."

"Look, you said—"

"Save it. I don't have the energy to listen to your excuses."

"My excuses? You're the one who lied."

"And I'd do it again, do you hear? I wanted my baby to have a life, and I won't apologize to you or anyone for what I've done to give that to her."

"And you think that's what I want, an apology?"

"I have no idea what you want, and frankly I don't care. All I care about at the moment is getting my daughter out of that cabin in one piece."

"*Our* daughter," Bjorn stressed.

"So how are we going to get *our* daughter out of there? Do you want to cover my ass when I go through that door, or would you prefer that I cover yours?"

"Neither. We're not moving in until morning."

"I can't wait all night to get Alzbet back. Prisca left on the helicopter a few hours ago. Alzbet will be feeling abandoned. Besides, I don't think I can last that long out here."

"Is the leg giving you problems?"

"Don't start, Bjorn. I don't need to hear how I'm the wrong agent for this job one more time."

"You are."

"Go to hell."

"Not before I send Holic there."

He saw her shiver and he shoved to his feet. "I've got a way to warm you up."

"I'll just bet you do. No, thanks."

"We both need to stay warm. We won't be making our move until five-thirty tomorrow morning."

When he reached for her, she scooted away. "Don't touch me."

"Suit yourself," he said, then stood and rolled out his winter sleeping bag. He stripped off his clothes, stuffed them inside the sleeping bag, then flashed her his bare ass and climbed inside the winterized bag.

Snuggling inside, his stocking cap still on his head, he said, "Who would expect that it could be this toasty warm at five degrees below zero."

She ignored him, and held out for an hour before she stood and shed her clothes. He heard her, but he didn't say anything. He just made room for her when she slid naked into his sleeping bag and turned her back to him.

The helicopter came back in the middle of the night, and then left again at five-thirty. But by then Bjorn had filled Nadja in on the plan he'd put together with Jacy yesterday. She didn't like it, but he didn't give a damn.

He was convinced it would work, and if it did it was going to give Holic the surprise of his life.

Holic was surprised to see Mady exit the helicopter first. His loving wife had lied to him, and that would not serve her well in the hours to come. No one betrayed him and lived. But how could he kill Mady?

Loyal, trusting Mady?

He stood in the open doorway of the cabin and swallowed another handful of pills as he contemplated what to do with her. Jakob was helping her keep her balance through the deep snow, and when she was on solid packed snow, he let go of her and she started toward the cabin.

Bjorn and Nadja remained seated in the helicopter, and he admitted he was anxious to see Mady's sister again. Sweet Nadja, the spy with a whore's body and the face of an angel.

When she exited the helicopter, he smiled to himself, silently vowing he would taste her before he killed her. She was all in black and she was stunning, although he couldn't see her face for the hat. But that would come off, as would everything else eventually.

When Bjorn Odell appeared, Holic's entire body stiffened. If it hadn't been for Odell pursuing him in Greece he would still have his hand and his career. But the Onyxx agent had made chase and they had ended up on a balcony that had collapsed. He was damn lucky that he'd survived at all.

Like the others, Bjorn had dressed for the weather—his hat was pulled low over his eyes, and his scarf was high, choking his neck.

To get things off to a winning start, and to set the tone for the morning games, Holic nodded to Jakob—when his mind was made up he never wasted time. His henchman didn't question the signal. He pulled his SIG out of his pocket and shot Bjorn in the leg, then tagged his gun arm high on the shoulder. His target dropped to the snow-covered ground.

Holic never tired of seeing a bullet drilling a body. And in this case it was sheer pleasure seeing Bjorn Odell go down. He wasn't about to take any chances where this particular Onyxx agent was concerned. Odell had been a thorn in his side for years.

He said to his wife, "Get in the cabin, Mady," then

to Jakob, "Tie up Odell and leave him there." He smiled at Nadja as she drew closer. "You must be anxious to be reunited with your daughter, sweet Nadja."

They went inside the cabin, and Jakob followed. Holic said to him, "Take Nadja to the bedroom to see her brat while I speak to my wife. Make sure she's unarmed."

Once Jakob ushered Nadja into the bedroom, Holic turned to Mady. He waited until she'd taken off her coat and hat before he hit her. The blow knocked her to the floor and split her lip. With his good hand, he hauled her back to her feet and then slammed her into a chair.

"Now, Mady, my sweet deceptive wife, I have a question for you. Think before you answer. And no tears. You know how I hate that. Why didn't you tell me that your sister was at Groffen, and that she was an agent for Quest?"

"I thought she worked for an insurance company. I don't even know what Quest is. And when she arrived I thought she came to visit Kovar because of his heart attack. You were suffering with your hand and I didn't think it was important. Please, Holic, tell me where Prisca is."

"My daughter has been sent away, Mady, far away. And I have no plans for her to return to you or Groffen."

"No, Holic, please…"

"The trust, my love, has been broken. And the price of your stupidity or betrayal, it does not matter which, is just beginning."

Mady started to cry again. Sick of the noise, Holic took a step forward and hit her again. The blow broke her nose and she screamed as blood began to flow.

He would have hit her again if not for the explosion
outside that rocked the cabin. Holic hurried to the window and saw that the helicopter had been blown to bits
and was on fire. He searched the surrounding area,
noted that Bjorn was no longer lying in the snow where
he'd fallen after Jakob had shot him. Where had he
gone?

"What the hell! Jakob, get in here!"

Holic heard a noise in the back bedroom, then footsteps. Jakob walked into the living room with an odd
gait. He was as white as a ghost and his eyes were di-
lated. More important, his sweater was the wrong color.
Instead of white it was red.

Blood red.

Nadja stood outside the cabin window chewing on
her lower lip. When she saw Casmir come to the window, her heart started to race. The window opened, and
then Quest's glamour girl handed Alzbet out the window to Nadja.

Nadja hugged her daughter. "Are you all right, love?"

Alzbet snuggled close. "I didn't like those men, Auntie Nad. Pris left me."

"I know. They didn't hurt you, did they?"

"No. But I was scared."

"But you're safe now." Nadja hugged her child again
and said a silent prayer of thanks.

"Everything is on schedule," Cass said, as she
slipped out the window. "Holic took the bait, like Bjorn
said he would. He didn't even know I wasn't you.
How's Pierce Fourtier? I was shocked when he was
shot."

"I think it was in the plan," Nadja said. "I believe

Bjorn knew that Holic would retaliate against him immediately because they have a history. Pierce's leg wound is minor. He was wearing some kind of special bodysuit, but the shot higher up dislocated his shoulder and he's in a lot of pain."

"The redneck and I didn't hit it off flying up here. He was an arrogant ass."

"When I left them in the woods, Bjorn was trying to put Pierce's shoulder back into its socket. Pierce was yelling, and Bjorn was yelling back. Two bulls who won't give an inch, is what they are."

"Men," Cass sniffed. "Can't live with them, and don't want to."

Bjorn's ill mood was an extension of what had transpired earlier that morning when Nadja had awakened to find his naked body curled around hers in the sleeping bag. She had welcomed his warmth and his strength—dammit!—and it had irked her at a time when she didn't need to be reminded of how much she had grown to love him.

Yes, it was love.

That's why she would have hated his plan no matter how ridiculous it was, and this one had been pretty wild. Surely Holic was too smart to fall for a pair of impersonators climbing out of that helicopter. But it had worked, and now she had Alzbet in her arms, thanks to Bjorn.

But it wasn't over yet. They still needed to retrieve the kill-file and capture Holic...alive.

"Let's get going," Casmir said.

Nadja's thoughts turned to Mady, and she made a sudden decision. "Here—" She kissed Alzbet, then handed her daughter to Cass.

Casmir took the child, unaware of what Nadja intended. But when she saw her climb back through the window, she freaked. "What are you doing? This isn't part of the plan. We're supposed to get back to camp as quickly as possible."

"The plan was Bjorn's, not mine, Cass. My sister is still inside. What would you do?"

"Don't ask me that."

"Holic killed my grandfather. He kidnapped my daughter and..."

Nadja hadn't meant to say the words, but there they were. She glanced at Alzbet and saw that her daughter's blue eyes were huge.

"I'm sorry, sweetheart. I would have picked a different time and place to tell you, but Mommy screwed up. You okay?"

Alzbet nodded slowly.

"So you're all right with it? Me being your mom."

Another slow nod.

"We'll talk about this later, okay? I love you."

More nodding.

"Cass, get going. Head for the woods. The camp is straight south a hundred yards once you reach the trees."

"You can be so damn stubborn, Nadja."

"This coming from the mule. Go on. Go!"

Casmir sprinted through the snow for the dense treeline while Nadja turned and assessed the bedroom, then walked quietly to the door. She listened, and when she heard running footsteps she had barely enough time to jump back before the door flew open. She was reaching for her Springfield when Holic rushed her and she lost her balance and fell backward.

Like a panther he struck fast, kicking her gun from her hand. It went flying and landed out of reach. Then Holic was there, a knife blade at her throat.

"Don't be stupid, sweet Nadja. I will kill you now if you wish. Make your move and die, or rethink your position."

She would rethink it; she had no wish to die. But that might be out of her hands now. She had made a careless mistake, and now it could cost her more than simply the mission. Mady's life still hung in the balance.

Holic glanced around, saw that Alzbet was nowhere in sight, and said, "Where's the brat?"

"She's gone. I sent her out the window."

"Mady! Get in here, now!"

A moment later Mady walked into the bedroom crying, her cheeks red and bruised. "I'm here, Holic."

"Sit over there in that chair and shut up."

Mady went quickly, trying to keep her crying muffled.

Nadja was careful not to react to the rage building inside her. Holic didn't appear to be as composed as his profile suggested. He was considered the most efficient, intelligent assassin in the business. She suspected that today he was again high on something.

He still had his balance and his quickness, but his hand was swollen, and he was guarding it close to his body. No doubt he was using the drugs as an attempt to escape the incessant pain he'd been forced to live with for the past month. But the drugs hadn't stolen his suffering completely. His eyes were bloodshot, as if he hadn't been sleeping.

She felt the knife slide down her neck to her left breast where her heart pounded. She looked up to see Holic grinning at her.

"Get up, Nadja. Off the floor."

She slowly came to her feet.

"Now take off your sweater and pants."

When she hesitated, he pressed the blade into her flesh.

"Do it. I want everything ready when Odell arrives. Even one-legged, and his arm broken, I imagine the bastard will find a way to ride to your rescue. After all, he's the father of your child, right?"

He knew Alzbet was Bjorn's child.

"Bjorn is like a bad toothache that keeps coming back. But this will be the last time. As for the brat, the weather is about to get nasty. There's a storm moving in, and my guess is she'll be dead by morning."

He had no idea that she had traded places with Casmir, and that her daughter was safe. Or that Bjorn would be a hundred percent healthy coming through that door.

Feeling more confident, she pulled off her sweater, then stepped out of her pants. She felt Holic's eyes on her, but she refused to let them bother her. She'd been in this position before and she wouldn't let this man win, not on any level.

"Lie down on the bed, sweet, sexy Nadja. Hmm… you do make a man instantly hard just looking."

Mady's crying became audible.

"Shut up, my lying wife, or I will be forced to hurt you again," Holic warned, never taking his eyes off Nadja's breasts. "I see that my knife cut you. Take off your bra and let me see how bad it is."

Pierce was in pain, and voicing it loudly in his Cajun accent. "I'm goin' to kill that son of a bitch. I'm goin' to put a hole—"

"I did it for you."

Both Bjorn and Pierce looked up to see Casmir standing behind them. She had Alzbet on her hip and she was out of breath.

"That's right," she said, eyeing Pierce. "I knifed Holic's muscle boy for you. I figured you'd thank me for it."

She waited.

He said nothing, just nodded then closed his brown eyes and leaned his dark head against the tree.

"Is this what they call redneck mentality? Okay, hotshot, have it your way. I never liked Frenchmen anyway."

Bjorn glanced behind her, expecting to see Nadja. When he didn't, he came quickly to his feet.

"She's not coming," Casmir said, as if she knew what he was about to ask. She set Alzbet on her feet beside her. "Nadja said she couldn't leave her sister behind. She's stubborn—maybe you already know that. When she sets her mind to something, I know better than to try to change it."

Bjorn was livid. Nadja had deliberately changed his strategic plan.

When Casmir finished telling him what had transpired at the back window of the cabin, he glanced at his daughter. She was staring at him. He crouched down and said, "You okay, Ally?"

She nodded, then said, "My auntie Nad is my mom."

Casmir cleared her throat and Bjorn looked up. "About that, uh… Nadja kind of slipped up back there. I'm sure she intended to tell her in a different way and in good time, but it just came out."

Alzbet tapped Bjorn's arm. "Can you go get my mom and Aunt Mady? Can you?"

He looked down at her little hand where it rested on his arm. It was small and very red. He took it in his hands and rubbed her icy cold fingers. She wore no hat and her coat wasn't all that warm. He scooped her up and her little arms went around his neck. Her breath touched his cheek.

He stood and went to where his pack sat in the snow. The survival blanket was coarse, but he wrapped it around her anyway. Then he whispered, "Stay with Casmir. I'll be back with Mommy."

She squeezed his neck and hugged him, then her cold lips kissed his cheek.

Chapter 21

Nadja tried to slip into her out-of-body-out-of-mind mode. It's where she went when she became Q. But it wasn't working, and she realized Bjorn was right, she was too close to this one—the mission was too personal.

She tried to shut out Mady's crying, to block Holic's hand on her body, but she couldn't do it.

Holic had the knife, and she wouldn't be so foolish as to make a move with it still in his hand. He would kill her. She knew that's what he intended before the day was over. He just wanted to play his sick game first.

He ran the knife blade between her breasts, then down her belly. Teased her navel. The tattoo distracted him for a minute. He touched it, looked up at her and smiled as if he knew why it was there.

He bent his head and kissed her stomach.

"There is something very beautiful about a woman's stomach," he said. "Yours, Nadja, is exceptional, even after having a child." He turned his head as if he'd heard a noise. "I wonder where Bjorn could be? Maybe he's having trouble hobbling to your rescue."

"He'll come," Nadja said. "Maybe not for me, but for the kill-file."

"Ah, the file. Yes, I suppose that has been of some concern to the intelligence world, as it should be."

The conversation had distracted him from touching her. She decided to keep him talking. "You killed Kovar."

"I had him killed, yes."

"Why?"

"He wouldn't answer my question."

"And what was your question?"

"Why he had put your daughter in his will as sole beneficiary."

His answer surprised Nadja. And in truth, she also wondered why her grandfather would do such a thing. But she would never know. Kovar was gone.

"You killed him for that?"

"Not really." He smiled as if he'd been caught in a lie. "That's how it began, but I hadn't seen a man die in at least two weeks and I was feeling anxious."

His answer made Nadja sick to her stomach, and she vowed she would have revenge for Kovar's senseless death. She had thought about killing her grandfather a hundred times, but she knew she never would have been able to do it.

"Where is the kill-file?"

"Tucked away in a place you will never think to look."

"It's on his computer." Mady stood, her voice suddenly stronger. "And if he's deleted it, there's an extra copy in the safe back at Groffen."

Holic came off the bed and angled his head to study his wife. "Have I ignored you for too long, my love? Do you crave my touch again?" He walked toward her, backing her against the wall.

The knife was still in his hand and Nadja was afraid he would use it on Mady. She scrambled for something to say. Anything. She came up with "In the file does it tell you how good I am? How many men have been blown away by me?"

Her choice of words, the innuendo, made Holic turn around. He was again smiling—amused by her, was Nadja's guess.

He tossed his head, his raven hair moving gracefully around his shoulders, then sent the blade of his knife over his crotch, stroking himself until his erection strained his jeans.

Now that she had his attention, she upped the stakes. "Did you know that no man has survived me. That I've killed them all. Afterward, that is. No, there were a few I killed before they…you know. Except for Bjorn Odell, that is. He's the only man who knows what it's like to be…there. The only man still breathing years later."

She knew she had just awakened the dragon with the words she'd chosen. Holic's eyes lit up like firecrackers. Mady forgotten, he strolled back to the bed. He set the knife down on the nightstand and, in that moment, Nadja knew she had him. Another few minutes and he would be hers.

He sat down on the bed, put a hand on her breast, and leaned forward and kissed her. She kissed him back,

teased him into wanting more—needing more. She
knew this game well, and suddenly she wanted to play.
Wanted to finish what Holic had started.

At that moment the door flew open and Bjorn joined
the party.

About time, Nadja thought as the noise jolted
Holic off the bed. He spun around and suddenly
pulled a gun from his pocket. A short-barreled .32
Seecamp.

When he saw Bjorn in the doorway standing on two
good legs with his .38 gripped in his gun hand he looked
momentarily stunned. It gave Nadja time to scramble
off the bed and retrieve her own .38 where it lay on the
floor near the window.

Suddenly Mady turned hysterical and rushed at
Holic, screaming, "You killed Kovar. You've sent Prisca
away. You plan to kill my sister. What else, Holic? What
else are you going to take from me?"

For an answer he grabbed her and spun her around
using his injured hand. It was obvious that it hurt him,
but he went with the pain as he used his wife as a human
shield.

"No!" Bjorn yelled, as if he knew what was coming
next. Nadja watched as Holic propelled Mady away
from him and into Bjorn, saying, "What more, Mady?
Your life, my love. Your worthless life." Then he fired.

Mady's knees buckled and she dropped to the floor,
and in that moment Nadja and Bjorn fired on Holic.
Their shots hitting him at the same time.

A week later Bjorn entered Merrick's office without
knocking. Polax was seated in front of his boss's desk.
They were waiting for him and Nadja. But Nadja wasn't

coming. Bjorn had had Polax's orders for her to fly to Washington intercepted.

"Where's Q?" Polax asked.

"She's sitting this one out," Bjorn offered. "But it doesn't matter. I've got what you need."

"Then you finally found the kill-list?"

"I have it."

Polax grinned. "That's wonderful. And Holic? Is he talking yet?"

"No. But he's pulled through his surgery. Too bad it didn't go too well. It looks like he's got a matching pair of useless hands. I'd say the assassin has retired."

"And Q's sister," Merrick asked, "what's happening there?"

"The bulletproof vest Mady was wearing saved her life. She's cooperating with us, and we've gotten some good information we didn't have earlier. We'll be releasing her in a few days."

"And Pierce?"

"Back at work in Hungary."

Bjorn eyed his boss. It was the first time he'd seen Merrick since his surgery. He said, "You look like shit, sir."

"Paul tells me once my hair grows back you won't see the scar. I guess I'll have to buy a hat."

They shared a smile.

Bjorn leaned against the wall and shoved his hands into his pants pockets. "So this is the deal. I'll hand over the kill-file, and you—" he directed the next thing out of his mouth to Polax "—agree to retire Nadja from Quest."

"What? Retire her? Impossible."

"Make it possible. She's done enough for Quest.

Now it's time you gave back. You've got ten days to get it done."

Polax screwed up his face, then looked at Merrick. "Is he serious? What kind of an agency is this, Merrick? Who's the boss?"

Bjorn held up his hand before Merrick could say anything. "That's not all you're going to do," he continued as if Polax's remarks were never made. "You're going to relocate her and her daughter. Send them someplace warm. A place where you can see a sunrise and a sunset every day. A two-story beach house. Expensive, but not too big."

Polax shook his head and again looked to Merrick. "Adolf, reign your boy in. He's way out of line."

"She did come through for us, Lev. And she was telling the truth about her double-agent status. She never compromised Quest."

To his commander, Bjorn said, "And from you, Merrick, I want Onyxx to start looking for Prisca Reznik. Mady's daughter is still missing. And I need a six-month vacation."

"Six months?"

"Back vacation. I've never taken a day off since I came to Onyxx. Check the records." Bjorn shoved away from the wall and headed for the door. Before he left, he asked, "Did we ever find out who Kimball was working for?"

"Not yet, but we're looking into it. I'll let you know what we find out."

Bjorn nodded. "In ten days, then."

"Wait!" Polax jumped up. "Adolf, stop him. Where's Q, Odell? What does she have to say about all of this? I want to hear her tell me she wants out."

"I'll have her give you a call." Then Bjorn left. He was whistling as he headed for the elevator.

* * *

Ten days later Bjorn delivered the kill-file to Merrick's office. Lev Polax was there to witness the delivery. Everything had been attended to, and to prove it he handed Bjorn a picture of a beautiful two-story beach house in the Azores.

"Satisfied?"

"If it's the one she picked, then I'm satisfied."

"It is. I gave her three choices. I don't like agreeing with you, Odell. You really do have a way of irritating the hell out of me, but after talking to Q I'm convinced that this is the best for all concerned. This mission has changed her, and I don't feel it would benefit Quest to retain her services any longer."

"Nicely put, Polax, but you sucked her dry and you know it. You expected too much, too often. And she gave it over and over again. You owe her more than a damn beach house."

"Don't push it, Odell."

Merrick cleared his throat. "There's one more thing, Bjorn."

He looked at his commander. "And that is?"

"We did get information on Kimball and it's not good. In fact it's damn upsetting. We believe Mace Kimball was working for the Chameleon at the time you shot him at After Shock."

"You mean working for his organization? The Chameleon's dead."

Polax said, "I learned that both Kimball and Moor were planted at Quest. Since Moor is still alive we were able to convince him to talk. He's claiming that the Chameleon is alive and well."

"That's impossible. He's in the lab morgue."

"I'll remind you that we don't have a confirmation on that body yet," Merrick said. "I'll keep you posted. Polax, do you have anything else you would like to discuss before we wrap this meeting up?"

Polax was fiddling with his watch. Bjorn suspected it was some new invention he was trying out. The Quest commander cleared his throat. "Actually, there is. When I talked to Nadja I forgot to ask about the phone. Do you know if she still has it?"

"The phone?"

"Yes, I gave her a special phone. A state-of-the-art invention of mine. I would like it returned. It was a prototype."

"Oh, that phone." Bjorn grinned. "Those explosives were ingenious, Polax. Remember in my report I said we blew up the helicopter?"

"Yes."

"That's how we did it, with the phone. Nadja set the timer, and tossed the phone to Holic's pilot."

"You mean the phone is..."

"History."

Polax looked sick. "A million dollars up in smoke," he muttered.

"But for a good cause, Polax. We recovered the kill-file."

Merrick said, "I've seen to your request for six months off. I know you plan to go out to Montana and see Jacy. Any plans after that?"

Bjorn shrugged. "Not anything concrete."

Merrick grinned. "Washington's chilly this time of year. I know how much you hate cold weather. Maybe you should find a friendly beach and warm up those old bones of yours."

* * *

Nadja was afraid that Alzbet was going to miss Austria's snow-capped mountains, but her daughter had never seen the ocean before, or a white sandy beach. Needless to say, when she saw both, she fell in love.

It was too good to be true, Nadja thought, and daily she had to pinch herself. She was free and sharing her daughter's life. Polax had truly become her white knight. His idea to retire her had been the perfect answer, although she worried about the KGB calling or sending someone to her door.

But she wasn't going to think about that now. She'd gotten a clean bill of health from Velich on her leg and she was good for another year.

They had moved into the beach house a month ago, and had settled in quickly. Being a mother to Alzbet was wonderful, and she cherished every day. Maybe it was because she'd been so afraid she would never have any days at all that she valued every minute.

The house was large and airy, with windows facing the ocean. There was a balcony off one of the bedrooms upstairs and she'd taken it for herself. She'd viewed a number of sunrises from the intimate place.

Had cried privately there. But she wouldn't let anyone see how her heart was breaking. There were so many blessings to be thankful for. Mady was beginning to smile again after weeks of tears, even though she knew that Prisca was never far from her sister's mind. As yet there had been no word on Prisca.

Nadja stood when she saw him and walked to the railing on the veranda. She wore a simple blue skirt, white tank top and slip-on sandals. When he was close enough to see her, she waved and he waved back.

Ruger was now working at a small church on the island and he came by almost every day. He often shared dinner with them, and he had been such a help to Mady.

He'd told her that it was Bjorn who was responsible for his rescue from the Italian prison. He hadn't talked about it much, but she knew he would in time.

She would have liked to have thanked Bjorn for finding her brother, but he hadn't come near her since the rescue of Alzbet and the capture of Holic that day in the cabin on Glass Mountain. Once they had located the kill-file in Groffen's safe, they had gone their separate ways.

"How was your day?" Ruger asked as he came up the steps.

He looked well, his blue eyes bright and his blond hair freshly cut. He wore white pants and a white shirt. He was thin, but his appetite was good. She was determined to put ten pounds on him.

"It was productive. I taught Alzbet to float and breathe underwater today. You know I want her to learn to swim as soon as possible."

"And what did she teach you today?"

"Patience," Nadja admitted, smiling. "This business of motherhood is hard work."

Ruger laughed as he sat in the swing, and patted the empty space beside him. "Where's Mady?"

"Taking a nap with my daughter. I just wanted to tell you again how grateful—"

"You are that I kept Alzbet," Ruger said. "Yes, I know. You've told me every day since I arrived. Let's put it to rest now. We're all here and everything is perfect, isn't it?"

"Yes, I suppose it is," she said, then leaned her head

on her brother's shoulder. "Are you staying for dinner?"

"I'm here to make dinner, and to watch over Mady and Alzbet for you, so you can catch your flight."

"My flight?" She sat up. "I'm not going anywhere."

"Yes, you are. I think it's time you stopped waiting for him to come to you. Go to *him.*"

"By him, I suppose you're talking about Bjorn?"

"Of course. You need to tell him, Nadja."

"I can't. If he wanted to find us he would have by now. He's very resourceful. Polax said my location would be considered classified information, but Bjorn found you within a week. What does that tell you?"

"Are you so sure you know how he feels?"

She didn't answer.

"Would it matter if I told you he knows where you're at? That he's the one responsible for all of this?" Ruger gestured to the house and the ocean.

"What are you saying?"

"It was his idea that you retire. He twisted Polax's arm. And he insisted that you have a house. I believe he even stipulated that it be someplace warm, with a view of the ocean."

Nadja stood. "I don't understand."

"That's my point. Maybe it's time you asked a few questions. You leave in two hours."

Nadja's flight to Washington, D.C., was nerveracking. At times she wished she could turn the plane around and go home. But by the time it landed, she was resigned. She was going to face Bjorn and ask him why he'd arranged for her to have a house and a life with her daughter. Was it to ease his guilt, or did he really care?

Dressed in jeans and a black leather jacket, and after waiting a long hour and getting the runaround, she entered Merrick's office. When he looked up from his desk he said, "I was notified that you were in the building. You shouldn't be here."

"Maybe not," Nadja admitted. "I'd like to speak to Bjorn."

"He's not here."

"Is he on a mission?"

"Not exactly."

"Then where?"

"He asked for some vacation time. I know he went to see Jacy. After that I don't know."

"Is it true?"

"Is what true?"

"My brother told me Bjorn made a deal to get me out of Quest. Was it his idea that I retire?"

"I can't disclose the details of your retirement, Nadja. If you need something clarified, call Lev Polax. I'm sorry but it looks like you've made this trip for nothing." He sat back in his chair, stroked his cropped silver beard.

"Just like that? I fly all this way and you're going to send me off without anything? Not even Bjorn's address?"

"If Bjorn wants to get in touch with you, he will."

"I need to speak to him. There's something important I need to tell him."

"He's been checking in every few days. I can let him know you stopped by."

At least that was something, Nadja thought. A very small something.

"I think it would be best if you flew straight back home and waited for him to call."

"Will he?"

"Call?" Merrick stood. "We didn't discuss you, if that's what you're asking. Go home, Nadja. It was Bjorn's wish that you have one, so enjoy it and your daughter."

It should have been enough. She would make it enough. She had her daughter, Ruger was safe, and Mady was alive.

It should be enough.

She could keep Bjorn alive in her heart, and he would be with her each day when she looked into her daughter's eyes.

"It'll be enough," she said as she climbed out of the car after her trip back from Washington. She avoided going inside the beach house and opted to head for the veranda to pull herself together. She didn't want to let Mady or Alzbet see that she'd been crying.

"You're home."

She turned to see Mady seated in the rocker. She was sketching the ocean and a sailboat in the distance.

"How did it go?" her sister asked.

"It didn't. He wasn't there."

"Of course not. He can't be two places at once."

"What?"

Mady motioned to the man walking along the beach, Alzbet racing around him as he came toward the house.

"He came yesterday afternoon. He was surprised when I told him you weren't here. He asked where you'd gone."

"Did you tell him?"

"Yes."

"Did you tell him anything else?"

"No. I do know that he told Alzbet he's her father."

"And?"

"And they've been inseparable ever since."

Nadja heart began to race, and she started through the open door that led back into the living room. "I need to go upstairs."

"I set out the blue dress. Wear your hair down."

Nadja stopped and looked back at her sister. "How did you know when I would be home?"

"I called the airport."

Nadja hurried upstairs and slipped into the blue dress, then brushed out her hair. Ten minutes later she was on her way back down the stairs when she saw him. He was at the railing looking out over the water. She ran her eye down the length of him and then back up to that memorable ass.

She had spent years seducing men and suddenly she was so nervous she could hardly swallow. She glanced around, wondered where Alzbet and Mady were.

He said without turning around, "Mady took Ally and went to Ruger's house for dinner." Slowly he faced her. "Hello, Nadja."

He was so handsome, and she was such a fool for falling in love with him.

"Hello, Bjorn."

She forced herself to move, crossed the living room and stepped out onto the veranda. She didn't join him at the railing, but kept her distance.

"So you came to see your daughter. Mady said you told Alzbet you're her father. I didn't tell her because you never did express how you wanted to handle that."

"I appreciate you letting me tell her myself."

"And how did she take the news?"

He smiled, and it lit up his beautiful blue eyes. "She's great, you know. She's tough like her mama. Resilient as hell."

He stepped away from the railing. He wore jeans and a white shirt. It was open and he looked wonderfully tough and sexy.

"I went to see you," she said. "Your boss told me you were on vacation. We've been here a month, Bjorn. Why didn't you come to see Alzbet sooner?"

"It took longer than I thought to settle things with the KGB." He slid his hand inside his back pocket, took out a paper and handed it to her.

"What's this?"

"Something I thought you should read."

She took it and read the letter. It was Kovar's handwriting. It was a request that she be dismissed from service to the KGB.

He'd planned to let her go. Nadja couldn't believe it.

"He told me he wouldn't do this, not ever." She looked up at Bjorn. "Where did you get this?"

"I went back to Groffen. I went through some of Kovar's personal things. I figured there might be something left behind. That's when I found the letter. He'd written it recently. He just ran out of time to send it. I figured it was worth a shot, that maybe they'd honor his wishes. Nadja, why are you standing so far away from me?"

"I'm not."

"Yes, you are." When he reached for her, she stepped back.

"No, don't touch me."

"Listen, I didn't come here just to see my daughter. I came because—"

"I'm pregnant."

"What?"

"Okay, we're pregnant, as in you and me. I didn't tell you about Alzbet five years ago because I couldn't. Circumstances being as they were. But now—" Nadja hurried to get through what she had to say "—things are different. I'm no longer in the business, as they say, so… So I'm telling you straight up that I'm going to have your baby…again. So now you know, and if you want to get mad, get mad. If you want to walk out, go. And—"

"If I want to stay?"

"Stay?" Nadja's heart began to pound faster.

"I have five months' vacation left before I go back to work. Five months to see if we can make this work."

"What work?"

"Us."

"Us? You're not feeling trapped suddenly, are you? Because if that's it, I don't need—"

He moved quickly, swept her up in his arms and locked her curvy body against him. "Me? Is that what you were going to say?"

He kissed her. Kissed her like she'd been dying to be kissed ever since she'd spotted him on the beach.

When he backed off, he whispered, "What if I need you? What if I want you and all of this? What if I took you upstairs right now and showed you how much I've missed you? How much I love you?" He kissed her again. "I do love you, Nadja. I think I've loved you since the beginning."

"Since the first touch," she said. "When you took my hand in the alley in Vienna. I felt it, too."

This time it was Nadja's turn to initiate the kiss, and

she did it intent on sealing Bjorn's fate forever. At the end of that kiss and before the next, she said, "Take me upstairs, Bjorn. Show me, touch me, love me, and I will be here in the morning when you wake up and every day after. Welcome home, my love."

* * * * *

Books by Wendy Rosnau

Silhouette Bombshell

The Spy Wore Red #32

Silhouette Intimate Moments

The Long Hot Summer #996
A Younger Woman #1074
The Right side of the Law #1110
Beneath the Silk #1157
One Way Out #1211
Last Man Standing #1227

*The Brotherhood

Coming in fall 2005 to Silhouette Intimate Moments.
Don't miss Wendy Rosnau's next book
in her Spy Games *miniseries.*

Turn the page for a sneak peek....

Chapter 1

It was a three-hundred-yard kiss-your-ass-goodbye shot. The rifle—an Austrian Steyr AUG with a history for accuracy at twice as many yards.

The assassin took aim as the red handkerchief drifted on the cool morning breeze. It floated, lifted, then settled to the ground in a graceful, almost poetic swan song. A synchronized second later, a slender finger with a neatly trimmed pale pink nail squeezed the trigger.

The bullet struck the British Intelligence agent in the right temple, and before Alton Bromly hit the pavement in the middle of Sloup svate Trojice, the assassin had disappeared off the rooftop of the Moravske Museum in Brno, mentally crossing number four off the kill-list.

Minutes later the assassin climbed into the passenger seat of a brown sedan at the end of the market square.

"An easy shot, this one," the driver said, wiping his forehead with a red handkerchief.

Otto liked to talk afterward—to analyze the kill, and what he called, the beauty of the descent. He reached for the compact leather gun case on Prisca's lap and lifted it over the seat and into the back. He was all about taking care of her—before the kills and afterward. He attended to everything. A multitasking expert, he had become her mother, father, friend, bodyguard and the controller of each mission.

Prisca swept her black stocking cap from her head and shook out her long raven-black layers—her father's hair. She tossed the cap into the back seat and it landed on the black leather gun case.

"The shot," Otto began, "was—"

"The shot was what it was." Prisca pulled the seat belt around her narrow waist and buckled up, then gave her partner a let's-not-go-there look, before turning to stare out the window.

He expelled a heavy sigh, reading her mood, put the car into drive and sped away from the curb. His mouth, again, open and on the move. "What the shot was, Miss Pris, was absolutely perfect."

She ignored the silly nickname he had labeled her with years ago, her sage-brown eyes searching the market square. She saw an elderly woman begin to scream. She was pointing to a body sprawled between two merchant vendors. Bromly lay on his side, a paper cup of spilled coffee beside him. His left hand still clutching a market bag. The soles of his shoes were visible, as well as his bare ankles—Alton wasn't wearing socks this morning.

"Yes, everything about you is perfect, Miss Pris,"

Otto continued. "A lucky man I am, to be here with you. Never think I take it lightly, your father's faith in my ability to care for you. Without fail I thank him daily in my prayers for the gift."

Prisca watched Otto tuck the handkerchief into his gray shirt pocket. Blind to the mayhem taking place in the market square, he steered the car past the gathering crowd and they left Brno and headed south for the Austrian border.

"That shot hit the old Brit dead square, Miss Pris. His cerebrum was turned to mush before his knees—"

"I don't need a forensic report on what just happened. Trust me, your descriptions are permanently embedded in my brain. As embedded as my bullet now in Bromly's skull."

"Trust you? Of course, Miss Pris. With my life. And you know you can trust me with yours. I would die for you." He glanced at her, his eyes full of emotion.

She knew it was true. Otto would die for her because he loved her. *Du*, it was in the eyes. She saw it each time she caught him staring. And she saw something else, too—hope that someday she would return his feelings.

She said, "Can we not talk? I have a headache."

"There are pills in the glove compartment, and water there." He motioned to the bottle between the seats. "You're right. Let's forget about Bromly. He's history, and next up, an American by the name of Walrich. He'll be in Florence in three weeks. Then we're off to Poland. Germany is after that, then Vancouver. At the end of the year we get a four-month vacation, so be thinking where you want to go. I vote for someplace warm."

Prisca didn't say anything. Let Otto think she was going to Poland with him after Italy. Let him make flight plans and all the arrangements for both of them as he'd done for each of the other kills—he was the controller, after all. The man who saw to the details and studied the files on each target.

Let Otto think she was content with the laid-out plan in the file. But things had changed since that file was composed.

It wasn't as if she was abandoning the killing schedule, just altering it slightly. They were all going to die eventually—those profiled in the kill-file were all marked for death.

So what if someone lived a few weeks longer and someone else died a few weeks sooner? So what if she set her sights and high-powered scope on number twelve and then twenty-one before she took out number five or six. In the end justice would still be served.

But not if she didn't address her anxiety. She wasn't sleeping well and it would soon start affecting her work. She needed personal satisfaction to put the future into perspective.

She hadn't mentioned it to Otto, and she wouldn't. He would not be happy with her decision. He would remind her of their promise to each other, and when he did she would get angry. Then tell him she knew the importance of their mission, as well as what she'd promised. After all, her father was in prison, her mother as well as Otto's father, Jakob, dead.

Prisca hugged herself, feeling the chill of loneliness wrap its cold fingers around her. In a matter of hours her life had been shattered. Her mother was gone and her father captured unjustly by some hotshot agency in the U.S. Otto had called Onyxx.

One day she'd been celebrating her reunion with her

father, and lunching with her aunt Nadja and her mother, and the next thing she knew her family had been wiped out of her life forever.

She had a right to her revenge. It may not be sweet, but it was necessary. Not for peace of mind—there would never again be room for solace in her heart. But justice would be served, and at her hands.

She was nineteen and alone, her legacy the only thing that hadn't been stripped from her. And no one could steal that away—she would always be the daughter of Holic Reznik. And it would be that legacy she would be remembered for.

Her father had always told her *practice made perfect*. And she'd proven it to him at Groffen the day she'd raised her gun and drilled the paper target with the accuracy of a professional twice her age.

"To my family I promise my loyalty," Prisca whispered, feeling her heart constrict. "And to those who took you from me, I promise death. Swift, final death."

FROM

DON'T MISS
DEBRA WEBB's
NEXT THRILLING ADVENTURE, ONLY FROM SILHOUETTE BOMBSHELL.

SILENT WEAPON
(March 2005, SB #33)

Her entire life changed when an infection rendered her deaf. But Merri Walters used her disability to her advantage—by becoming an expert lip reader and working for the police. Now, her special skill was needed for an extremely dangerous undercover assignment—one that put her at odds with the detective in charge...and in the sights of an enemy.

If you enjoyed what you just read,
then we've got an offer you can't resist!

Take 2 bestselling love stories FREE!

Plus get a FREE surprise gift!

Clip this page and mail it to Silhouette Reader Service®

IN U.S.A.	**IN CANADA**
3010 Walden Ave.	P.O. Box 609
P.O. Box 1867	Fort Erie, Ontario
Buffalo, N.Y. 14240-1867	L2A 5X3

YES! Please send me 2 free Silhouette Bombshell™ novels and my free surprise gift. After receiving them, if I don't wish to receive any more, I can return the shipping statement marked cancel. If I don't cancel, I will receive 4 brand-new novels every month, before they're available in stores! In the U.S.A., bill me at the bargain price of $4.69 plus 25¢ shipping & handling per book and applicable sales tax, if any*. In Canada, bill me at the bargain price of $5.24 plus 25¢ shipping & handling per book and applicable taxes**. That's the complete price and a savings of 10% off the cover prices—what a great deal! I understand that accepting the 2 free books and gift places me under no obligation ever to buy any books. I can always return a shipment and cancel at any time. Even if I never buy another book from Silhouettte, the 2 free books and gift are mine to keep forever.

200 HDN D34H
300 HDN D34J

Name	(PLEASE PRINT)
Address	Apt.#
City	State/Prov. Zip/Postal Code

Not valid to current Silhouette Bombshell™ subscribers.

Want to try another series?
Call 1-800-873-8635 or visit www.morefreebooks.com.

* Terms and prices subject to change without notice. Sales tax applicable in N.Y.
** Canadian residents will be charged applicable provincial taxes and GST.
   All orders subject to approval. Offer limited to one per household.
   ® and ™ are registered trademarks owned and used by the trademark owner and
   or its licensee.

BOMB04   ©2004 Harlequin Enterprises Limited

Silhouette® BOMBSHELL™

BRINGS YOU THE THIRD POWERFUL NOVEL IN

LINDSAY McKENNA's

SERIES

Sisters of the Ark:

Driven by a dream of legendary powers, these Native American women have sworn to protect all that their people hold dear.

WILD WOMAN

by *USA TODAY* bestselling author
Lindsay McKenna

Available April 2005
Silhouette Bombshell #37

Available at your favorite retail outlet.

COMING NEXT MONTH

#33 SILENT WEAPON by Debra Webb

Her entire life changed when an infection rendered her deaf.
But Merri Walters used her disability to her advantage—by
becoming an expert lip reader and working for the police.
Now, her special skill was needed for an extremely dangerous
undercover assignment—one that put her at odds with the
detective in charge...and in the sights of an enemy.

#34 PAYBACK by Harper Allen

Athena Force

Dawn O'Shaughnessy was playing a dangerous game—
pretending to work for the immoral scientist who'd made her
a nearly indestructible assassin, while secretly aligning herself
with the Athena Force women who had vowed to take him
down. But when she discovered that only the man who'd
raised her to be a monster could save her from imminent
death, she had to choose between the new sisters she'd
come to know and trust, and payback....

#35 THE ORCHID HUNTER by Sandra K. Moore

She was more hunter than botanist, and Dr. Jessie Robards
knew she could find the legendary orchid that could cure
her uncle's illness—Brazil's pet vipers, jaguars, natives and
bioterrorists be damned. But the Amazonian jungle, filled
with passion and betrayal, was darker and more dangerous
than she'd ever imagined. This time it would change her,
heart and soul...*if* she made it out alive.

#36 CALCULATED RISK by Stephanie Doyle

Genius Sabrina Masters had been the CIA's favorite protégée—
until betrayal ended her career. Now she'd been called back
into duty—to play traitor and lure a deadly terrorist out of
hiding. Only she had the brains to decode the terrorist's
encrypted data, which was vital to national security. But when
the agent who'd betrayed her became her handler, the mission
became more complicated than even Sabrina could calculate....

SBCNM0205